The
Shoe Shine Boy

Andiel
Thank you for
your Friendship
Best wishes

David Mucci

Also by David Mucci

The Cardiac Cartel

A medical thriller where Cardiologists who have pledged the Hippocratic oath would rather kill than expose their secret society.

What the critic's say about David Mucci's first book
"The Cardiac Cartel":

New York Post
"...peppered with so much gunfire and mayhem...the gang warfare of the 1990's seems like a trip to a bakery."

CU CITYVIEW Champaign-Urbana's News and Entertainment Weekly

"Strap yourself in and set aside several hours because once you start Cardiac Cartel, you won't be able to put it down."

The Hartford Courant

"A bombastic cardiologist...murders patients and hires assassins, all to maintain a monopoly in the multibillion-dollar coronary angioplasty business."

The
Shoe Shine Boy

David Mucci

Dedication

This book is dedicated to the men and women fighting the War on Terror that are part of the American Military, Coalition Forces, and Homeland Security organizations. Special thanks to those who are doing, or have done, active duty in the Middle East and Persian Gulf, to free the thousands that were repressed and make this world a safer place for us all to live in. And our deepest gratitude to those who have sacrificed their lives to defend the right for families to live free.

May God bless all of you and your families, and may God Bless America.

David & Jeanne Mucci

1   Chapter One

The rail yard was stark and cold, warmed only by the steam that hissed from an arriving train. The oppressive silence was broken by the harsh commands that cut through the air. It was business as usual for the Nazi officers. With military efficiency they herded groups of prisoners towards various destinations. By the hundreds, the Jews walked in despair. The days they'd spent in the depths of dark trains had stolen their courage, their hope, and for many, their lives.

The incoming train screeched to a stop. A few moments later the moldy rotting wooden door opened. The occupants laid or sat inside, crushed together. The stench that emitted from the car was vile. For those inside, the sunlight was so bright all shielded their eyes.

"Out! Out of the cars, you filthy excuses for human bowel waste!"

Abraham was one of the first. Squinting, he rose painfully. Those with enough strength left to walk slowly shuffled towards the open door. At the age of eleven Abraham felt tired and bitter. His emotions were that of an old man at the twilight of his life. He and his companions helped each other onto the dirt a few feet below. They steadied the oldest and caught the youngest. The S.S. officers stood nearby, arrogantly tall in their black uniforms and finely polished black boots, sneers of derision on their faces.

Head down, Abraham meekly obeyed orders. He and the other prisoners found themselves herded a few feet away from the cars. The staccato sound of automatic guns suddenly cracked through the air. Abraham jumped and turned his head.

He saw black uniformed S.S. officers murdering the helpless victims left alive in the cattle cars.

"You and you." The commander of the brigade walked over. He pointed to the two men next to Abraham. "You two. Climb into that car and clean out those filthy carcasses."

Abraham kept his eyes riveted to the ground. One of them who was barely able to stand spoke up, "I don't have enough strength to lift them. I've had no food, or water, in two days."

"Then you're of no use to me." The commander pulled out his luger, raised it and pulled the trigger.

"You!" He pointed to Abraham. "Are you also too weak?"

"No." Abraham fought to keep his voice steady.

"Then get in that car and clean up that mess!" He turned and stormed away.

Abraham slowly climbed back into the cattle car that had been his prison for the past three days. He'd only been outside in the fresh air for a short time. Nonetheless he found himself repulsed by the stench, which minutes before he hadn't noticed. The sickening odor that mixed with the acrid smoke from the gunpowder filled his nostrils. He fell to his knees and gagged, but wretched up nothing but bile.

"You have to get up or they'll shoot you. We must work. Now!"

Abraham looked up into the steady dark eyes of a boy, not much older than himself. He had, though, a careworn demeanor. Abraham took his outstretched hand, a gesture of help, friendship, and sympathy, and stood up.

For the next half hour, Abraham helped his companion gently stack bodies onto a pushcart. He was overcome by the need to treat them with dignity. His new friend seemed to feel the same.

"Take them over to that field and bury them!" An officer pointed with the muzzle of his gun to a nearby field.

As they struggled with the cart, Abraham averted his eyes. He looked to his left. There he saw a field of tall grass filled with thousands of wild flowers. A soft breeze rustled through the meadow, causing the grass to sway and the flowers to dance. Abraham wondered how two worlds so different could exist side by side.

The pushcart got heavier with every step. Abraham's weakened muscles strained and burned to keep his body moving forward. Behind him was a guard. His gun aimed at their backs, his finger on the trigger. When they pushed the cart around a large pile of dirt the guard ordered them to halt. In front of him, he saw a tremendous hole in the ground.

"My God!" Abraham's knees started to buckle. His nameless friend reached out and supported him.

"Come. When we're done we'll say a prayer for them…and us."

"Why?" Abraham stared into the death pit. "What have we done? Why are they doing this to us?"

"Because we are Jews. No other reason."

Throughout the afternoon, the two of them emptied out multiple railroad cars. Three hours later, emotionally and physically exhausted they finished. They soon joined a group of twenty prisoners under the watchful eyes of the guards and their dogs.

"Sergeant! Take these men to Lab five."

"Actung!" the Sergeant bellowed. "You will walk two by two. There will be no talking. If you disobey, you will be shot!"

They walked through the rail yard in utter silence. Abraham caught a glimpse of another train arriving out of the corner of his eye. That train quickly unloaded its human cargo and the men, women and children were lined up. With slow and methodical deliverance, an officer walked in front of them. He would occasionally stop and tap a man or a woman with the riding crop he held in his gloved hand. Those tapped were immediately pulled out of line and marched away. Abraham's final glance caught sight of the rest being herded down the cobblestone path. The same path he was currently on.

High hedges on both sides now obscured Abraham's view. Eventually, he and the others came upon a wooden gate. High above it a hand carved sign hung.

WILKOMMEN AU AUSCHWITZ-BIRKENAU

"Move! Walk faster!"

They passed under the sign. Abraham now could hear orders that were barked to a separate group of frail prisoners. "Take off all your clothes and jewelry. Place them in the bins provided. You will all take showers. Pile your clothes neatly so you can find them when you are done."

Abraham and his group, however, were directed past the shower line. He soon found himself standing ankle deep in mud behind a small single story building. He glanced from side to side ever slow slowly. The silence was absolute. Each prisoner was lost in his own thoughts, with arms hung limp at their sides. For Abraham the sights and smells he had endured over the last few hours made him wish silently for a quick death. His heart and spirit were broken. His faith in mankind swept away with the noxious odor of death, inflicted by the ruthless on the helpless.

The building's rear door opened and two S.S. officers emerged. A young man in his early twenties wearing a white lab coat followed them. One of the Nazi soldiers walked through the mud and stopped in front of the group of prisoners. Without hesitation, he picked four of them. "Captain, take these four to the Lab." He looked down at the mud on his otherwise highly polished boots and shook his head. "Young doctor, I hope your little experiment works as well on those men as it does on rabbits. The Fuhrer is growing very impatient with your lack of results. If I were you, I would not report too many more failures." He again looked at his boots.

"The Fuhrer will get his results soon. He's waited this long. I'm sure he has the patience to wait a few more weeks. Unless you want to take the responsibility for false, inaccurate results?"

The General spun around and faced what remained of Abraham's group. His face was flushed. He pointed to Abraham. "You! Come here."

Abraham walked to within five feet of him and stopped.

"Jew boy, can you shine boots?"

"Yes," Abraham said in a low voice.

"Little Jew boy, listen to me. Your life depends on how well you clean my boots. If you do a good job..." he turned his head and shot a glance at the young inventor. "Doctor, he can help clean up your lab. Follow us, Jew boy."

They walked off towards the door. "Private!" he called out over his shoulder, "Take the rest of those Jews into the field and shoot them." He entered the lab last and closed the door behind him.

Inside the lab, the General sat perched on a stool in front of a large glass window. He stuck out one leg. "Jew boy, pull my boots off and clean them."

Abraham trembled, knelt before him and pulled them off. He used some old rags he found and started to clean the mud off them. The fine black leather slowly shined. He glanced up occasionally at the activity in the room. Each time his eyes came to rest on the young scientist. He found this man's arrogant stance and cynical attitude mesmerizing.

"General, let me explain this experiment," said the scientist as he flipped a switch. The room on the other side of the glass window became awash with light. On the other side of the window stood the four men led off earlier. "Two of these men are without protective clothing." He continued, "They wear what they did when they arrived here. The other two wear gas masks, and modest protective clothing. Nevertheless, they still have a small amount of skin exposed."

Abraham cautiously looked up from cleaning the General's boots and saw his friend that had helped him in the railyard, standing behind the panel of glass. Fright and anticipation was on his friend's face. For a moment their eyes locked. Abraham could see his lips moving, over and over again, mouthing words as he stared intensely at him. Finally Abraham understood what his friend was saying.

"PRAY FOR ME, MY FRIEND. PRAY FOR ME."

The only comfort Abraham could offer was a nod of recognition for his friend's dying plea. With that message understood, a small peaceful smile came to his friend's face.

Abraham heard the high-pitched hiss of gas. He watched his friend try in vain to hold his breath but to no avail. Though it lasted only moments, Abraham knew the horror he just witnessed would stay with him every moment of what little time he had left on this earth. All he could do was bow his head in horror and pray.

When he looked up he saw the two other Jews still alive, protected by their gas masks. Both cowered in the corner in terror, their hands holding their masks tightly against their faces.

"Doctor! That was one frightening exhibition of death."

"General, you surprise me. You haven't watched those you condemn out there die in your great chambers? There are glass-ports built in for that sole purpose. I'm surprised you haven't spent your evening there, sipping your after dinner Cognac." His eyes bore into the General. "What do you think happens hundreds of times a day in your shower rooms? You see them walk in alive, and when the doors open they're all dead! How do you think they die? You think they just lay down and fall asleep? No, General, you've just witnessed death by cyanide gas. The same gas you use in your chambers. That, General, is the reality of your work." The scientist pointed his finger at the two dead Jews.

"How interesting, Von Wilbert. You make me out to be such a butcher. Yet you turned the valve. I have no illusions as to who I am or what I do. And, no, I don't indulge myself in the amusement of their deaths. But I think you do. You are as much a butcher as I am."

"Wrong, General!" he snapped back. "I kill out of the need to experiment, to save German soldiers. If a few dozen pitiful Jews die to save thousands of German soldiers, then it's worth it. But you...you just exterminate."

The young scientist turned his attention back to the control panel. He flipped a switch and fans whirled, flushing the small gas chamber with fresh air. "Enough of politics and philosophy, back to the experiment, General. You will notice the cyanide gas left the men with the gas masks unaffected. Cyanide gas is good in closed rooms like this one, and the ones you use. It is useless though as a tactical weapon in the field. However, a short time ago, through one of those unplanned mistakes in chemistry, I came upon a new gas that is a derivative of cyanide gas. Watch its effects."

Abraham watched Von Wilbert shut off the fans. This sealed the room from outside air. Next he turned a second valve. The two remaining victims still wearing the gas masks suddenly died.

"General, despite the protective gas mask they are dead. The gas entered through the small exposed area of skin on their wrists and killed them. But what is remarkable is that in approximately one hour this gas will become non lethal. It decomposes into...nothingness."

Von Wilbert kept his eyes on the General, who had no immediate response. He simply stared at the grotesque sight behind the glass window. When he spoke it was with excitement. "Yes, safe for the German Army to enter and occupy the battlefield. I commend you!" The General snapped his head towards Abraham. "Jew boy! Give me my boots and in one hour get rid of those carcasses in there. Doctor, you can have him as a cleaning boy. When he is through, do what you want with him."

A few hours later, a guard led Abraham to a wooden barracks and threw him inside. He stumbled and fell to the filthy floor. He lay there, too weak to move. His eyes slowly grew accustomed to the dim light. He saw wooden bed-frames, stacked to the ceiling filling the room. Hundreds of them were lined up row after row with only inches of walk space between them. Abraham could hear rustling sounds. Too tired to move he waited for the rats to come and eat him alive.

A voice called out from the dark, "Is this the traitor who cleans the boots of the butcher?"

Abraham couldn't answer. He could do nothing other than lay on the floor, his face in the dirt. His eyes bore into the darkness. He came to realize there were hundreds of men, their faces shrunken, looking down on him. A shuffling of feet stopped next to him and Abraham looked up. A man stood over him with his skeletal hand extending downwards toward him. Abraham gathered all his strength, reached for the hand, and slowly stood up.

"Ignore them, boy. My name is Joseph." The skeleton turned and spoke into the darkness. "He's only a boy! If cleaning mud off boots keeps him alive, who here will deny him? He faces the same horrors we do. Who here will deny him the chance to grow older?"

"The Nazi swine's will," a voice called back.

"Yes. But we won't!" He turned back to Abraham. "Come, you can share my small bunk."

Over the next few days Abraham witnessed the death of countless Jews. Many of them he recognized from his barracks.

The word quickly spread throughout the camp's S.S. officers that the small boy who cleaned the lab would also shine their boots. Daily he sat in a corner of the laboratory shining boots and watching his fellow Jews perish. He came to envy the workers who cleaned the bodies out of the showers. At least they didn't have to view the deaths. They didn't have to see the choking, the horror of the last moments of life.

Day after day the Nazi scientist donned a sardonic grin while he watched the Jews die. Abraham knew this image would also stay with him forever.

His daily tasks blended from one day into the next until there was no real distinction between them. At night he looked to his bunkmate, Joseph, for a small escape. The two shared bittersweet memories of life before the camp. Even that soon came to an end. One morning one of the bodies Abraham dragged out of the lab was Joseph. It was almost too much to bear. Yet Abraham knew Joseph was one of the lucky ones. He had quickly learned the anticipation of the future in this place was far worse than death.

The next morning the guards broke their routine with sudden frantic pounding on the doors and walls. They shouted orders to each other, and to the prisoners. Abraham tried at first to hide in his bunk but he quickly realized he did not want to be singled out, so he exited the barracks as ordered.

"Stand in two rows shoulder to shoulder. No talking."

He watched soldiers walk down the rows with their pistols drawn. They systematically shot those who appeared old, weak, or unfit. His heart pounded when one stopped in front of him for a quick review. He shut his eyes and waited. When he heard the loud report of the gun near his head he jumped. Terrified, he forced his eyes open. The skeleton of a man who had stood next to him lay dead at his feet in the dirt.

"Take these dead carcasses and place them inside the barracks. Then return to line!" the soldier screamed at those left standing.

One hour later Abraham and the others marched out of Auschwitz with guns at their backs. They marched by the lab, and by the crematoriums. They walked along the pits that had been recently filled in with dirt. They marched across the railroad tracks leaving the confines that had brought them so close to hell. Behind them rose a black cloud of smoke. Explosions rocked the ground, and the smell of burning wood and dead flesh drifted above the flames that consumed the camp.

Abraham turned his head for a moment. The Allies must be near, he thought. The Nazis were trying to destroy the camp, and the evidence.

They marched for days down the main road out of Poland and into the heart of Germany, to a destination unknown. When they walked through small towns the villagers ignored them with total indifference. He and the others were a pathetic sight. They were nothing more than dirty, filthy shells, with loose skin draped over their bones. Not one villager acknowledged their presence. Not one villager threw them a morsel of food, a scrap of bread, or offered them a drink of water.

Abraham felt like he and the others were ghosts walking down the street unseen by all. He asked himself *how can they pretend not to see us? What kind of animals are they?*

For some prisoners it became too tempting with the woods so close. Abraham could see it in their eyes. They had lived as animals in the camps. The woods could not be more difficult. One occasionally would make a run for the freedom that was only a few feet away. The crack of a rifle shot would inevitably be heard and the running body would fall to the ground. Those who couldn't walk fast enough and slowed the group were also left behind, shot in the head.

With their numbers reduced, their forced march ended at Buchenwald just outside Weimer, Germany. This concentration camp was smaller than Auschwitz. Because of the influx it was filled far beyond its capacity. Food was scarce and the treatment handed out by the guards was as brutal. The days dragged on. The prisoners, as well as the Germans, felt the Allies were near. The tension inside the camp mounted. The guards stepped up the process of mass extermination. They would indiscriminately fire pistols and machine guns into the barracks at different times during the day. The Germans refused to allow the removal of bodies from the barracks. Where they fell, they stayed. In order to survive the shooting sprees, the living took refuge behind the dead. Rat infested cabins were doused with gasoline and burned. All those still alive found themselves locked inside the inferno. For the first time, the prisoners sensed their captors were in a panic.

Abraham stirred one morning when he heard the door to his barracks being locked from the outside. He wondered *is today the day I will die?*

He waited for the barracks to burn. He prayed the smoke would render him unconscious before the flames melted his skin. He sat peacefully and waited. He was not afraid. He contemplated what he had endured in his short life. Yes, he was ready to die. He was ready for this nightmare to end.

The day wore on and the camp remained quiet. The flames never came. The anticipation became more terrifying than the actual fear of death. Still, Abraham continued to sit and wait with the few men left alive in the barracks. They rarely spoke. Their despair was too overwhelming.

The day became night, and then quietly flowed into dawn. Abraham waited for the guards to burst through the locked door. The sun was up now and a new day of death had arrived.

The morning rolled on and Abraham wondered what had happened. The camp was quiet. The guards never came.

Then, faintly at first, with increasing intensity he heard the rumble of artillery and small arms fire off in the distance.

"The Allies were coming", rejoiced Abraham and the others. Nevertheless, would they get here in time, or would the Nazis kill them first? They all wondered aloud.

There was commotion throughout the camp. The door to his barracks suddenly burst open and soldiers rushed in. Abraham held his breath, not knowing whether to expect freedom or death.

"Sergeant!" a strong voice barked in English. "Take every man in this barracks and give him food and water. And if any of them can't walk, carry them out. Is that understood?"

"Yes, Sir!"

Abraham strained to remember the English he had learned in school. It seemed so very long ago.

The Commander took a quick glance around. The odor and stench that those inside had grown accustomed to, overwhelmed and overpowered him. As he turned to leave he spoke softly to the Sergeant, "I think I've seen enough. I need some fresh air."

"No! You can't go," Abraham called out to him, but his voice could barely whisper. "You have to see what they did to us and how they made us live. You must punish them."

The Commander reluctantly took Abraham's hand and allowed him to be led away from the door. They went deep into the barracks. The Commander held a white handkerchief tightly to his nose as he followed the boy from one side of the barracks to the other. He saw how they survived. How they had stacked the bodies to protect themselves from the carnage of bullets.

He shuddered while Abraham pulled a blanket off a bunk. Abraham pointed silently. Bile rose in the Commander's throat as he witnessed sights he knew would haunt him for years to come. When he was finally outside, he fell to his knees and heaved his breakfast onto the ground.

He looked up and as his eyes met Abraham's said, "Now I've seen enough."

Hours later Abraham sat in the back of an open troop truck with thirty other death camp survivors. It was hard for him to grasp that in the blink of an eye his horror had ended. He had survived physically. Emotionally he felt crippled. Questions swirled in his mind. How many had he buried? How many thousands had died? Would they ever know? What would he do? Where would he go? The only thing he knew was that he wanted to go far from this land of death.

A jeep pulled to a stop a few feet from him. In it sat Claus Von Wilbert. Their eyes met. Abraham noticed a smirk on his face.

Abraham reacted immediately. "Killer! Murderer! Butcher!" Abraham half climbed, half fell out of the truck onto the dirt below. "He is a Nazi killer!" He screamed repeatedly in a frail weak voice as he made his way to the jeep.

An American solder stopped him ten feet from the jeep.

"You must arrest him! He is a killer of Jews!"

"He's already under arrest," the soldier said. "Look, he's in handcuffs. We also tied his feet so he can't run away. Don't worry boy, the only place he's going to is in front of a firing squad."

"He's a killer, he's a killer," Abraham said. He wanted to leave no misunderstanding in the soldiers' mind.

"We know what he's done. Please come with me back to the truck."

"Sergeant, what's the problem here?" The Commander approached.

"Nothing, sir. This boy saw our prisoner and got upset."

For a second time Abraham looked into the eyes of the Commander. "He's a killer. He killed a lot of Jews. Please punish him, please." Tears rolled down his cheeks for the first time in many months.

"We will son. Don't worry. We will. Go with the Sergeant. He'll take you back to the truck."

Abraham sat in the truck as it drove away. His eyes met Von Wilbert's again, but this time Abraham was the one with a smile.

Shortly after Abraham's truck had disappeared, a second jeep approached and stopped. A Second Lieutenant jumped out and approached the Commander.

"Sir, I understand you are transporting Claus Von Wilbert."

"That's right. That's the bastard in the back of that jeep."

"Sir, these orders give me custody of your prisoner. I'll be taking him for interrogation before his processing."

The Commander checked the orders and shrugged. Then he waved on the Second Lieutenant to complete his assignment.

2   Chapter Two

June 15, 2001

Slightly less than a five-hour drive from the city of Taipei, Sun Moon Lake sat high in the rugged mountains of Taiwan. A thick forest of camphor, pine and eucalyptus surrounds the lake. Each evening at dusk, a mist descends from the mountains and hangs over the lake. Then in one swoop the mist envelopes the countyside. Those lucky enough to witness this event feel a unique harmony and serenity as they watch heaven meet earth.

Tucked away at the far end of this massive lake is the Evergreen Hostel. The isolation and enhancement of this lodge lends itself to a romantic hideaway. Each room's large windows give occupants a splendid view of the sunset, highlighting the distant dark green mountaintops. Each room also has an enormous balcony that overhangs a beautifully sculptured garden. Beyond the garden a finely landscaped lawn is terraced down to the water's edge.

Inside the hostel, three men sat around a finely polished mahogany table. They talked casually while sipping after dinner drinks, the landscape's enchantment lost on them. An air of anticipation surrounded the men. They planned to spend the next few days in hard negotiations. They eventually hoped to strike a deal.

John Gordon, the United States' Secretary of State, reflected for a moment in silence as he sat at the table. The world had changed dramatically over the last decade. Fundamentalist religious groups had attacked United States' interests on American soil in 1993 with the marginally successful attack on the World Trade Center. In 2000 a suicide bomber's attack on the U.S.S. Cole in Yemen, as the war ship was entering the harbor, reminded the world how effective a few small groups could be if they were willing to sacrifice their lives to kill others. In all accounts, the United States' support for Israel over the Palestinians was one of the root causes blamed for the attacks. In early spring of this year, the U.S. intelligence community felt that something big was in the making, though they had no idea what was being targeted. Europe had turned a blind eye at previous attacks on the United States. Europe's position was that the anger of the Islamic community toward the U.S. was one of the American's own making and would be fixed only by a change in U.S. position. The President of the United States, President Andrew Rhodes, thought differently. He felt the Israel-Palestinian issue was a convenient scapegoat for the terrorists. President Rhodes vowed that in the summer of 2001 he would resolve the Israeli-Palestinian issues, forcing the world community to take a strong stand against further terrorism. So there the three men were, as a result of the U.S. President's resolve, negotiating peace.

Gordon looked down from his six foot five inch frame upon his two shorter adversaries that sat round the table with him. Born and raised in Texas, Gordon had the inbred attitude that bigger is better. This attitude, complemented by his height and stocky presence, added an intimidation factor that helped him through many tough negotiations. Gordon hoped this negotiation would be no different. Gordon stood and picked up his drink. As he walked the short distance around the table his Texan string tie swayed below his neck, and his highly polished formal cowboy boots clicked on the hardwood floor. He brushed his left hand through his wavy silver hair as he stopped in front of the two men seated facing him. His smile appeared genuine. However, in reality, it was well polished and rehearsed. His brown eyes constantly made contact with those of the person he was talking to at that moment. He raised his glass and spoke with a distinct Texas drawl. "I toast both of you on your foresight and political acumen."

The Palestinian and Israeli sitting at the table nodded as they raised their glasses.

An hour later Gordon visited Mateusz Adar, Israel's Defense Minister, at his room. The Israeli sat at a desk piled with official dispatches. Adar was much smaller than Gordon. His five foot four inch wiry frame was dwarfed by Gordon's size. Adar's glasses sat perched on a long thin nose. Gordon spoke from the middle of the room. "I've gone through a lot of soul searching on this issue. You and I have met about nine times, and every time we've ended in a stalemate. It can't go on like this. There is too much at risk. This time I'm going to handle it in a different way, an unorthodox way. One would say a very undiplomatic way. These negotiations should have been handled this way a long time ago."

Adar got up quickly and walked over to the window. When he spoke, it was always rapid. However, each word was clearly enunciated. This along with his quick body movements gave him a nervous appearance. "I think you need to clarify yourself."

"Plain and simple, the American public is sick and tired of watching their tax dollars go toward policies that are NOT in our country's best interest. It is time to stop biting the hand that feeds you."

Adar spun around. His glasses almost flew off his nose. "The State of Israel will not allow any government, and that includes the almighty United States, to interfere with our domestic or international policy. We are a sovereign country!"

"That's fine," Gordon said. "Then don't expect us to invest our money on a bad bet. You can sit on your holy pedestal if you want, but let's face facts. Your country...your people are very dependent on the kindness and the money my country gives you. And if you don't like the rules we set then leave...but without our money." He stopped for a moment and stared at Adar. Then he continued, "My country, also a sovereign country, has the right to decide where to invest their fifteen billion dollars. And frankly, at this moment Israel and its sovereign policies is not looking like a good investment."

"This is blackmail! We won't stand for this!" Adar screeched, taking a step towards Gordon and pounding his fist into his hand.

"You won't stand for what? It's our money, our sovereign money! You decide what's good for you, and we'll decide what's good for us."

Adar turned away in disgust. "You're no better than anybody else in how you deal with Jews. We are expendable to you also. How dare you!" he screamed. "How dare you! We are not expendable! We will not be pushed into gas chambers anymore!"

"Stop the melodrama. The Holocaust was abominable, but it's behind us. Let me remind you, yours isn't the only suppressed or slaughtered race." He swept the air with the back of his hand. "What about the Armenians at the hands of the Turks, the Bosnians at the hands of the Serbs? No, yours isn't the only race that's been singled out for extermination. That's past history. We shouldn't forget it, but it's time to move on."

Adar walked over and sat down in the chair opposite Gordon. "You are a sanctimonious ass. What gives you the right to tell Israelis to move on? You want us to make peace with the Palestinians. Give up land that we have won in wars forced upon us! These savages of the earth kill our women, children, and old men. They attack farmers that work the fields in the desert. The same fields that we, not they, turned into fertile land. They attack unarmed buses and synagogues! They storm beaches and shoot innocent people in the back! NO, NO, we will not ever trust them. We will never give them land to launch attacks against us!" His voice was now raised two octaves above normal. "Look, Mateusz, the Jews aren't angels either! Let me remind you of a little history. On September 15, 1982, the Israeli army surrounded the refugee camps of Sabra and Shatila in West Beirut. No one entered, no one left without passing through Israeli checkpoints. That afternoon both refugee camps were shelled from the hills above. The next day with the Israeli army standing guard, the Phalangist militia was allowed to enter the camps to find and kill terrorists. Over the next two days your forces stood by and watched as a large number of unarmed civilians, mostly children, women and elderly people, were raped, killed, and injured by the Phalangist militia. Then your Israeli army stood by and watched, and at times helped, as there were systematic roundups that resulted in dozens of disappearances. Reports vary but some say as many as 3,500 innocent people died. How can you disown the innocent people who died there? No, your soldiers did not pull the triggers, but they had the means to stop it. Instead, they stood by and watched the Palestinian massacre.

"No, Mr. Israeli Defense Minister, your Jewish race is as guilty of atrocities as all others. You want to play the game? You want fifteen billion dollars and access to U.S. technology? Then you play by our rules. Negotiate and cooperate with the formation of a Palestinian state. Or you can stand-alone with your sovereign country and all that goes with it. I'll be waiting for your answer." As he turned and left the room he was pleased to see Adar red-faced and breathing fast.

Ten minutes after receiving the Israeli Defense Minister's reply that his government would sit and negotiate for the creation of a free Palestinian state, John Gordon met with Hassan Abba Shaar, Minister of the Palestinian Liberation Organization. Gordon felt his margin for success was far greater now that he had the Israeli's agreement to negotiate and hopefully cooperate. Nevertheless, he knew dealing with the Palestinians would not be easy. They were as blindly stubborn concerning concessions with the Jews, as the Jews were with them.

Shaar stood stiffly in the entranceway of the Gazebo that sat on the manicured lawn overlooking Sun Moon Lake. Though the light was low when Gordon approached, he could still make out the large girth around Shaar's waist. Gordon had never seen him smile. He wondered if Shaar was capable of it. Gordon approached and immediately set the tone of their conversation. "Let me give you the bottom line, Mr. Shaar. The political situation in the P.L.O. is far more acute than you wish to admit. Since the 1991 Gulf War the P.L.O. has lost its support from the Arab Gulf states, losing millions of dollars in aid. The P.L.O. is on the verge of bankruptcy, and your power is slipping away. The P.L.O. has enemies, Arabs and non-Arabs everywhere. Your Chairman has a bull's-eye painted on his chest. The only question is who will put a bullet through it first. The Jews or the Arabs."

The P.L.O. Minister replied, "If you are convinced we are through, there is no reason to negotiate with us." He spoke with a thick Middle East accent. He turned his back to Gordon and walked to the opposite side of the Gazebo. Though more than one hundred pounds overweight he carried himself with smooth fluid steps that were diametrically opposite his Jewish counterpart's quick jerky movements. He stopped at the railing and appeared to stare out over the lake.

Gordon ignored the comment and continued, "Here's the deal. The Israelis will stop the settlements in the West Bank, and they will allow the Gaza Strip to become a Palestinian state under the Israeli flag for five years. At the end of that term the Palestinians can have their independence. The only conditions are those I laid out the last time we met. And yes, the P.L.O. is close to its demise. That is why you will negotiate."

"I am impressed by your ability to force the Jews into such negotiations," Shaar said. "But what gives you the right to pass judgment and force political agreements, especially agreements that concern Palestinian land? Land held illegally by the Israelis?"

"You can call it your land from now to eternity. The fact is, the Israelis occupy and control it. In addition, neither the P.L.O., Syria nor Jordan will be able to displace them militarily, now or in the near future. Therefore, either you compromise and cooperate or this deal, and any in the near future, is dead. Even worse, the world will know that the Israelis finally agreed to a Palestinian State, but the P.L.O., who bills themselves as the defenders of all Palestinians, declined. In addition, you will sign openly and unconditionally a peace treaty with Israel, recognizing Israel as a sovereign country that has the right to exist and live in peace. And lastly you will put a stop to all suicide attacks." Without another word, John Gordon walked away.

The following evening they gathered in the dinning room. John Gordon was pleased. Negotiations had started. Though tense, they were at least talking.

Gordon raised his glass. "Again...I toast both of you. I..." The sound of gunfire and the thud of large explosives interrupted the peace of the night. The door to the dinning room burst open and a guard ran in. "Come! Take cover in the basement! We are under attack!"

The walls suddenly exploded in a spray of splintering wood as a shower of bullets ripped through the large picture window. The guard, struck multiple times, died before he hit the floor.

"Duck! Take cover!" yelled Gordon as he threw himself onto the hard wood floor.

Silence quickly descended upon the Inn. The attack had not lasted very long. The terrorists were professionals. They left nothing to chance.

The diplomats stayed huddled in the corner, shock and fear bonding them in a way no treaty could. The silence was oppressive, until three men burst into the room. The dark scarves wrapped around their heads covered their heads and faces with only their eyes showing. Each held an AK-47 machine gun. Their eyes darted around the room as their guns stayed pointed at the three cowering diplomats.

"Anyone moves and I will kill you!" one of them called out.

"Arab terrorists!" Adar, the Israeli Minister, spoke up, his voice trembling. He looked first at the terrorist, then at Gordon. "This is why we can never trust them. They have no honor. They don't know what peace is."

"Quiet, Jew pig! No talking!"

They heard the sound of footsteps approaching on the hardwood floor. Through the archway, a fourth masked terrorist entered and stopped. He was slightly above average height with coal black eyes that bore into the victims as he surveyed the room. "I am Mohammed Khanum." He spoke in fluent accent free English. Khanum slowly walked over to the diplomats until he stood in front of Hassan Abba Shaar, the P.L.O. Minister. "So it is true. You sleep with swine, with sons of whores."

Gordon pulled himself to his feet. He stood eight inches taller than the terrorists and looked down onto him. "I am John Gordon, the Secretary of State to the United States of America. You are undertaking a very serious act. My country will not tolerate this barbaric deed!"

"You are the United States Secretary of State?"

"Yes."

Khanum's pistol hit him in the mouth and he fell to the floor. "Now you are dog meat."

He turned to Shaar as Gordon slowly wiped his mouth. "It is true. They tell me you sit and talk to dogs, and sniff their backsides. You disgrace our people, our cause! You are too vile a swine to let live. I will kill you now!" He raised his pistol.

"No!" Adar dove towards Shaar, and threw him out of the way as the shot rang out. Moment's later the Palestinian lay under the Israeli. Shaar was dazed and confused, but unhurt. Adar, though, had a bullet in his left shoulder.

"So, Shaar, you are such a weak woman you need the protection of a Jew whore!" The terrorist kicked Sharr in the side repeatedly. "So be it, for soon you'll all be dead! For now you can hide behind his skirt!" After one final vicious blow to Shaar's side, he left the room followed by the others.

Adar, the Israeli Defense Minister, sat on the floor, wincing in pain. He pressed his right hand tightly over the bleeding from his left shoulder.

"Lay still. Let's take a look." Gordon approached him.

"I think I'm all right. It hurts like hell…but I'll live."

Shaar knelt beside him. "You saved my life, and risked yours."

"Sometimes," Adar sputtered, "we do things we swore we'd never do. I couldn't stand by and watch him murder you."

"Your gesture moves me, my friend. You have given me my life…though it seems for just a short time. I am in your debt."

Adar turned his eyes towards Gordon. "I thought more about what you said last night. They were words most people are afraid to say to us because we are Jews. It is time to move on, time to try." Adar glanced at his bleeding shoulder then continued, "But I am afraid this gesture will be in vain."

"Yes, I fear my idiot compatriots plan our deaths to further their own cause…denying us any hope of ours," Shaar spoke to no one in particular as he looked around the room.

*   *   *   *

Washington, D.C.

In the bowels of the National Security Agency building, the first indication of a problem was the coded message that flashed onto the screen. Passed through many satellites and relay stations, the high frequency message that emanated from John Gordon's belt buckle indicated he was alive, but taken hostage. Many emissaries had carried this security system on secret missions, but this was the first time someone had needed to activate it.

*   *   *   *

On the fourth floor of the Central Intelligence Agency in Langley, Virginia, Abraham sat at his desk reviewing satellite photographs of the Bering Strait. The Japanese had recently been caught over fishing their salmon quota. The government had asked the C.I.A. to help track the many small vessels they used.

Abraham, now seventy-two, was highly regarded by the intelligence community. After World War II, he had resettled in the United States and developed a keen skill for photo interpretation. While working on his P.H.D. thesis in photo analysis of migratory birds to help predict long-term weather patterns, he had been tapped by the government to interpret satellite photographs of the Soviet Union, a crucial job during the cold war. Abraham was a quiet person who rarely showed emotion. His colleagues and friends interpreted that as a scholarly persona that his white hair and closely cropped beard reinforced. Abraham knew different. He was afraid if he opened up even a little, he would be unable to deal with the flood of sorrow he carried in his heart. So when he talked it was with a gentle demeanor.

The phone rang, but he methodically finished his notation before answering it. Much to his surprise, he was summoned to Al Niddiem's office. The Director of the agency wanted to speak to him personally. Abraham reluctantly closed his notebook, and then put both it and the photos into a locked drawer.

When he arrived at Niddiem's office, the secretary immediately ushered him in. He took a seat across the desk from the Director. Niddiem was completely bald and when he spoke he was very animated with his hands. His face was round and full. His fingers were short and plump and when he talked while standing his portly belly jiggled. He had given up on a belt a long time ago trading it in for suspenders.

"Abraham, it appears we have a very delicate, very crucial hostage situation in Taiwan. Terrorists took the Secretary of State, Israeli's Defense Minister and a high-ranking P.L.O. Minister hostage. We do not know who they are.

"Here are some background pictures of where they were staying. I cannot tell you the nature of the meeting. But, I will tell you this meeting is so critical we are immediately moving forward with a hostage rescue. What I need from you is your best analysis of the latest satellite photos. We'll have the photos downloaded within the hour. I want to know if you can tell us anything about the size and strength of the hostile force. And if they have any reinforcements in the vicinity."

"How soon do you need it?" Abraham asked with a poker face.

"I want as much as you can give us in four hours. Then I want you to meet with Colonel Burnhall. His men will be conducting the hostage rescue. Burnhall requested your participation in the briefing of his team in case they have any questions."

Before Abraham could object Al had his hand raised, cutting him off. "I know you're leaving for Israel in the A.M. We will get you down to Fort Bragg and back by helicopter. I promise you will have plenty of time left to pack. We need you on this one."

"Megan can do it." Abraham said. "She's excellent and I think she's more than ready for her own team."

"I know she's good. However, Burnhall requested you. I promise you won't miss your flight."

Abraham got up slowly as if deep in thought but inside he was emotionally tired. This was his first vacation since his wife, Clara, died.

*   *   *   *

A third of the way around the world from the beauty and serenity of Sun Moon Lake sits a small patch of land that has little beauty left, the Bekka Valley in Lebanon. Years of war and civil unrest have taken its toll on what was, many years ago, an alluring countryside. The meadows that once held wildflowers in abundance are now gutted with craters from artillery shells and bombs. Their haphazard appearance contrasts dramatically with the neat rows of ditches found along the one dirt road that runs through the valley. These ditches were dug by men and contain the carcasses of men, women and children, all innocent victims of the falling artillery and random gunfire.

Not far from this field sat a bombed out, bullet-riddled farmhouse, long abandoned by a family now rotting in the ditch by the side of the house.

General Kazem Malek stared through a jagged hole that once was a window. He reached up and touched a hideous scar that started on the brim of his nose and swept down to his left cheek. The cut had partially severed a nerve and a portion of his left cheek did not move when he talked. The past few years had been a wild roller-coaster ride for this forty-year-old Iraqi soldier, emotionally as well as professionally. He and his people had been led from relative peace and security into hell's fire. However, the quirks of fate that sent some to their deaths propelled others forward in their careers. Such was the case for Kazem Malek. His rise in the Iraqi military was impressive. He still felt the personal pride of being the executioner of General Akkad, his commander. General Akkad had been a fool. If Akkad had only listened to Lt. Colonel Malek the '91' Gulf War might have ended differently. Kazem had pushed and pressured Akaad to launch at Israel the Scud missiles filled with chemical weapons, the same weapons that still lay hidden in the sands of western Iraq. Akkad had no spine. He had dismissed Kazem's repeated requests and pleas to send the Jews to their well-deserved deaths. Akkad had feared the Jews' response, and worse, that of the United States.

Malek would later say at Akkad's trial that Akkad was blind, a man with no vision. Couldn't Akkad see that by killing Jews in such a barbaric way they would have been forced to retaliate? Certainly, the Jews would have attacked innocent people with nuclear bombs. All Islam could then have united against this unholy act.

Lt. Colonel Malek had enjoyed the process of charging that foolish Akkad with stupidity and treason. Malek had savored the sentence, "immediate death", handed down personally by Saddam Hussein. Saddam had honored Malek by choosing him to carry out the sentence. He was the one who brought the fool to trial. It was only right he should shoot him.

Most executioners choose anonymity. Colonel Malek, now General Malek, did not. Malek walked up to Akkad and stood in front of him. Malek looked into Akkad's eyes with contempt. One can only imagine the horror Akkad felt. In a strident voice Malek read the charges of treason. With little ceremony, he raised his pistol to Akkad's face and pulled the trigger.

Now the war was officially over, but General Kazem Malek would exact his revenge. Though it was too late to change the course of recent history, he would make sure the future was bathed again with the blood of Jews.

Malek turned from the slight breeze that floated through the open hole in the wall and faced two zealot Palestinians. They had been ranting and raving non-stop during his self-reflection.

"We must slaughter all these Jew pigs!" Moustafa said. "We will not stop until we have replaced their filth with a righteous Islamic Palestine state that is governed by the laws of Islam." Moustafa paced, punctuating his words with his fists. "Sheik Arash calls for all members of Hamas to elevate this holy war against the Zionist Jews to its bloodiest level. We will not let the deaths of our past martyrs be in vain. Those cowards will pay. They think they can simply send their helicopter gun-ships and tanks anywhere and kill without any repercussions?"

Malek let him rant. He is pleased with his choice. He remembers presenting their files to the Iraqi Security Council for approval.

At nineteen, Adan Moustafa was already a seasoned fighter...or terrorist, as some prefer to call him. His fanaticism was rooted in the deep religious belief that his cause was just and righteous. Adan had no political hatred for Jews or the state of Israel. His fight was based on religious matters and becoming a martyr for the cause was his ultimate wish. He had become an extremely dangerous opponent. One would never have guessed that from his appearance. He was overly thin, almost malnourished with dark hair and bony fingers. Adan talked in an annoying singsong whine that grated on most people's nerves. His thinness made his small five foot six inch body seem taller when he was at a distance.

Adan's brother, Ehaib, two years younger and two inches shorter was a carbon copy of him. Ehaib had long ago been indoctrinated to the cause by Adan, having killed seven people before the age of fifteen.

Malek smiled remembering how the council approved them unanimously.

General Malek, on the other hand, cared nothing for their religious cause. His hate was political and personal. As far as he was concerned, the Jews had manipulated people and governments against his own people. General Malek simply wanted the Jews annihilated.

Malek had had enough of their ranting. "Enough! If the two of you want to continue spouting your rabid hatred, then do it on your own time. When you are ready, join me in the next room." He stepped over the rubble and debris and walked into the adjoining room.

"What a pompous idiot," Adan said to his brother. "We will tolerate his attitude for the time being, but he better not push us." They then joined Malek in the next room.

General Malek stood next to a table made of a piece of war-scarred wood that sat on top of a small pile of broken bricks. "Near the seaport of Haifa, at this address," he handed Adan a piece of paper, "the two of you will pick up a small shipment of bricks similar to this one." The General held up a brick with his left hand revealing only four fingers, the little finger had been shot off in a gun battle. "They've already arrived by boat and are at the brick yard at this address." He handed them a piece of paper. "You'll then drive to Jerusalem. There you will go to the Russian Orthodox Church. It is off Jaffa Road, near Zion Square. On the top of that church the bricks that face west have been destroyed. The two of you will replace them with the bricks that you pick up in Haifa."

"And how do we kill the Jews," Adan asked? "Do we drop the bricks on their heads as they walk by?"

General Malek's jaw tightened. This contorted his face to the right, away from the paralyzed side. A moment later, he relaxed and continued, "It is very important that when you position the bricks and mortar them in place, the side that has this small blemish is facing out. Inside each brick is a canister that contains a powerful, lethal gas. The timing device will be set automatically when you leave Haifa. At midnight of that day each brick will release its gas. All those within a few blocks will die. They will not be able to trace the gas to the bricks or to us.

"There will be massive death, but no destruction. I will have my revenge and you will be that much closer to regaining your land." Malek looked at the two men, then handed them a small pouch as he continued, "Here are the papers that will allow you passage through Israel."

Malek smiled as he watched them grip their documents.

Adan and Ehaib looked at each other with fire in their eyes and chanted in a high-pitched screech. "Allahu Akhbar!" (God is great.)

3   Chapter Three

Sam Davon took his time and slowly made his way through the thick underbrush. He moved through the woods silently, undetected by anyone or anything. His small stature of only five feet seven inches made him even harder to spot. Sam had learned long ago that height and pure brawn didn't necessarily make you the best warrior. His cinnamon skin and black hair stereotyped him upon sight as a Native American Indian but his facial features had a sharp noble quality that hinted of Polynesian ancestry many generations ago.

Sam had spent a large amount of time in the wilderness when he was younger. Growing up he had studied the old ways of his Sioux ancestors. The tales his now-deceased great grandfather Chieftain had told him had fascinated him. Chief Gluscabi, had been leader of the local tribe. He was a Lakota, or western Sioux, from the plains area. Sam had sat at his great grandfather's feet many times listening to him talk of the rights and wrongs of this world, and the after world. As he listened to the tales, he learned how to respect and communicate with nature. At thirty-six Sam put what he had learned to good use. With 20/10 vision and the skills passed down to him from his Grandfathers Sam could move around the woods with tremendous stealth.

Sam advanced through the woods. He placed each step with care. His foot sensed the ground beneath him, applying the right amount of pressure, avoiding any sound.

It had been a good day. Sam had tracked his prey with skill and tactical cunning. He was confident the deer heard only the sounds of nature and none of the sounds of his human presence. This was Sam's gift. He and nature could be one.

Sam watched the eleven-point red deer as it strutted back and forth in a small clearing. Any hunter would prize its velvet-covered antlers for their wall. The deer pranced proudly around his three females, each with a new calf. He rocked his head armor back and forth, showing them they were safe to tend their offspring, his offspring. It was the calves' feeding time. This tended to be a vulnerable time for them because the females paid attention only to their calves.

Sam froze as the stag walked near him, its ears and eyes sharp, ready in an instant to lower its antlers and attack to protect its calves and hinds. For Sam, this moment of approach was the most dangerous. If discovered the stag would gore him and stomp him to death in an instant. This added danger made the hunt even more challenging and intriguing for him.

He lay motionless, his breathing slow and shallow, as the stag walked to within five feet of him. Sam had his human scent disguised with the perfume of flowers. Sam was indeed a chameleon. He looked through the eyepiece and brought the feeding calves into focus. His trigger finger held steady as he waited for the appropriate time to shoot.

The stag walked back to his family and stopped. Sam watched the stag's head rise high, proud of his family. There was one moment when all eyes were upon their male protector. That was the moment. Sam took the shot. Nothing moved, nothing was disturbed. The camera was made for complete silence. Even the fine click of the shutter had been suppressed. Frame after frame he captured a moment in nature rarely seen by man.

As he concentrated, he felt a fine vibration. He carried a message beeper that never left his side. Today it was on silent mode. He knew his was not the only beeper going off right now. An unknown number of other beepers were simultaneously vibrating or beeping. Sam had two hours to assemble with the others and find out where and into what hell they would be sent.

With a sigh, he withdrew. Sam used as much care and silence in his retreat as he had used in his approach. He was satisfied. He had his trophy. These pictures would hang on his wall and the walls of his friends. He was indeed a great hunter. However, he did not kill animals. Sam only killed when he hunted humans. To him humans were the most savage beasts on Earth.

*   *   *   *

The barbed wire fence had only one entrance, and next to it was posted a solitary blue sign that read "SECURITY OPERATION TRAINING FACILITY". Within this compound in an isolated part of Fort Bragg, North Carolina sat the headquarters and training area of the clannish and insular "Delta Force". This team was so special the United States government and military would not officially acknowledge its existence. The men who trained within this inner sanctum were not muscle-bound Rambo show-boaters. They were warriors whose intelligence was as dangerous as their fighting ability. Their kind had replaced the snake-eaters who survived the Vietnam War.

Six members of this elite force sat talking quietly amongst themselves. They talked mostly about family and friends. Most of them were family men, teetotalers and extremely religious. They believed strongly in their convictions, and assignments.

Colonel Burnhall, the Commander of Delta Special Forces, entered without fanfare. He wore full combat fatigues and though reaching the later part of his fifth decade, his body was rock hard. The Colonel had salt and pepper hair that was in a regulation military buzz cut. At five feet ten inches, he filled out his uniform with a forty-eight inch chest and biceps to match. He could and did on many training missions keep up and even surpass his men. It was rare for him to conduct a briefing, so they knew something extremely urgent was going on. The Colonel had spent twenty-seven years in the Special Forces. He started as one of those lone-wolf dirt-eaters who roamed the jungles of North Vietnam on suicide missions. However, early on he learned the importance of teamwork, camaraderie and mental, as well as physical, toughness.

Burnhall started speaking before he reached the small podium that stood in the front corner of the room. "I would like to get started. Please open the files in front of you." His voice projected a pride and confidence in his men.

All six broke the seals on the files in front of them in unison. They opened to the first page, which was an extremely clear, crisp photograph of Sun Moon Lake. Though taken from sixty thousand feet, even the vegetation could be clearly distinguished.

"This is a picture of Sun Moon Lake," the Colonel continued. "It is two hundred and seventy-six kilometers west of Taipei, on the Island of Taiwan. As you can see, the building in the lower left is isolated. The only direct access is by boat. There is a road and a dock in the northern end of the lake. That is visible in the middle of the picture. At 03:20 Eastern Standard Time the occupants of this resort were taken captive by unknown hostiles. Next three pages please."

They turned to three eight by ten-color glossies of three different men.

"These are the known captives. The first picture you should recognize as John Gordon, the Secretary of State. The second is Mateusz Adar, Israel's Defense Minister. And the last is of Hassan Abba Shaar, the Defense Minister for the P.L.O.

"Their condition is unknown. We have no idea who the assailants are or what they want. For now, we will go on the assumption that all three are alive. Next page...this is a copy of the floor plan of the Inn. We have no onsite intelligence. We have no idea which room, or rooms, the hostages are in."

The six looked back and forth between the pictures.

"Unfortunately, this is all we have in such a short period of time. I think you realize the urgency of this mission, as well as the danger. You will not have time to practice. You will have to rely completely on your training, instincts, and intelligence. The speed and completion of this rescue necessitates our deciding here and now how the assault will proceed. You will then depart immediately. Lieutenant Commander Stone is here to help with the planning." Burnhall stepped away from the podium and Commander Stone replaced him.

The briefing lasted close to two hours. The Lieutenant Commander reviewed the multitude of problems that faced them, one of which was complete lack of intelligence on who and how many terrorists were within and around the hotel. They were all concerned, not knowing what type of firepower the terrorists had. Did they have pistols and rifles, or bazookas and grenades? There were many questions with no answers. The Lieutenant quickly devised a plan of attack that maximized this small group's mobility, firepower, surprise factor and survivability.

Finally, the Lieutenant introduced Abraham, "Lastly I want to introduce Abraham Feinstein. He will review the topography of the region and answer any questions concerning the visible strength of the terrorist group that has been spotted."

Abraham took the podium and for the next thirty minutes he reviewed the topography and ground cover of the area around the Inn. He unfortunately had to tell them that in none of the recent satellite photos had he spotted any signs of movement. He could not provide any answers to their many questions. They were flying into the unknown, and he could only tell them where the biggest rocks and shrubs were for their protection.

At the end of the briefing the six members felt satisfied that they had devised, in such a short amount of time, the best possible plan to execute. The briefing ended. There was no milling around for chitchat. They would leave in one hour. They had packing to do and equipment to acquire and check.

4   Chapter Four

Two UH-1N Huey helicopters, the kind made famous during the Vietnam War, hurtled along at one hundred knots in the dead of night at one hundred and fifty feet above the tree tops. The cargo bay of the first lay empty and dark. All lights inside and out, including the navigation lights, were off. The pilots sat in darkness as they sped into the black moonless night in front of them. During the day, the forest west of Sun Moon Lake appeared as an expansive ocean of green trees. But in the dead of the night it blended with the dark sky, producing a black wasteland with no boundary or horizon to guide the pilots.

The Delta team had borrowed these two older styled Hueys from Taiwan's Royal Air Force. They were concerned that bringing their own high tech copters would arouse unnecessary attention.

It was a slightly overcast evening, which made the members on this mission ecstatic. The two pilots had trained for this type of proficiency flying for years. They flew guided by the navigational display illuminated on their Night Vision System (NVS) Helmets. The co-pilots, also wearing NVS Helmets, kept a sharp outlook for unknown obstacles, such as the power lines that crisscrossed the countryside. The NVS Helmets illuminated the blackness of night, making it as clear as day. Although only a little starlight filtered through the overcast evening, the NVS amplified what little light there was twenty-five thousand times. The projected image on the pilots' face shields clearly detailed the land below in phosphorous green.

A small red light illuminated the inside of the second copter's cargo bay. A canvas covered the open cargo bay door, stopping any leakage of light. Sam Davon and his partner, Willie, sat checking their equipment. Willie was an African-American man from Tennessee. At thirty-two, he had mastered four languages other than English. At five foot eleven inches, Willie carried himself with pride and confidence. His muscular frame was agile and fluid in his motions. Willie's brown eyes were as sharp as his jaw was square, and they could penetrate a crowd to find his target without hesitation. For now, he and Sam focused on their equipment.

For this mission they took the M25A assault rifle in place of their M16A2 assault rifles. This piece of equipment had revolutionized weaponry for the Special Forces. Made of poured polymer plastic it was only thirty inches long. It fired a hollow point piece of lead that was encased in a rectangular propellant. It was caseless ammunition. The magazine held fifty shots and the total weight of the gun with five hundred rounds was only ten pounds. With a built in silencer, and a laser site, it was the most deadly assault rifle in the world.

The noise of the copter's rotating blades was deafening inside the cargo bay. Sam and Willie wore earphones and microphones that deadened the noise. This allowed them to talk with the pilot and each other. The copters bounced up and down in violent jerks as the pilots kept close to the treetops. The two pilots flew on skill and instinct. The urgency of the mission had necessitated their immediate departure. There had been no time to review in detail their flight plan, or the ground terrain.

Willie and Sam's chatter tapered off. Intuitively they knew they were close to the drop off point. Their attention was now isolated and focused. They concentrated on their equipment, tightening gear attached to their camouflage suits and rearranging, if only minutely, the weapons and ammunition attached by Velcro straps that surrounded their bodies. There would be no time for opening pockets. The Velcro enabled them with one motion of a hand to pull a full ammo clip from its anchor point and insert it into the vacant slot in their gun. Satisfied that things were in place and properly secured, the two sat back and stared into space meditatively. This was their last private moment to make peace with themselves.

"Three minutes to L.Z. (landing zone). One minute to Hot Guns," the pilot notified them over their headphones.

The co-pilot nodded to Sam and Willie as he climbed into the cargo bay and pulled off a tarp revealing a mini mobile version of a twenty-millimeter Vulcan cannon. This addition was made to the Huey before take off. Its spinning six barrels spewed six thousand rounds per minute and decimated anything in its path. When fired, its enormous muzzle flash belched flames, giving the copter the truly mythical image of a flying fire-breathing dragon.

Next, Sam and Willie removed the black canvas sides to the copter and extinguished the red light. The cargo bay, now exposed to the open black night, filled with the intense noise of the rotors above them and the rush of warm air.

The co-pilot had moved to gunner position. He swung the cannon on its pedestal, aiming its barrel outward. Sam and Willie adjusted and activated their NVS Goggles illuminating the surrounding countryside. The goggles were smaller and lighter than the pilot's NVS Helmets, and just as effective seeing through the night. Individual trees took form and the valleys rolled as far as they could see. The Huey continued bouncing up and down, jostling them.

They looked out to see the second Huey flying parallel to them fifty meters away, its cargo bay open with a gunner operating a similar cannon. The gunner's silhouette was distinctly depicted on their NVS Goggles.

"Let's go to hot guns," the pilot announced over the headphones.

The gunner flipped a switch on his gun. An electric motor whirred, spinning the six barrels clockwise. This gave the illusion that it was now one large cylinder. Sam and Willie flipped the safety off their M25A and activated the infrared strobe on their helmets. The strobe could only be seen using NVS equipment, thus avoiding a friendly fire accident.

"We are hot guns," the gunner announced. The wind whistled through the open bay and the violent bouncing of the craft seemed to increase as they flew closer to the treetops. Sam and Willie took their positions in the opposite open bay door. They stood with their feet wedged against the landing skids, their left arms looped through holding ropes. Their copter suddenly lurched to the right and dropped to within ten feet of the treetops. The other helicopter banked to the left and flew out of vision.

"L.Z. in thirty seconds," the pilot said.

Sam and Willie took off their earphones and instantly ear-splitting thunder assaulted their eardrums as the rotor and engine roared a few feet above their heads. There was no quietness for stealth built into these copters. Sam and Willie concentrated on the terrain as it sped by them despite the wind that pulled at their trousers. They peered at the phosphorous screen that hung inches in front of their faces and searched for the distinct infrared silhouette of the enemy below. Their goggles completely covered their faces, allowing them no direct vision of the outside world. The scene in front of them resembled a futuristic video game, painted in shadows and outlines of phosphorus green and black. They scanned the terrain looking for different shades of purple and red that signified warm-blooded animals…the enemy.

Without warning, their forward momentum stopped and the skids hovered inches above the grass. In that instant Sam and Willie jumped down to a field. They stooped low and in a full sprint made their way towards the perimeter of the landing zone.

"Multiple Tangos (terrorists) at your ten o'clock!" The call came to the copter on the ground from the second Huey flying picket patrol.

No sooner had the warning been issued than the pilot heard the resounding pings of bullet strikes. He pulled on the control lever and the pitch of the whining rotors changed. The copter rocketed into the air. He turned the craft and brought the targets into view. The gunner in the cargo bay squeezed the trigger on the spinning gatling gun. One hundred rounds per second spewed towards the silhouetted shapes now projected on their NVS visors. The field lit up in a frightening light show. Every third bullet was a tracer. That showed the gunner where his aim was truly going, and it terrified the enemy who could only watch the tracers passed over them, decimating them in a deadly volley of lead.

Sam and Willie made their way toward the opposite corner of the perimeter already engulfed in the firefight. For the first few seconds of the attack they were only spectators. An instant later, that changed. From the brush thirty feet to their right distinct muzzle flashes of fully automatic machine-guns illuminated the area. The enemy had spotted them.

Both men reacted immediately, firing off multiple three shot bursts at the group. Willie hit one sniper in the chest, whose gun tumbled through the air as he fell to the ground. The other three, hidden by trees, stayed momentarily out of harm's way, firing from the protection of the tree trunks.

The second Huey spun to the left and brought its gunner into view of the three that were firing at Sam and Willie. The gunner squeezed the trigger, but quickly released it, stopping the deadly barrage. The flashing strobes on Sam and Willie's helmets were too close.

Two snipers took the momentary pause from the arch of tracers angling towards them to dive into deeper brush for cover. Willie quickly centered his laser sight onto the third and squeezed off a three shot burst.

Sam suddenly could not see. The screen of his night vision goggle became awash in a sea of white. A powerful flashlight had illuminated it. He knew he only had an instant before he would die. Instinct took over. The next few seconds seemed to slow to minutes as he crossed the threshold from conscious to subconscious thought. All external input...the roar of the helicopter engines, the thumping of their rotors, even the blasts from the spinning barrels of the gatling gun...ceased to register in his mind. His right thumb flipped the selector switch from triple shot to fully automatic. His index finger pulled the trigger and held it tightly in place. He could feel each individual shot leave the end of his barrel as his weapon slightly recoiled back. He swung his arc of fire from left to right.

Sound and reality returned to Sam as quickly as it had left. His NVS again registered the scene in front of him. Two flashlights flew through the air with their beams now harmlessly directed away from his optic input lens. Only one and a half seconds had elapsed. He had fired fifty shots. With his vision restored, he saw two terrorists sprawled on the grass with their lifeless bodies spilling blood into the dirt. He had escaped once again.

Overhead, the two copters traversed the clearing. Their pilots and gunners scanned the perimeter and the adjacent woods for any further contacts. Sam and Willie also scanned, ready to resume the battle instantly. The copters took positions at opposite ends of the field. When Willie and Sam were satisfied the danger had been neutralized they flickered hand held strobes that were the size of a Zippo lighter. In unison, each copter gunner responded with his own infrared strobe signifying agreement. The Landing Zone was clear. They used no other communication. Radio silence would not be broken unless absolutely necessary.

The copters landed parallel to each other, their guns aimed out and their barrels still spinning. The whine of the engines slowly ceased, and the pulsing of air under the rotors subsided as their rotations diminished. When the noise of the engines finally stopped, the only sound inside the cargo bays came from the whirling gun barrels.

Satisfied the battle had ended, the gunners switched off the electric motors and the spinning barrels slowly stopped. "Guns are cold," was the call over the intercom.

Willie approached Sam, who stood near the two terrorists he had just killed.

"Close one, Sam. Very close." He looked at the bodies then at Sam. "Someone was watching over you."

"It wasn't my time to die." Sam picked up one of the flashlights and shined it for a moment into Willie's NVS goggle, blinding his vision. Willie ducked.

"I see the problem."

"Yeah. It's amazing. All the money they spent on Research and Development for this Night Vision System and a simple flashlight makes them useless."

"We can't worry about that now," Willie said shrugging his shoulders. "Let's get more ammo from the copter and get going."

Gino and Jay stood opposite each other in the belly of a C-130 plane. These two members of the Delta Force Team were to parachute into the lake. Gino grew up in the Italian section of Brooklyn. His large hooked Roman nose offset his curly black hair, green eyes and pearly white teeth. Gino was a devout Christian and always wore a gold cross along with a Saint Christopher medal around his neck. Growing up on the streets of Brooklyn had taught him to throw a punch long before his opponent had consciously thought of it. Being very street smart, he also realized early on that he wanted a better life. His survival skills had led him into the Special Forces where he flourished. Jay on the other hand grew up in Midwest Ohio where he was raised to always be clean cut and polite with a "yes maam, no maam," or "yes sir, no sir" response. He stood five feet eight inches and was prematurely balding at the age of thirty-three. His smile and blue eyes were infectious and easily placed a lesser opponent at a disadvantage.

For the moment Gino and Jay stood safely enclosed within the plane's cocoon. This abruptly changed moments after the red lights above them blinked on and off. As the rear of the plane opened into the black void of night, they held tightly onto the hand rings attached to the hydraulic lifts at the very end of a steel platform that slowly extended behind the plane. Both men were dressed in black neoprene wet suits. Their torsos were loaded with lightweight space age weaponry. At thirty thousand feet the thin air necessitated supplemental oxygen, which was supplied by small bottles attached to their parachute harness. On their feet were oversized diving fins, making even small steps awkward. Despite the equipment Gino knelt down on one knee bowing his head in prayer.

The gantry settled into its open extended position as the wind pulled at both of them, trying to rip them free from their precarious perch. Jay was forced to grab his mask before it was nearly ripped off his face by the wind. Their enhanced images projected sharply onto the screens of each other's diving mask. Along with the Night Vision System that was incorporated into their masks, a digital read out of their position was displayed, constantly updated by the Navstar Global Positioning System Satellite high above. This projected their coordinates to within three feet of their actual position.

The Shoe Shine Boy

They focused their attention on the coordinates displayed on their diving masks. When they had reached their designated jump point, they both took a waddle step into the cold dark sky and plunged earthward. The altitude projected on their diving masks reeled downward with every foot they fell. Presently they were five miles east of their target. Gino spun in the air until the image of Jay came into view, in vivid phosphorous green. Beneath them, their view of the surrounding countryside, its rolling hills and sharp jagged rock ledges were clearly projected on their masks. To the east Gino easily identified their splash point, which was the far end of Sun Moon Lake.

They extended their arms, which made a triangle wing of the cloth between their elbows, armpits and sides. They looked like overgrown bats extending their wings. Their aimless plummet earthward suddenly turned into a glided descent, as they quickly closed the five-mile gap to where they intended to land. The end point was one of the lake's small inlets, which was hidden from the view of the Evergreen Hostel by a sheer peak that rose twelve hundred feet from the water's edge.

In a short time their digital read out informed them they had reached their designated coordinates. They then assumed a wide left hand spiral, corkscrewing downward. When they passed below twelve hundred feet and were hidden by Sun Moon Lake's highest peak, they opened their parachutes. There would be no second chance, no time to pull a reserve chute. At one thousand feet they were too low and traveling too fast for any backup system to work. Both chutes opened with a thump and a snap. Pulling on the shrouds, they guided their rectangular chutes to land them as near to shore as possible.

Gino felt a wave of relief upon entering the cold dark water of Sun Moon Lake. For him the hardest part was over. He hated these HALO (High Altitude Low Opening) jumps. He jettisoned the chute and let the oxygen tank fall to the lake's bottom. He then tugged at the mouthpiece of his closed circuit breathing apparatus peeling it off its Velcro mount, and placed it between his lips. No bubbles were released when he exhaled. This self-contained unit allowed him to swim undetected by those above. He slowly swam five feet beneath the surface until Jay's figure came into view. Even underwater his Night Vision System allowed him clear vision, and his GPS Receivers still picked up data from the Navstar Global Positioning System Satellite orbiting thousands of miles above them. He communicated with Jay through hand and finger signals. They were ahead of schedule. There was no need to rush. They would be early for this party.

Sam moved cautiously along the infrequently traveled, overgrown path that led him and Willie from the landing zone toward their target...the Evergreen Hostel. Every thirty yards he assumed a stable firing stance. With his right knee bent to the ground he scanned the empty path in front of him, gun aimed and ready.

Moments later Willie quickly moved by, making his way thirty yards further down the trail and assuming a similar position. Willie stayed to the left side of the trail, out of Sam's line of fire.

The evening was warm and dark with the occasional whisper of a breeze. To anyone else the trail appeared nondescript, void of any form, shape or shadows. To Sam and Willie, though, every detail, every branch, leaf and rock, projected in full clarity on their Night Vision Goggles. And so it went, back and forth, the two of them leap frogging their way down the trail in complete silence, closing in on their destination.

John Gordon opened his bloodshot eyes and looked around the room. It had been stripped of all its furniture and its second story windows, which sat thirty-five feet above a cement patio, excluded that route as an escape. Nonetheless, Gordon's hands and feet were tied behind his back, as were the two ministers. Early on he realized the terrorists weren't about to take any chances. They had important plans for their eventual deaths.

After a day of tense interrogation, involving physical as well as emotional torture, Gordon was allowed to rest. Rolling onto his buttocks, he swung his feet in front of him. This contortion increased pressure on the rope that bound his wrists tightly behind his back. Gordon had to see how Mateusz Adar, the Israeli Defense Minister, was, for he had just been returned from his interrogation and beating session.

"Mateusz, they didn't spend much time with you. But it appears they gave you your share of the beating." The left side of Adar's face was swollen. It was becoming bright red from the bleeding caused by multiple blows.

"That bastard was just starting to enjoy beating me when another one came in." Adar's speech was slow and labored instead of his typical fast paced and staccato. His lips were parched, and his shoulder bullet wound was bandaged with a bloody cloth. "He said they couldn't make radio contact with the group at the clearing. He left, telling two of them to take new radios to the field. Then they dragged me back here. Something is going on."

"Mateusz, my friend," Hassan Abba Shaar, the P.L.O. Minister, spoke quietly. "I'm so sorry for your pain. I am embarrassed by what my people are doing. I am here to take steps forward...not back. We have to put this hatred behind us so our people can move on. We must open a new chapter in history, a chapter of peace." Shaar lowered his eyes to the floor.

Sam moved instinctively. Each step was placed with gentle quick precision. He was alert, his senses on overdrive. Sam spotted them first, and quickly knelt. His left hand signaled

Willie not to advance. Two figures emerged from around the bend fifty feet in front of Sam and walked toward him in single file, each carried a heavy-duty flashlight, which illuminated the trail at their feet. The vision of the two approaching Sam was limited to the beam of light shinning in front of them, and they had no chance of noticing the two crouched figures up ahead.

The two approaching figures were illuminated in detail on Sam and Willie's screens. Sam, being the lead man, designated his target. The instant the two had come into view, he had activated his gun sight. He brought the beam onto the center of the lead's forehead. Willie took the second one. The infrared lights from their guns, visible only to them, centered on the terrorists' foreheads. As if on cue, Sam and Willie pulled the triggers simultaneously. In the instant it took to aim and fire, the battle was over.

Sam and Willie stepped over the bodies and continued on.

Northwest of Sun Moon Lake, Roger and Carlos sailed in wide circles at twenty thousand feet. Their hang-gliders were fitted with lightweight single piston engines and carbon fiber propellers. They were the third leg of the assault triad. They would be responsible for isolating and protecting the hostages prior to an open assault. Roger and Carlos were to make a silent landing upon the roof of the Evergreen Hostel. They knew the chances were good. The roof was slanted only slightly, providing an ideal landing spot, and it was unlikely that, without the tell tale thump-thump of helicopter rotors, anyone would gaze skyward. All eyes would be scanning the surrounding woods and water for an assault.

The air at this altitude was cold. The men wore tight black flight suits, black gloves, flight masks, and a thick coat of black camouflage grease where their skin was exposed.

Carlos and Roger grew up in Los Angeles but it was impossible to tell that they had grown up less than twenty miles from each other. That was the nature of Los Angeles. Growing up in East L.A. Carlos developed a fiery Mexican temper that was explosive, especially when he was referred to as a Puerto Rican. This was a constant obstacle since he moved to the East Coast with the Special Forces Team. Carlos aggressively and without hesitation defended his Mexican heritage.

In contrast to Carlos, who stood only five feet seven with dark black hair and brown eyes, Roger stood six feet tall. He sported bleached blond hair, blue eyes and a soft baby face smile. Roger's demeanor was laid back and interspersed by a reply of 'cool'. He emanated the attitude that there was no problem insurmountable. On occasion Carlos would try to raise Roger's dander and get him mad. Carlos would inevitably end up as the one enraged when the only response evoked from Roger was 'Chill Carlos'.

Carlos and Roger hung in harness with their hands gently grasping the control bar. They wore one of the most sophisticated flight helmets designed. It incorporated a Night Vision System, all flight data, altimeter, air speed, and positioning from the Navstar Global Satellite. All readings were displayed on one screen within the mask.

They banked to the left and kept a constant altitude of twenty thousand feet with airspeed of forty-five miles per hour. In the dark void of night, each man's infrared image was projected on the other's screen. They breathed supplemental oxygen from a mask and ignored the cold wind that tugged at their faces. The countryside below was clearly defined, and in the upper right corner of their screens the digital clock read out turned from 03:59 to 04:00. It was time. They simultaneously shut down the turning propeller and jettisoned the engines. Their airspeed slowed and their rate of descent picked up. They glided in radio silence. There was nothing to talk about. They had gone over this countless times.

With a slight pressure on the bar, Roger made a subtle course correction to the right after glancing at the two numbers projected in the left corner of his field of vision. One number represented the direction he needed to fly to reach the target. The other number represented the direction he was traveling in. When both matched, he was heading correctly.

Under any other circumstance, he would have been ecstatic flying this high tech glider. This was work though, not play. This was a deadly game. No sense of exhilaration in flying came to him today. He glanced over to Carlos whose infrared image was still easy to see. Their courses were matched.

His chronograph read 4:21 and his altimeter passed below one thousand feet. Forward air speed was forty-three miles per hour. Directly in front of him was the Evergreen Hostel with its rolling lawn and walkway that led to the dock by the water's edge. It was decision time, to land on the roof, or abort and land on the lawn. It looked good. The wind was still, and there was no sign of the terrorists. Roger looked at Carlos, who gave him a thumbs up sign. Agreeing, Roger depressed a small button on the glider's bar. On the visor of all six squad members a small green light blinked for ten seconds, and then went out. The mission was a go. There was no aborting from this point on.

Three minutes earlier, Sam and Willie had made their way on their stomachs to the rear lawn of the hotel. They kept fifty yards between them at all times. By now they could identify the guards at the building's perimeter. One hundred feet to Sam's left, protected by the roof of an ornate gazebo, stood one terrorist. Sam's laser sight illuminated the right side of his target's head that stood in profile. Sam's gun slightly pushed against his shoulder as its three burst shot spit out silently. A perfect head shot. The guard fell lifelessly to the wooden floor, the opposite side of his head missing.

The Shoe Shine Boy

At the lake's shore, Gino surfaced ten feet from the dock. A terrorist stood there staring out across the water, unaware of the laser sight pointed at him from Gino's gun. Death came before any recognition of danger could register. The front of his face and the back of his skull disappeared. As the terrorists fell silently earthward the two masked creatures from the deep shed their breathing tanks and pulled their way onto shore.

Each assault group on the ground now held its position. Stage one was complete. High above, Roger took the lead. He slowly spiraled down towards the far end of the building. At one hundred feet he banked left, then after a short straight run, banked hard right, gliding over the roof. The screen in front of his face changed quickly giving him instant readouts of speed, height and direction. He fell to within six inches of the clay tiled roof and pushed up on the bar, stalling his forward motion. Aided by thick soft rubber boots, he stepped lightly onto the tile, and, just as gently, placed the glider into its resting position. Before he had unhitched himself from the harness, Carlos had duplicated the soundless landing.

The two of them made their way slowly and silently to the edge of the roof. Carlos pulled a plastic tube from his small pack and extended it. He lay on his stomach and lowered the periscope over the edge. With his eyes pressed against the viewfinder he peered through it into the room below. Their analysis of the building had been correct. They had purposely landed on the highest part of the building. They assumed the terrorists would put the hostages on the top floor to discourage escape. Sure enough, all three were bound and gagged, alive but much abused. Carlos saw one of them had a shoulder wound. Carlos scanned the room, but saw no one else.

John Gordon was the first to notice a man wearing a futuristic helmet covered with optical lenses lower himself through the open window. He wore a black flame resistant suit, and a lightweight bulletproof vest with numerous accessories held in place by velcro strips. Gordon watched him kneel and hold up a blackened hand to his mouth gesturing for silence. He nodded his understanding. He wasn't surprised. He'd expected them. But he was astonished at the silence with which he entered. Gordon watched in amazement as the man ignored them, and instead knelt facing the closed door with his strange weapon raised and aimed.

Within moments he saw a second identically dressed figure enter. This one immediately approached him. A razor sharp hunting knife appeared from nowhere and his ropes were cut. "We're here to get all of you out alive," the rescuer whispered into his ear. "But you are our first priority. Please do exactly as we tell you. Do not try to help us, or your companions in any way. That's our job. Do you understand, Mr. Secretary?"

"Yes," replied Gordon nodding.

Mateusz Adar, the Israeli Defense Minister, stirred and noticed the intruders. "If you must kill me do it quickly. Let me die like a man…with dignity," his voice squeaked.

"You must keep quiet," Roger whispered into his ear. "We're not here to kill you. We're here to free you. You must do as we say without question or you and the rest of us might die. Do you understand?"

Roger cut his bonds and received a nod of acknowledgement. Next he released the P.L.O Minister, Hassan Shaar.

With all three free, Roger quickly took note of their injuries and assessed how they would hinder the rescue if they needed to move fast. He decided only the Israeli would need help. He motioned with his hands for the three hostages to lie flat on the floor in the far corner of the room. Then he took his position against the wall to one side of the door. Carlos remained ten feet in front of the door with his gun aimed at it.

Roger broke radio silence for the first time since the rescue was declared a go. He swiveled the small microphone on his helmet in front of his mouth and said quietly, "Hawks have hit a Home Run."

Outside, Sam raised his right hand, signaling Willie to move into position at the rear door. He then watched for Willie's signal. When it came, he moved with graceful swiftness across the manicured lawn with the infrared strobe on his helmet barely bobbing with each step. The laser sight from his gun always pointed at the house.

Gino and Jay heard Roger's code words and similarly started to move across the grass that led from the dock to the other side door. However, upon rounding a statue, they ran head on into a two-man patrol leisurely making rounds. Both terrorists fell silently to the ground with bullet holes in the side of their heads. When in position at the side door, Gino activated a ten second signal that blinked a green light in everyone's visor. Moments later, Sam activated his signal. All were in position.

After again reminding the diplomats to stay down, Roger removed two stun grenades from their attachments and pulled the pin on one. He opened the door slightly, and then tossed it over the railing onto the floor of the main living room below. Seconds later he pulled the pin of the second, which had a longer delay, and sent it flying in the same direction.

Two terrorists were on the first floor. One saw the grenade land six feet from him but couldn't react fast enough. There was an enormous flash, then a tremendous bang. The entire Inn vibrated, and the concussion threw them upside down towards the rear of the large room. Though stunned, they were still alive.

Within seconds, two other terrorists ran out of a bedroom on the first floor. They were confused and slightly disoriented. Their sleep had been abruptly disturbed. Nevertheless they

David Mucci

had their weapons ready as they searched for targets. As they entered the room, the second grenade exploded. Sam and Gino, with their teams at different entrances to the hostel, then blew the doors off their mounts with small charges and entered.

Sam and Willie rushed the living room and found themselves in the middle of a firefight. The advantage, though, was theirs. The terrorists shot aimlessly and randomly across the room. Their senses were still trying to cope with the disruption from the stun grenades and the unexpected intrusion. Sam moved slowly on the first floor. His laser sight cut through the darkness, and centered on a silhouetted image in the middle of his screen. With a squeeze of the trigger the image fell. Willie spotted two more in the dark recesses of the hall. With his weapon on full automatic he unleashed a deadly barrage of lead that decimated both terrorists.

"Kill the hostages!" came a cry from the second floor, down the hall from where Roger, Carlos, and the hostages were.

Roger threw the door open and fell prone on the floor. This gave Carlos, who hadn't moved from his kneeling position, an unobstructed aim. They both unleashed an impassable wall of lead as one terrorist attempted to run down the hall towards them.

Sam and Willie moved deeper into the dark living room as Gino and Jay moved up the opposite hallway towards them. Their flashing strobes clearly identified them to each other. Willie froze when Gino's infrared sight beamed directly onto him. In the last instant it lifted off his shoulder, and three rounds rushed by his left ear, striking their mark only feet behind him. One of the terrorists originally stunned by the grenades stood up, gun in hand. Now he lay dead.

Sam and Willie spun around in a 360-degree arch, firing. They ended any possibility that the others stunned on the floor might interfere with this rescue operation. Their orders were clear. They were to take no prisoners if there was any danger to the hostages. Sam and Willie emptied their clips, and without missing a beat, replaced them with full ones. They then proceeded down the hall.

When all the rooms on the first floor had been searched, the four moved up the stairs. They leap frogged the same way Sam and Willie had done in the woods. When they reached the platform, they broke off into two groups to search and secure the remainder of the Inn.

"YOU WILL DIE!" came the scream from one final terrorist as he dove through a doorway and onto the floor, his weapon wildly throwing bullets haphazardly. Before he hit the floor to take better aim he was dead.

Sam entered the hostage room and looked around. Carlos rose from his kneeling position.

"Gentlemen, are you all able to walk?" Sam asked.

"Yes," their voices were shaky.

Adar stood but his legs buckled and he fell to the floor. Shaar instantly hoisted him up and wrapped his log-sized arm around him. "I will help you my friend," he said in a deep voice. "It is the least I can do." Shaar pulled Adar into his soft large girth. "We can go now," he said to Sam.

"Stay between us as we move down the stairs. If we yell, dive towards the floor. Do you understand?"

"Yes."

Sam and Willie took the lead far ahead of the group. The three diplomats were sandwiched between Gino and Carlos in front and Roger and Jay in the rear. At the front door Sam and Willie stopped them momentarily. Seconds later they heard the distinct thump-thump of helicopter rotors. Both copters landed simultaneously in the yard outside, their rotors spinning at full speed, the gunners manning the spinning gatling guns.

"Let's go! Now!" Sam yelled.

The entire group ran out of the Inn and across the lawn. As they ran, each member of the rescue team spun and turned, giving maximum coverage and observation to their surroundings. They would not allow a sniper to ruin a picture perfect operation.

Once in the helicopter, John Gordon leaned over to Sam, who stood on the copter's skids, and yelled in his ear over the roar of the engine and the blast of the rotor. "I want to thank you for saving our lives. Who are you?"

"I am nobody, Mr. Secretary, and this didn't happen. We do not exist! You will forget you ever saw us! And I trust you'll impress this upon the other diplomats."

"I understand, son. I understand." He extended his hand and they shook.

With barely enough time for Sam to step off the landing skid, the copter was up and beyond the tree line, and out of harm's way. Sam and the five others climbed into the second copter and in an instant were in the air. Eleven minutes had elapsed from the time the first stun grenade had gone off to the second copter leaving the Inn's lawn. It had been a flawless exercise. Just as fast as it had happened Sun Moon Lake returned to its tranquil existence.

5   Chapter Five

While New York was considered the melting pot for America and the modern world, Jerusalem has always been the true city of immigrants. People from parts of the Middle East, Africa and now the states that were once part of the former Soviet Union, flocked to this city, which has endured for thousands of years. What brought them here was difficult to pinpoint, for it was different for everyone. Some ran from persecution. Others felt an inner need to be at the world's religious center. Christians, Jews, and Muslims alike have held this city in reverence.

The atmosphere of Jerusalem was as difficult to describe as the varying social cultures that inhabit it. The mixture of fragrances and smells that are distinct to any given culture permeated the air, varying from street corner to street corner. Arab women, covered head to toe by hand embroidered dresses, slowly strolled the same streets as the bearded Hasidic Jews, who scurried around under their broad black hats and garments. But every inhabitant of this ancient city had one thing in common, fear. Fear for their proud city, and for their own survival. While death and violence were not strangers to the people who lived here, few left willingly. Instead more and more immigrants flocked to Jerusalem every week.

For Abraham, Jerusalem was where he would see his family and share his grief. He had long since come to terms with the unimaginable horrors experienced in the death camps of Auschwitz. He'd spent the years after the War trying to cope, sunk in self-pity, but when he was twenty-three his life changed. He met Clara. She was three years younger than he, beautiful and gentle. She'd lifted him out of his self-absorption and eased the bitterness in his life since Auschwitz. They married, and she gave him a wonderful son, Joshua, who'd gone on to marry a native Israeli woman, Sarah. Now he had a lovely granddaughter, Susan, who was four years old. But Clara was gone, lost to breast cancer just months ago.

Abraham appreciated Joshua's invitation to visit. He knew Joshua was worried about his depressed state of mind. Since meeting Clara, his life had revolved completely around her. He had been there by her side, over the last year, as his lovely "Little-one" slipped away. He was no stranger to death, but this was different. This was his Clara. She had been his reason to live.

It was mid afternoon. Abraham had arrived five hours ago and after a short nap he wanted to get some exercise. He and Joshua walked the streets of Jerusalem. They talked about many things. It was good for Abraham, for during the last two hours the conversation had moved from self pity to bereavement and now they seemed to be talking about politics. Though father and son, the two couldn't be further apart on their feelings about Israel's domestic and regional policies. Now they engaged in a heated debate about the Palestinians.

"Dad, with the success of Yerushalayim Hashlema we can finally worship where it is our right. Before 1967 we couldn't go to the West Wall, which is our birthright."

"Yes, my son, I cannot argue or defend the wrongful quarantine of this wall, one of our faith's holiest sights. But what about the Muslims? Do we have the right to restrict their mobility and access to their own holy shrines?"

Abraham looked around at the wealth of cultures all mixing as they passed in the street. "I wonder why this intermingling can't coexist politically. How can such a holy place be the center of so much hatred and violence? Guns are everywhere, carried by Jews from all walks of life. Why? The answer, my son, is because they're afraid. We've forgotten the past Joshua, and that frightens me."

"We have forgotten nothing, Dad. That's why Jews, for the first time in history, are relatively safe."

"If you call ducking suicide bombers safe," Abraham replied.

"We protect ourselves. We are not weak," Joshua snapped back. "People fear us, instead of us being the cowards."

"Yes, I know the slogan, 'Never Again'. You forget I was there. That gives me the right to speak out." Abraham felt no malice. He spoke like a scholar teaching a student.

"So, what have we forgotten?"

"What? Let me tell you. Innocent men, women and children pulled from their homes, displaced because of prejudice and discrimination. They were told they were scum, they didn't belong, and it wasn't their birthright to be there, that they tainted the purity of the society.

"Some were dragged away by their hair screaming, tied together only to be shot. Others were mutilated, their bodies ripped apart, the soldiers not caring if they were dead or alive before they were dismembered."

Abraham glanced at Joshua walking quietly beside him, and then continued, "Occasionally, a soldier would stop to smoke a cigarette or have a candy bar, tossing the wrappers at the feet of their next victim. Some prisoners escaped only to be stopped at gunpoint by the regular army. They turned them around, sent them back to the ones trained for such atrocities. Some murders were casual, a bullet to the head, a throat slit. Others though were calculated and planned. Groups were lined up and segregated by sexes. But in the end they were all led off to a sure death."

He again stopped and caught his breath. Then as abruptly as he stopped he continued, "After the screams and bullets stopped, volunteers were sent in to lift the bodies one by one, or to bulldoze them into ditches. 'Never Again', we cried." He threw his hands into the air then grabbed Joshua's shoulders. "Yes, my son we have forgotten."

"How can you say we've forgotten? When everything you've mentioned is the basis of our strength so that it will never happen again. You recount what the Nazis did to the Jews and then you accuse Jews of forgetting. How can you say this? Look around you."

Abraham shook his head, a sad, gentle smile on his face. "I was not talking about what the Nazis did to the Jews." His voice was low and solemn. "I was describing the bloodbath, the massacre of Palestinians, at the Shatila and Sabra refugee camps. And the soldiers that stood by and watched...soldiers that forced men, women and children back to the slaughter at gunpoint were Jews, not Nazis. That day, my idealistic son, this nation lost its moral superiority over other nations. Jews transformed themselves from the David into the Goliath. The actions that day were counter to everything Judaism stood for. It was the absolute antithesis of our traditions. And, my son, what frightens me most is not only have we forgotten that we were actively involved in such an atrocity, but we have since dismissed it as an aberration. Yes Joshua, we've forgotten the lessons of the past as quickly as we've forgotten Shatila and Sabra. And this is one of the reasons I cannot live here. At least in America, we know and admit what we are!"

He wasn't sure if his son, who walked alongside him quietly, had accepted any of his feelings and convictions. They turned down a side street and entered the doorway that led to Joshua's apartment. Their walk was over, now it was time to sit and eat and then sleep, they were both tired.

*   *   *   *

The Shoe Shine Boy

Though it was only five thirty in the morning and still dark, the day was already muggy and hot. The Mediterranean Sea breeze would not spring up for a few hours. Even then it would only bring slight relief from the heat.

Adan and Ehaib joined the long line of Palestinians who stood side by side at checkpoint Erez. Each day hundreds of Palestinians stood waiting for permission to pass from the Gaza Strip into Israel to work.

"Soon, very soon, my brother, we will not have to present identity cards, travel permits, or working papers to sentries. We will be able to travel freely." Adan double-checked their documents as he spoke. He knew if they weren't in proper order, or if anything was missing, they'd be denied passage.

"Your transit and identity card," an armed Israeli soldier demanded as he approached Adan. Without comment Adan handed them to him.

The soldier scanned the magnetic strip on each card. Instantly the small computer cleared them. "Your work permits." He held out his left hand. His right index finger never left the trigger of his gun.

Adan gave him the papers General Malek had given them a few days earlier in Lebanon.

"Where are you going?" the soldier asked as he scanned them.

"I travel to Haifa," Adan answered without hesitation.

"What is the address and reason of your visit?"

"1427 West Dheisheeki. I am a brick layer."

Apparently convinced, the soldier handed the papers back. "Your travel papers only allow you travel until eight tonight. You must return through this checkpoint before that time."

Adan's eyes looked into the soldier's in a hard stare, acknowledging their mutual hatred.

Moments later, he and Ehaib boarded a crowded, non air-conditioned bus and made their way to Haifa.

By seven thirty a.m. Adan and Ehaib were driving out of Haifa towards Jerusalem. The open bed of the Toyota pick-up truck was filled with bricks. Their cargo had made its way from Baghdad to Jordan. From there it was placed on a freighter and shipped to Cyprus. From Cyprus it was shipped to Haifa. Along with the bricks came two fully loaded AK-47 machine guns that had been placed behind the truck bed's inner panel. A tug at the loose panel allowed easy access to them.

Adan and Ehaib hadn't spoken much during the bus trip. They had been careful and watched what they said. It was well known the Israelis had spies everywhere. In the last few month's Israeli forces, also known as Sayarot, had stepped up their offensive against "Hamas," the militant group to which Adan and Ehaib belonged. Hamas had exchanged their rocks for guns, bombs, and belts filled with explosives. With clandestine operations and open attacks by the Sayarot against the Palestinians, many Palestinians were found with a bullet in the head or a lethal rocket shot into their car.

Once in the truck and on their way, Adan broke the silence. "Allahu Akhbar! (God Is Great) It is fitting, my younger brother, that our journey towards justice starts from this town."

"What do you mean?"

"How soon you forget your history," he said. "It was here, in this city, that the Jews started their persecution of our people. Haifa was the first city they forcibly took control of, starting them on their road to subjugating innocent Palestinians."

Ehaib watched the rolling hills pass by. He hesitated for a moment then responded. "Yesterday I spoke with Shocat Musa. He said we are wrong. He said what we're doing is wrong and the problems the Palestinians face are caused by us." His voice was low, and his eyes looked away.

"Musa is a fool! It's his weakness that causes Palestinians problems! We're innocent, victimized people!" Adan retorted snapping his head towards Ehaib. "You didn't tell him our plans?"

"No! We can't trust him." Ehaib said.

"What else did that weak pig say?"

"Just trash, my brother, he spoke lies and garbage."

"Tell me! What else did he say! I need to know if he's a threat to us! I need to know if he must die!"

"He said we are militant fools. He said it's our attitude that has stopped us from living in peace all these years. He also said it is people like us that refused the United Nations plan to divide Palestine between the Jews and Palestinians, forcing us into refugee camps where we live like caged animals today."

"That's it! He is a dead man!" Adan cried slamming his fist onto the dashboard. He took a deep breath and continued, "Now, let me tell you of things! In 1947 the United Nations, under the pressure of the Jews who controlled Washington, voted to divide our Land! Our land! They voted to take half of it away from us! What right did they have? What right?"

"None," replied Ehaib.

"That's right! It's people like Musa who've accepted this. We will not accept the annexation of our country. No! Praise Allah, there were Palestinians with convictions like ours in 1948 that attacked those filthy bastard Jews. If we had been stronger we would have won, and driven those bastards out. But no! They forced us to fight with inferior weapons. That's why we lost. Then what did the Jews do? They declared their independence and said all of Palestine was theirs. They even changed the name from Palestine to Israel. You see my brother, that was their plan from the very beginning. They always planned to take over. And what do they call us?"

"Terrorists."

"Yes! Terrorists! Barbarians! Butchers! They say we murder and maim innocent people. That we are animals! They're so wrong! We are peaceful people. We don't want war. They're all so blind. They can't see all we want is to live in peace in our own land. We are a peaceful society. But no, they push us to kill. They force us to fight for our land. And if they won't live with us peacefully, we'll see all of them dead!"

In time the rhetoric subsided. Ehaib closed his eyes, and drifted off to sleep in the passenger seat of the pickup truck.

Adan drove on, taking in the scenery as it sped by. They took the long route south from Haifa, along the coast to Tel Aviv, instead of the newer four-lane highway from Tel Aviv east towards Jerusalem. The countryside was inspirational for its beauty, as well as its history. As they entered the Latrun area, in the Judean Hills, Adan hit Ehaib on the shoulder, startling him.

"What's the matter?" Ehaib said.

"We're near Fort Latrun."

"So what?"

"So what! It is here that thousands of Jews were slaughtered years ago as they tried to control the pass. Just think, my brother, of the awesome picture of slaughtered Jews falling with their blood spilling and fertilizing the soil." He looked over at Ehaib. "Are you hungry?"

"Sure. But where can we eat that's safe?" He motioned over his head towards the cargo stacked in the truck bed.

"We'll stop at the Latrun Monastery and get some cheese and wine."

The monastery, centuries old, sat peacefully beyond the Fortress Latrun. It sat undisturbed by the conquerors and invaders who had traversed the pass on their way to victory, or defeat. The Latrun monks had always lived in quiet meditation under a vow of silence. In their tranquil environment they made wine and cheese to sell or give away to passersby. Even the most barbaric invaders couldn't bring themselves to harm this peaceful group of monks, who had taken a lifelong vow of silence.

Adan pulled off the road and stopped. He and Ehaib walked in the bright sun to the roadside stand and purchased a snack. Returning to the parked truck, Adan noticed an Israeli security patrol. "Remain calm. Here, eat some cheese." He handed Ehaib the lightly wrapped bundle.

As they drove off, Adan looked in the rear view mirror and muttered over and over again. "This unjust system will change." With no reply from Ediab he again became engrossed in the passing countryside.

In Ramallah, they turned onto a road and began to climb steep inclines. The hairpin turns wound around hills terraced out of the mountainside. During the final portion of their drive, close to Jerusalem, they passed old, rusting military equipment strewn on both sides of the road. There were trucks and tanks, burned out relics left as reminders of past wars, past defeats of invaders.

Finally in Jerusalem the traffic slowed and became congested. They turned onto Jaffa Road. "My brother, we have arrived. Wake up. This is our day...our moment! Today we become part of the history we've passed on our drive here."

"Allahu Akhbar!" replied Ehaib as he sat tall in his seat.

"Yes, Allahu Akhbar!"

Adan turned left and passed Zion Square, then pulled onto the sidewalk in front of the Russian Compound that held the Russian Church. He looked up at the green-domed cathedral.

"Look up, my brother." Adan pointed to the brick vestibule that was below and to the left of the main cathedral dome. They saw the broken bricks, strategically damaged to be an eyesore to the church. Damage such as this was evident throughout the city, and was rarely repaired. But, to the church's surprise and delight, an anonymous gift had been received to pay for the complete restoration of the church, starting with the bricks.

Moments later the two brothers stood on the church steps.

"I expect the two of you to work quickly and quietly," the building's curator informed Adan and Ehaib as he ushered them in. "We will be open for tourists. While you work I do not want them inconvenienced." As they walked, the caretaker shook his head and muttered. "First they do the damage, and then we pay them to fix it. Oh well, someone has to do it."

Without any fuss, Adan and Ehaib got to work, first they removed the broken bricks, and then they replaced them with the ones they brought. The day wore on as they made progress. Adan made doubly sure that each brick was placed properly, with the necessary side facing out. A bricklayer by trade, he was also concerned about the neatness of their work. More than once he chided Ehaib for sloppy mortaring.

"But Adan, as long as the bricks are facing the right way who cares?"

"I do. And you should too. This is our true profession. Always do your work with pride. Years from now these bricks, and your handiwork, will still sit here, for all to see. Be proud my brother, be proud."

"I will, after the gas in them spills out and kills those below."

Adan took a moment and stared out over the city. "Soon the Palestinians will again be in charge of this wonderful place."

Three hours later they were finished. They packed up their masonry equipment and departed the church. As they exited they noticed a small group of Palestinian children playing in and around their truck.

"Bang, bang." One child called out as he ducked and hid in the now empty bay of the Toyota. A second mimicked him, returning play gunfire from behind a lamppost.

"Bang, bang! I hit you in the arm!"

"I hit you in the chest first. You're dead, fall down!" The first boy demanded from the truck.

"No! You always say you got me first."

"But I did!" He kicked the side panel in anger and it popped open. "Hey! Look what I found!" He bent down and removed the loosened panel. When he stood up there was an AK-47 in his small hands.

"Wow! Let's keep it!" His friend ran to the truck.

Before Adan could stop him, Ehaib dropped his masonry tools and raced towards the truck. "Drop that gun!"

Ehaib hadn't noticed the two members of the Israeli Defense Force watching from across the street until he had wrenched the loaded weapon out of the unsuspecting child's hands. By then it was too late. Both he and the weapon had been spotted. Ehaib spun around and leveled the weapon at the soldier.

"No!" Adan yelled.

Ehaib jerked violently as both he and the boy were engulfed in a hail of bullets. As he fell to the pavement, he squeezed the trigger, spewing bullets randomly across the road.

"NO!" Adan screamed in a high shrill as he ran towards his fallen brother and grabbed the assault rifle. "I will kill you all!"

A bullet struck Adan in the left shoulder, throwing him to the ground near his bloody brother.

Ehaib glanced up towards the newly laid bricks. The sun was setting, casting long rays around the dome of the church. A smile fell across his face as his eyes met Adan's. "Allahu Akhbar," was Ehaib's last words, as his breathing labored, then stopped.

"Yes...Allahu Akhbar my little brother. Allahu Akhbar."

"Don't move, if you want to live!" a voice barked at Adan. A foot stomped violently on the nape of his neck and a gun barrel was jammed into his back.

The street was completely silent and still. All those who had been innocently walking by moments ago now lay prone on the pavement, not knowing if the danger was over or just beginning. The Palestinian child, who minutes before had been playing with his friend, also lay dead. His lifeless twisted body slumped in the back of the pickup truck.

One of the Defense Force members called out to those on the street, "No one move! For your safety, everyone stay on the ground until we secure the area!"

A brigade of reinforcements soon arrived and fanned out. The soldiers found three bystanders had been hit by the random burst from the terrorist's gun. Two women lay dead. Near them an older gentleman lay in a pool of blood, a non-fatal wound to his leg. The Israeli Defense Force (I.D.F.) was brutally efficient. Adan was hand cuffed and taken away. Ehaib's body and that of the Palestinian child were tossed into the back of a military vehicle and driven away. The bodies of the dead Israeli women though were treated with respect and dignity. First they were covered with clean white sheets, and then they were gently lifted into stretchers and carried away.

The commander in charge approached the wounded man and knelt down beside him on the pavement, momentarily interrupting the care the ambulance team was administering. "I am Commander Kleinman. Are you hurt anywhere other than your leg?"

"No." Abraham looked at the wound. He'd seen far worse in his time. The actual sensation of being shot surprised him. It happened so fast. It felt like a sharp kick in the thigh. It had taken a few moments for the intense burning to start. "I think I'll survive, but it feels like someone's sticking a red hot poker into my leg."

"Yes, you'll survive. I'm sorry to say the two ladies who were also shot weren't as lucky. What is your name?" the Commander asked in a soft tone.

"Abraham Feinstein. I'm visiting my son Joshua. He lives two blocks from here. I need to tell him what happened, and that I'm all right."

"I'll have one of my men bring him to the hospital and meet you there"

"Thank you."

"Shalom." The Commander gave him a warm handshake, and then the paramedics hoisted the stretcher into the ambulance and took him away.

*   *   *   *

"Dad, now do you see why we can't trust these people? They'd kill us all if given the chance!" Joshua spoke passionately to Abraham, who now lay comfortably in a small but functional hospital room.

"So, you would condemn all Palestinians for what a small group of radicals do?"

"I just don't understand you! They shot you, almost killed you. And yet you refuse to condemn them. I can't believe how blind you are to reality!"

Abraham looked down at his leg, then at his son. "They shot me, not you. In reality, you are the one who's blind, blind to condemn an entire race. Would you wipe them out like the Nazis tried to wipe out the Jews? Then where would you be on the scale of atrocities?"

"Let's not get into that argument again!"

"Fine. Then what right do you have to condemn anyone on my behalf? I was the one shot. So don't lecture me on whom to condemn or forgive!"

"Then why can't you forgive the Germans? They weren't all Nazis!"

"Because the Germans turned their backs!" Abraham said. "They turned their backs as we dragged each other through the streets!" Tears streamed down his checks. "They wouldn't help us! Not one of them helped us! But there are many good Palestinians who help Jews daily." Abraham buried his head in his hands and wept. "They wouldn't help us."

Joshua reached out and embraced his father. Together, they cried for each other, and for those who couldn't.

*   *   *   *

Every time John Gordon walked into the Oval Office it amazed him. The most important person in the world had such a small office space.

"John, I can't tell you how happy I am that you're safe." President Rhodes clasped one of John's hands in both of his in an expression of friendship. "I know you're tired, so I won't keep you long. How successful do you feel you were, despite the attack?"

Gordon was indeed tired. He had spent most of the long flight home writing the report he would present to the National Security Council tomorrow. Despite such pressure, he knew he owed the President a personal briefing. It was with relief that he saw the President walk to a comfortable side chair. They both sat.

"Very successful, we reached an agreement on structure and principle ideology. I did have to twist some arms. I think, ironically, the attack brought both parties closer. They had to cross an ideological boundary to help each other. Their survival gave them a common goal and they quickly developed a personal bonding. They now embrace each other as old friends."

Gordon had spent the twenty-four hours after the assault cementing an ideological common ground between the Israeli and the Palestinian. It had been relatively easy. All parties wanted to come to an understanding, and return home.

The President reflected for a moment, and then grunted in amazement. "It's hard to believe the attack furthered our aim. Suddenly two enemies have become allies. Well, I know we've been brief, but you're tired. Thank you for stopping by. Go home and get some rest. See you in the morning."

*   *   *   *

Although Abraham's wound was only a grazing of the flesh, the doctors were keeping him in the hospital overnight, more for observation than any real medical need. That was fine with Abraham. He embraced the thought of a quiet night. As much as he loved his little granddaughter, life at Joshua's house was hardly peaceful.

"Okay, Dad, I'll pick you up in the morning. We'll have a big breakfast waiting for you. Sleep well." Joshua embraced him and left. The frustration they felt towards each other was far less than the love and respect they felt and showed.

*   *   *   *

Adan was thrown violently through the corridor and fell to the floor in front of a cot in a cell. He had been brought to the local police jail for processing. As he lay on the cold cement his shoulder continued to ooze blood from his poorly treated bullet wound. He gasped for air and held his chest tightly with his right hand trying to brace his newly broken ribs. He'd been viciously beaten and he could no longer differentiate the pain in his shoulder from the pain in his abdomen. Despite the agony he was proud of himself. He had told them nothing.

He rolled onto his side and slowly pulled himself onto the cot. Every movement, every breath seared through him. Despite the pain, he knew he would die comfortably. The cell was only three blocks from the church. He was on the fringe of the expected gas ring but definitely within its kill zone. He fell onto his back, on the pillow less cot and stared at the ceiling. It was moments before midnight.

"Soon. Yes...soon. Martyrdom...holy martyrdom," he muttered. He would die happy. His place in heaven was secure. Contentment now replaced the pain in his body. He would not see his people free. Instead he would be the cause of it. He'd made peace with himself. Now he waited.

Soon he felt a funny tingling sensation come over him. He knew what it was and he was not afraid. What surprised him was how painless it was as the dark shroud of death fell around him.

For Abraham's son, daughter-in-law, granddaughter, and all those who lived within three blocks of the Russian Church, life ended quietly. Death came as they slept. Their dreams simply stopped.

6   Chapter Six

The sirens wailed without interruption, echoing off the walls of mosques, churches and synagogues. Not since the terrifying moments during the '91' Persian Gulf War had the sirens of Jerusalem heralded such disaster. The people of this ancient city awoke confused and disoriented. They heard no explosions. They'd seen no lights from fires, or destruction, but the sirens kept on raging. The population of Jerusalem knew something had happened...something bad. They turned on their radios and televisions and tried to make sense of the chaos.

The sirens from vehicles converged in a tightening ring to within three blocks of the Russian Compound. At the periphery of that ring a group of soldiers stopped people from entering. It was the demarcation zone. Everything on this side was alive, but on the other was dead. The soldiers acted very professional, keeping order. Yet each one was terrified. There had been no explosions. There was no smell in the air. Everything was quiet, too quiet, except for the sirens.

The Commander in charge, a solid block of a man named Kleinman, kept his orders short and concise, setting the example for an unemotional, detached investigation. If he acknowledged the extent of the devastation he knew he would be inviting instant hysteria. The initial report was that everything, human and animal, within a three-block radius had died.

"How many chemical protective suits do we have here?" Commander Kleinman asked a junior officer.

"Eleven, sir," he replied.

"Fine, until you hear otherwise, only those completely protected can enter."

"Yes, sir."

Over the next two hours the Israeli Defense Force ran a multitude of tests on the air, water, and even the dirt on the street. That confused them more for they found no evidence of any toxic chemical. None-the-less, Kleinman wasn't taking any chances. He had dogs walk through the empty streets and observed them for thirty minutes. Only then did he feel the area was safe for unprotected entry...by the military. The public would still be kept out. He didn't know what had happened, and the scientists, bringing in more sophisticated equipment, had asked that nothing be disturbed.

For hours the streets remained empty. People stayed indoors both at the request of the government and out of fear. Some donned their gas masks. Many sat in groups and prayed.

With the nations military on full alert, the horror of what had happened shot around the world. All told, over one thousand seven hundred had perished that morning.

Eventually, a small crowd gathered in spite of the requests of the soldiers to return home. They stayed well within the safety zone and watched men with equipment go in and out of buildings. The soldiers and scientists moved from apartment to apartment, street to street. The crowd hoped and prayed that just once a rescuer would exit a building with a survivor. It never happened.

The military searched each house, but each one was the same. It was as if someone had simply turned off a light switch, shutting off life. They found no signs of struggle. People appeared to have died instantly, most in bed. Yet, no cause could be found.

No one noticed the elderly gentleman limping up the slight incline in the street towards the small crowd of onlookers. If anyone had, they would have noticed the pain on his face went far deeper than the discomfort he had walking on a leg that had recently been ripped open by a bullet.

"Who is in charge here?" Abraham asked the nearest soldier.

"Commander Kleinman. He's over there." He pointed to the other side of the street.

"Commander Kleinman." Abraham called out as he limped up to him.

"Yes." He looked up. "I'm sorry. I'm very busy and can't answer any questions." He started to turn away, but then turned back. "You're the man that was shot in the leg yesterday?"

"Yes." Abraham looked down one of the blocked off side streets, then at the Commander. "My family is down there. They're dead, aren't they?"

After a long hesitation, Kleinman said, "We don't know. We can't be sure how many have survived at this point."

"Thank you for your kindness, Commander. They're dead. If you'll excuse me, I must tend to my family."

"I'm sorry. I can't let you into this area," the commander replied. "We're still not completely sure it's safe. Also, I don't think you want to be the one to find your family."

"Commander, when I was a boy, I survived Auschwitz by cleaning the muddy boots of the German S.S. officers. When I wasn't cleaning boots they forced me to clean out the bodies of those who died from the experiments the Nazis were doing with nerve gas. I'm no stranger to death. I carried many close friends from the death chamber and treated them with the dignity they were denied in life. Commander, I intend to walk to my son's house and tend to him and his family...my family. If I die from the same poison that killed them, so be it. There's nothing left for me here anyway." He walked past the Commander and started up the street.

"Soldier!" Kleinman called. "Stop that"...then Kleinman paused and restated, "Take that jeep and help that man with his family."

"Yes sir."

Moments later, Abraham and the soldier climbed the stairs to the second floor. The slam of the fire door echoed like thunder through the still air. It was followed by a deafening silence that filled the apartment building's hallway, causing their footsteps to resound off the walls. Abraham stopped in front of the third doorway. The soldier stopped a few paces back. It was obvious he didn't want to enter first. It was obvious he didn't want to be there at all.

Abraham hesitated before the door. "I don't have the key," he said.

"I'm sorry, sir. What did you say? I didn't hear you."

"I don't have the key to the door. It's locked," Abraham spoke calmly, but looked at him with pleading eyes. "I can't open the door. Can you help me, please?"

The soldier reached both hands into his own pockets, and then pulled them out...also empty. "I don't have a key either."

"Then would you break open the door, please?"

"I'm not sure I should," he said.

"What is your name?"

"David."

"David, this is my son's home. He, his wife, and their daughter are inside. They are dead. I am their only relative. I give you my permission to break open the door. Please, I must get inside."

David hesitated then gave the door two swift kicks with his boots. The wood around the lock splintered and the door swung open.

Abraham walked to the very center of the living room. It was small, sparsely, but tastefully decorated. The furniture was of simple wicker design, very functional, and adequate. "We sat here two nights ago and played games."

"I'm sorry, what did you say?" David stepped forward.

"I said we played here two nights ago. Come in please."

David followed Abraham into a small side bedroom, but stopped at the threshold. Abraham sat down on his granddaughter's bed, and gently brushed her hair with his fingers. Her skin felt cool to touch. Then, with a corner of the bed sheet, he wiped the vomit from her face. He turned to the soldier. "Would you please go into the hall linen closet and get me a clean white sheet?"

"Yes sir." He left quietly and returned with clean white linen.

Abraham gently placed her little body on the sheet and carefully wrapped her in it. Without a word he lifted her into his arms and walked out. David silently followed Abraham, who limped out to the jeep with his only grandchild cradled in his arms.

Ten minutes later they again stood in the living room, this time they approached the open door to Joshua's room. Abraham's resolve seemed to waiver for a moment, and David reached out to grab his arm when he saw him lean against the doorframe.

"Do you want to sit for a moment?"

"No, no. I'll be all right. Thank you." Abraham stood up straight and shook his head.

They entered the master bedroom. It was so peaceful. A small ceiling fan slowly turned, causing a slight current of air. Joshua and his wife lay on the bed under a thin sheet, their hands touching. Abraham's eyes filled with tears at the sight of this final embrace.

"I might need your help, please," Abraham said.

David helped him lift the cold naked woman from the bed and wrap her in another clean white sheet. Together they carried her and placed her in the jeep beside her daughter.

Back in the bedroom, Abraham sat on the bed next to Joshua's body. He stared at him without saying a word. David approached to help him again, but was stopped with a hand gesture. "Thank you, no. He is my son, my flesh, my blood. I'll bring him myself."

With tears in his eyes, David stood motionless and watched Abraham place his son, with difficulty, onto a clean sheet and wrap him up. "El maley rachamim. Lord full of mercy...El maley rachamim..El maley rach..." Abraham looked up at David, bewildered. "I can't remember...I can't remember the words. What comes next?"

"I'm sorry, I don't know. What is it?"

"It is a prayer song. The prayer I used to say when I tended the bodies at Auschwitz. It was the only prayer I could remember at that time," his voice was tremulous. "But now, I can't remember. I can't remember."

"Here, let me help you." He stepped forward as Abraham wiped a tear from his cheek.

"No, no...I'll be all right." Abraham stood and tried without success to lift Joshua's body. Joshua was too heavy for him to carry, especially as his leg burned with searing pain.

Without prompting, David helped raise the wrapped body into Abraham's arms, and then stepped back respectfully, allowing Abraham to carry his son alone. His limp became more prominent with every step.

When they reached the curb outside, Abraham stumbled. He and Joshua tumbled onto the pavement. David rushed to his aid, but was helpless to do anything. Abraham sat on the ground with Joshua's head cradled in his lap and all pretenses of strength and composure left him. "El maley rachamim...Lord full of mercy please help me remember...El maley rachamim...El male rach..." He looked at David. "I can't remember!" He threw his hands skyward and wailed, "Please help me remember, please!"

Overcome with grief, David knelt down and held Abraham, who in turn held his son.

Though this moment of torment and anguish was personal and private for Abraham, a photographer near by had different ideas. She focused her telephoto lens from three hundred yards away and clicked off frame after frame. Finally lowering her camera, she could hardly contain herself. She had just captured every photographer's dream, the picture that would win her a Pulitzer Prize.

7   Chapter Seven

At first the bells were part of John Gordon's dream, clanging incessantly and annoyingly. Ever so slowly, though, his mind slid back to consciousness. On a normal day by the middle of the first ring he'd be instantly awake, lunging for the receiver. This time, jet lag had done him in, and age was slowly catching up. The phone was on its twentieth ring when he finally snapped on the bedside light. The clock read one-thirty in the morning. He'd gotten only four hours of sleep. In a hoarse voice he said, "Hello."

"John." The voice was that of Steve Albridge, the Secretary of Defense. "There's been an incident in Israel. It's bad. The President's called a meeting of the N.S.C. in forty-five minutes. We'll send a car for you." The line went dead.

Gordon sat on the edge of his bed for a moment and rubbed the sleep out of his eyes. Then, acting on instinct, he quickly showered and dressed. When he walked outside he found a car waiting.

The members of the National Security Council gathered in the west wing of the White House. Upon entering, John poured himself a large cup of hot black coffee, the first of many, and sat down in his designated chair.

Steve Albridge came over immediately to greet him. "Welcome home," Steve said. "Sorry you couldn't get the sleep you need. God knows, you deserve it after what you've been through."

"Thanks, Steve. I'm so tired I can't believe I'm here and functioning. If I start snoring, wake me."

Unannounced, and unceremoniously, President Rhodes entered. He was casually dressed in a pull over shirt and slacks. Despite his casualness there was no question that he was in charge. Members of his Cabinet likened him to John Wayne both in looks and in confidence. He walked to his chair and sat down. His face was impossible to read. "Shall we begin?"

All eyes focused on the thirty-five inch television in the wall cabinet, which for the next fifteen minutes replayed a CNN report that had aired only an hour earlier. It detailed everything known about the massacre that had just taken place in Jerusalem. After it was over, the room was momentarily quiet. Its occupants were all stunned.

The President broke the silence and set the tone for the meeting. It was not to be one of open discussion and opinions. Rhodes had many questions, and he wanted answers. "Al, what else can you tell us? And I am referring to information CNN can't get their hands on, if that's possible."

Al Niddiem had been through many foreign policy crises. He'd been the Director of the C.I.A. through the terms of the last two Presidents. Now nearing sixty, Niddiem still had youth and vigor, which he projected with his can do attitude. He had made it clear long ago that his allegiance was to the protection of the American people, and not any political party. This doctrine secured his longevity in the beltway of Washington long ago. He also knew how to play a crowd, and waited until all eyes were on him to answer. "It appears every living creature in a three block radius died from exposure to a chemical weapon. The point of origin appears to be the Russian Church. Coincidentally, two Palestinian terrorists were involved in a gun battle yesterday just outside its gates. One died at the scene. The other unfortunately was thrown in jail…within the three block death zone."

"What kind of gas caused this?" the President asked.

"We don't know."

"You don't know?" The President leaned forward. "Are the Israelis withholding information from us? Are they playing games?"

"No, not at all. They're cooperating completely. Basically, I think, because they need our help. They've found no trace or residue of any toxic chemical. The area appears completely safe now. Whatever killed those people has completely dissipated, without a trace. It's too early for autopsy information. Hopefully tissue samples will help us."

"So we're dealing with a gas that kills and then dissolves without leaving a trace?"

"It appears so."

The President stood up and began to pace.

"Ben, do we have anything like that in our arsenal?"

Ben Wildemen was the Chairman of the Joint Chiefs of Staff. Like Al Niddiem, he was a veteran of numerous administrations. In his mid sixties, he had had his share of conflicts in the global arena as well as those distasteful battles with the Commander in Chief in the Oval Office. He was always honest and forthright with his opinions. Because of that attribute many people thought he belonged behind the desk in the Oval Office. Ben was from New England. He had a weathered face from growing up on the water that was complemented by his salt and pepper hair and mustache.

"Yes, Mr. President, we do. It is called YB520," he replied with a Boston accent.

"Make sure it's all accounted for. And if not, when, where, who and how it's missing."

"We'll have that by morning."

"Al, what do we know about the Russian's capability in this area?"

"Well for one thing they haven't been completely honest with us in this regard." He had anticipated the question and prepared a file.

"Tell me something I don't know."

"Through the seventies and eighties the former Soviet Union engaged in the research and development of offensive biological weapons."

"I guess they forgot they had signed a treaty forbidding such R & D in 1972," Steve Albridge, the Secretary of Defense, added.

"As did we." The President shot him a warning glance. "Please continue."

"In 1989, a Russian microbiologist, Vladimer Kernig, defected while in London at a scientific conference. What we learned from him was frightening. The Soviets had a civilian research program known as "Biopreparat". It was represented as research and development for medical cures of chronic devastating diseases. We learned that this so called "civilian research program" employed twenty-five thousand people to create lethal diseases that couldn't be cured by present day means. They also were developing deadly nerve gas concentrations. We know that the officials who ran the Biopreparat Project were open to giving certain terrorist groups access to these weapons. Fortunately, after the fall of the Soviet Union, Yeltsen shut down all chemical and germ warfare projects. They placed General Antily Kurtsevich in charge of overseeing this order. But under the old Soviet Union, he was the head of the very project they were now asking him to shut down."

"Asking the fox to guard the hen house," the President retorted.

"Exactly," said Niddiem nodding. "And not too long ago a second official in the Biopreparat project defected. He was higher than Kernig and informed us that the dismantling of the germ-warfare division was a hoax. The Biopreparat Project continued." Niddiem closed his file and stared at the President.

"Do we know if Yeltsen was aware of this when he was Russia's President? But more important, Putin is running things now. Do we know if he is aware of any of this?"

"No, we don't, nor did the second defector know."

The President made no comment for a moment, and then said, "Al, CNN estimated eighteen hundred to two thousand deaths. Is that accurate?"

"Yes, that's about what we and the Israelis estimate."

"So at the moment we can assume the Russians aided the Palestinians by giving them chemical weapons."

"I think it's more plausible the Russians aided the Iraqis, who used the Palestinians as their surrogates," Niddiem said.

"Why the Iraqis?"

"We already know most of Iraqis military hardware came from the Russians. We also know the Russians helped the Iraqis develop chemical weapons for years."

"I'm sure that same observation hasn't been lost on the Israelis. What's the present status of their military?" Again the President stood and paced, his eyes focused on the floor in front of him.

"Full alert," Niddiem replied. "Even worse, they've activated Plan Goliath, a nuclear alert. They have planes loaded with nuclear weapons. Their pilots only need their flying orders and they're off to war."

"Are you certain? I need to know that your interpretation of Plan Goliath is one hundred percent accurate. And I mean no margin of error." The President glared at Niddiem.

"We have...through our own means, come to possess a copy of the Israeli code and retaliatory plan book. Yes, Mr. President, Plan Goliath stands for a retaliatory nuclear strike."

"Let me make this perfectly clear. Under no circumstances can we allow this atrocity to escalate to nuclear warfare. Effective immediately, I'm issuing an order quarantining the Israeli Air Force to within its own borders. Ben," he pointed a finger, "you will issue that order to the Pentagon. I want a show of force in the air at all times to enforce it. I do not want any planes to slip through."

"We have enough planes based in Saudi and Kuwait. With support from the task force in the Mediterranean and the Persian Gulf, we can completely blanket Israel," Wildemen said with stoic New England confidence.

"Al, is there any relationship between this terrorist attack and the attack at Sun Moon Lake? Are the groups interlinked?"

"No, Mr. President, we already know they're not. The two Palestinians killed in Jerusalem were members of the Hamas group. The group that attacked John at Sun Moon Lake were not Palestinian at all."

Gordon's head snapped up. "What! Then who were they?" he asked with a Texas twang.

"They were Israelis, ultra right wing Jews, members of the Kahn group. They, as well as many right wing Palestinians, want the peace process to fail. Killing you then blaming the Palestinians for the murders would have had dealt the peace process a fatal blow."

Everyone in the situation room appeared momentarily shocked, but none more than Gordon who ran his fingers through his silver hair.

"Sorry, John," Niddiem continued, "I was going to tell you in the morning, after you slept. We just learned this at the agency."

"Do the Israelis or the P.L.O. know?" the President asked, his tone hinting of an idea.

"No," Niddiem said.

"Good." The President turned to Gordon. "John, I know how tired you are, but I need you. I want you to inform the Israeli Defense Minister that, as of this moment, we are quarantining their air force. I want you to use whatever influence you have to get them to stand down. Inform him about the identity of the terrorists that attacked you. Put a doubt in his mind. Make him uncertain as to who's behind all of this. Link both incidents or make him uncertain of their linkage. Also, inform him that we know about Plan Goliath, and that this is unequivocally unacceptable to us. That information must come from you, not me. I don't want to appear to threaten the Prime Minister when I speak to him, at least not initially. I want to give him the chance to back down without losing face."

"Mr. President, I essentially will be telling Israel we have their code and retaliatory battle plans." Niddiem said.

"I really don't care! We obtained them for a purpose. That purpose was to help us in formulating opinions and options towards whatever action they may take. If we use our knowledge to get them to stand down, then it was knowledge well spent." There was no room for discussion in the President's voice. "Why don't we wrap this up now. We all have calls to make. Let's meet back here at seven thirty A.M. At that time I'll entertain thoughts on our next step. There are only a few hours left to the night and we have a lot to do. Till seven thirty." He stood and left the Situation Room.

The west wing of the White House remained illuminated throughout the remainder of the night. The President spoke on the phone with the Israeli Prime Minister. He expressed his profound sympathy for the tragedy. They also discussed working together to find and bring the perpetrators to justice. Plan Goliath was never raised.

On another line, Gordon spoke with Mateusz Adar, Israelis Defense Minister. Their conversation started with a sympathetic tone given the nature of the attack in Jerusalem but after Gordon informed Adar of the identity of their attackers in Taiwan it suddenly turned far less congenial. Gordon then laid the proper groundwork for the real reason behind his call. First he informed Adar that Plan Goliath was unacceptable and that the Israeli Air Force was, for all intents and purposes, quarantined to Israeli air space.

Wildemen also made his calls. He woke up the necessary officers, and gave the orders that immediately implemented the quarantine of the Israeli Air Force.

In a quiet moment, after all the calls were made, Al Niddiem and Ben Wildemen sat down for a private talk about the true problem they faced.

"Al, what are the chances that it wasn't our gas?"

"None. We know what the Russians have. Their gas leaves traceable toxins. Their process isn't as clean as ours. Only the British are as advanced as we are. No, it was our gas." He rubbed his forehead. His eyes were tired and his temples throbbed from tension. "I don't see any way to avoid briefing the President."

"Not yet." Wildemen held up his hand. "Let's see what happens in the next few hours. If necessary, we'll brief Gordon first, and then proceed from there. Let's wait and see how the seven thirty meeting goes."

Niddiem reluctantly agreed. Moments later they left for their individual offices. They still had a lot to do before the meeting.

The group gathered at seven thirty sharp in the Situation Room. Without exception, they looked haggard and tired. Only the President had rested a short while, though sleep hadn't come. After his call to the Israeli Prime Minister his mind had raced, full of potential disasters and crises.

"Okay, where do we stand? What have we accomplished, and what do we know?" The President poured himself a cup of black coffee. "Ben, Let's start with you since you're Chairman of the Joint Chiefs of Staff. How's our military position?."

"As of four a.m. the Israeli Air Force has effectively been quarantined within their borders. We have the carrier group headed by the J.F.K. in the Eastern Mediterranean, a task force group led by the Coral Sea in the northern Persian Gulf on full alert, and A.W.A.C.s from Saudi bases with our F-16s from Saudi and Kuwait flying air patrols along the Israeli borders. They haven't challenged us yet, although we have monitored flights along the borders."

"Are they testing for holes?" Gordon asked.

"Could be, or they're just making sure we're there. Doesn't matter, they can't get through. Israel is a small country and we have it blanketed."

"Good." The President nodded. "At least we don't have to worry about that part of the problem. John, how did your conversation with Mateusz Adar go?"

"He wasn't pleased. At first he refused to back down. I had to play real hard ball." Gordon smiled. "He was speechless when I informed him of the identity of the terrorists in Taiwan. He adamantly denied any retaliatory strike was in the works and he even became indignant. When I informed him of our knowledge of Plan Goliath he denied its existence and declared they have no nuclear weapons."

"What do they think we are, stupid? How did he react to the quarantine?"

Gordon leaned back and crossed his legs. "He went ballistic. You know the typical rhetoric about interfering in a sovereign country and all of that bullshit. I've heard it from him before. But in the end it didn't amount to a hill of beans next to our threat. He understood, and took it seriously."

"Good. I don't want them questioning our resolve." The President threw a glance to Niddiem and nodded. "Al, what do you have from the C.I.A's end of things?"

Niddiem took a moment to adjust his right suspender strap that had slipped down. "We're having much better cooperation from the Israeli intelligence group. They need our knowledge and expertise. They're out of their league with this one, much as they hate to admit it. They found the point of dispersion of the gas. It was from hollow bricks that had just been laid at a repair site in the Russian Church."

He passed out pictures of the church that he'd received only moments earlier. "The two Palestinians involved in the gun battle outside the church were the masons who'd delivered, and placed the bricks. The truck they drove originated, with the bricks, in Haifa. The bill of lading for the bricks showed they traveled from Jordan to Cyprus, then to Haifa. Backtracking from Jordan, though, has been a problem. The Jordanians aren't cooperating with us. However, the Israelis found the electronic timing mechanism that activated the gas. The circuitry had been cannibalized from an I.B.M. computer. The computer was one the Iraqis took from Kuwait after their invasion in '91'. The piece happened to have a serial number on it and we were able to trace it."

The President stood and walked to a window, staring out in silence for a moment. "I had two conversations with the Prime Minister." He continued to face the window. "The first one was filled with sympathy and understanding. I called him that time."

Now he turned to face the group. "My second conversation occurred shortly after John talked with Adar. This time he called me. He was filled with anger and threats. I couldn't blame him. I wonder how any of us would react, if we were told our Air Force was quarantined within our borders. I let him talk. I didn't try to stop him. I figured I owed him that much. After a while, he calmed down." He walked over and took his seat. "The bottom line is he wants Saddam Hussein's neck. He agreed to try it my way, only for a while though. He does agree that blasting Baghdad back to the Stone Age would be counterproductive. He's agreed to step down from Plan

Goliath, but I still want our planes airborne and ready. Anything can still happen."

After taking a gulp of coffee, he continued, "It appears the gas came from Iraq with the help of the old guard in the now defunct U.S.S.R. We agreed that what's left of the gas must be destroyed. The Iraqis have obviously done a good job of hiding it from the U.N inspectors.

We will," the President said pointing at Niddem, "find it, and destroy it. And we will bring back hard evidence that this was the gas used in Jerusalem. If we can prove that Russia was involved, it will be a very big bargaining chip in the future. Moreover, Saddam Hussein will stand trial, even in abstentia."

He looked around the room, making eye contact with everyone. "Whatever sentence is handed down to that bastard must be imposed on him. We'll leave that to the Israelis. But they can only go after him, not the entire Iraqi population. I'll use whatever information we have to keep the Russians in line. Ben," the President continued turning towards Wildemen, "I want you to coordinate a Special Forces group to destroy the remaining gas and return with evidence."

"That's if we can find out where it is," Ben replied.

"Al, how long before our C.I.A. team can pinpoint the storage facility?" the President asked.

"A day, a week, a month. Who knows? Maybe never. It could be hidden ten feet away from us, buried in shifting sand, and we'd never know it."

"That answer is unacceptable!" The President's voice rang across the room. "You will find the storage site, and find it fast! I can only keep the Israeli Air Force grounded for so long. What am I supposed to do, shoot down their entire Air Force? Frankly, I don't know why they've bought our line so far. Al, soon! Now if you'll excuse me, I have to prepare for a press conference." The President stood and abruptly left the room.

Most of the group filtered out quietly. The President's unofficial inner circle lingered, Al Niddiem and Ben Wildemen stayed behind by design. John Gordon stayed behind by a quirk of fate, a fate he would bear the burden of for a long time. Niddiem and Wildemen conferred in a low tone, nodding in agreement. Niddiem then approached Gordon who was still in his seat reviewing papers, and spoke softly to him. "John, Ben and I need to have a word with you privately."

"Fine, how about my office in five minutes?"

Niddiem nodded and walked away.

Gordon's office was small by corporate standards, but it was functional for his needs as the Secretary of State. He sat behind his desk rubbing his eyes as Niddiem and Wildemen entered. Exhausted, he planned to lie down for a nap after this short meeting.

"John, we have information you need to know," Niddiem said.

"Does the President know?"

"No. We're not sure he should just yet," Wildemen added.

"Really?"

"Let me start with a little history," Niddiem said. "First, remember the anger and hysteria within the administration during the early eighties concerning Khomeini and Iran. The Iranians were out of control. They held our citizens hostage. There was great fear in Saudi Arabia and Kuwait that Islamic fundamentalists would not only spark but also succeed in fundamentalist revolutions. The United States imports twenty-five percent of its oil from the Saudi fields. Can you imagine what it would've done to our economy if Islamic fundamentalists controlled the pricing on the oil in Iran, Kuwait and Saudi Arabia? Our economy was already depressed because of high OPEC oil prices.

"Saudi Arabia's economy was also in a slump," he continued. "Their market share of OPEC oil was depressed. They, along with Kuwait, were financing Iraq in its war with Iran to the tune of billions of dollars. Iraq was losing and that frightened everyone."

Niddiem glanced at Wildemen who nodded his support to continue. "The United States and the Saudi government entered into an agreement...no, it was more of an alliance...based on oil. They secretly fixed oil prices at a level that benefited the United States economy. With the jump start to our economy there was an increase in oil consumption. The Saudis then boosted production of oil and increased their market share. In return, the United States was to aid and assist the Iraqis in their war against Iran. We did so in many ways, both legal and covert."

"Covert, bullshit! What you really mean is illegal," Gordon said.

"Yes, if you must use that term," Wildemen interjected.

"Al! You're not saying we supplied Iraq with chemical weapons?" Gordon asked.

"No. Absolutely not! But we did assist them in developing their gas."

"What! Were you people crazy?" Gordon leaned forward in his chair.

"No! Those were hysterical and paranoid times. At the time there were two schools of thought. One was to assist Iraq to become the military equal of Iran. Then they'd be at a stalemate."

"And the other?" Gordon asked.

"To fry Iran!" Wildemen stated.

"You god damn fools! I can't believe what I'm hearing. Do you have any idea the position you've placed us in?" Gordon fell back in his chair.

"There's more, actually."

"How much worse can it get? Tell me, Al, how much more is there?"

"It was a very paranoid time."

"Enlighten me."

Niddiem made eye contact with Wildemen again before continuing. "At the end of World War Two there was a major push by both the United States and the Soviet Union to benefit from the research and development the Germans produced during the war. As the war wound down the intelligence service in Washington heard about chemical weapons, specifically a nerve gas that was developed and tested in Auschwitz."

"On Jews?"

"Who else? Anyway, at the time the Russians were scooping and running with as many scientists as they could find. We were paranoid. Though Roosevelt felt that Stalin was a man we could mold and work with, the military and intelligence community had their doubts. So we targeted a young chemist named Claus Von Wilbert, amongst others, for retrieval. He was in charge of the experiments at Auschwitz.

"We brought him to the U.S., gave him a new identity, and he continued his research here. In the late seventies, he retired. But when the Iraqis needed help developing their chemical weapons program we reenlisted him. We set him up with a wealthy German industrialist, and together they developed the gas that was to be used against the Iranians. The war ended though, and it looks like now that gas has been used against the Israelis."

Gordon's face was buried in his hands at this point. He looked up at them. "Do the two of you understand...do you have any idea of the consequences, if what you've just told me ever gets out?"

"Yes, I think we do," Wildemen replied.

"No! You don't!" Gordon stood up behind his desk knocking his chair over. "Let me spell it out for you. Instead of bringing a murderer, a contributor to the Holocaust, to trial, we hid and protected him. Then we, the United States, helped this man, this butcher, years later by finding him German financing to kill more Jews! No, I don't think you understand what this could do to our government! This country! This President!"

The room was quiet for a moment as Gordon regained control and began to pace. Neither Niddiem nor Wildemen said a word. After a long moment, Gordon spoke, "All, and I do mean all, of that gas must be found and destroyed."

"We know that," Wildemen replied. "I plan to speak to Colonel Burnhall. Once we locate the gas a Delta Squad will go in and destroy it."

"At present that's all we can do." Gordon's mind was racing through the options. "Other administrations made those decisions. For now we'll tell the President nothing. I'll coordinate any damage control."

"A cover up?" Wildemen asked.

"I don't give a fuck what you call it. This President was not, is not, and will not, be involved in this mess. Is that understood?"

They nodded in agreement.

"I want honest assessments from the both of you."

"When Al tells us where the gas is, as sure as the sun will rise in the east, I'll ensure it is destroyed." Wildemen stated looking at Niddiem.

"The Agency will find it, Ben. We'll find it for you."

They rose to leave.

"Al," Gordon said. "I need a word with you. Ben, we'll speak this afternoon."

After Wildemen left, Gordon spoke quickly and to the point. "One, we will destroy the gas. Two, under no circumstances can that Delta team return with any evidence implicating the United States."

"What are you saying?"

"I'm saying the Delta team cannot return from their mission. After they have destroyed the gas, they are to be taken out."

"What do you mean taken out?"

"Look, don't make this any tougher for me. I have no choice. Our country can never be implicated in this disaster. The Delta Squad will not return from their mission! They are to be eliminated after the mission!" Gordon stated with fiery determination in his eyes.

"And how am I supposed to see to that?"

"It's up to you. I don't like this any more than you do, but it has to be done."

Moments later Gordon sat alone in his office. All desire for sleep was long gone. He wondered when he would rest peacefully again.

8   Chapter Eight

The day had been aimless for Abraham as he wandered the streets of Jerusalem. He looked disheveled with his white hair haphazardly going in all directions and his shirt wrinkled and stained with underarm sweat from walking in the Middle East heat. The pain in his wounded leg was completely overshadowed by the emotional pain inside. His mood, as was the mood throughout the city, was one of grief, confusion, and fear. Many people stayed inside. Those who did venture out carried gas masks close to their sides.

Without any preconceived plan, Abraham found himself walking along the Avenue of the Righteous Among the Nations, as it slowly climbed the Mount of Remembrance. It was lined with trees that had been planted to give thanks to all the non-Jews, who through their own courage and sacrifice saved many Jews from death during World War Two. At the top of the hill the Israeli government had constructed an imposing memorial museum that housed the story of the Holocaust. The main building, rectangular in shape, was constructed of large natural uncut boulders and stones. Abraham walked into the main foyer.

"Oh, no." Abraham stopped and raised a closed fist to his mouth. In front of him were images of horror and anguish recreated and depicted in jagged twisted steel. They captured the essence of terror he'd left behind many years ago. A solitary candle lit the huge room. Its flickering rays danced off the hand carved names of the death camps that had been cut into the rock: 'Auschwitz', 'Dachau', 'Bergen-Belsen'. He stopped in front of each name. He wondered, would anyone bother adding Jerusalem to the list?

The room was quiet. It offered no speeches or sermons. A few people moved around its perimeter. They refrained from weeping or shouting damnation against those responsible. The memorial said it all. It spoke eloquently for the pain inflicted upon the Jewish people.

Abraham wondered if he would find peace within these walls, or further torment. Still he continued his tour, and soon took a garden path that led to the next building.

Upon entering it, he held his chest with both hands. "Oh my God!" he muttered. In front of him row after row of pictures hung of the camps, the death, and the horror. That period simply known as the "Holocaust" reached out and mercilessly grabbed him, as it did every viewer. Mesmerized, Abraham stopped and forced himself to look around. The sights, the sounds, the smells, flashed vividly in his mind. They were as real as the days he had spent in the camps.

'WILKOMMEN AU AUSCHWITZ-BIRKENAU'. He shivered as he gazed upon that photo. His palms began to sweat and he trembled. Ever so slowly, though, he moved from picture to picture.

"Yes, I remember you," he occasionally said to individual faces in the pictures. He could remember their faces, not their names. Pictures of the camp, individual buildings, gates and guard towers rekindled the emotions he thought he had put to rest many years ago.

"Hall of Names," Abraham muttered out loud, reading a small sign with an arrow under it.

"Excuse me," he said to one of the museum curators. "What is the Hall of Names?"

"Original documents," the guard replied. His voice strained. Then he said, "Yesterday's massacre...These halls are supposed to be a reminder of past hate. So people would learn.

But they have learned nothing!" He hung his head and tears welled up in his eyes. "I'm sorry. I just don't understand any of this sometimes. You…you had a question…yes, the Hall of Names holds original documents of over three million Jews recounting their experiences at the camps."

"Thank you." Abraham entered the room and looked around for the section labeled Auschwitz. Finding it, he sat in one of the private cubicles provided for reading, meditation and grieving. He slowly started to leaf through books and diaries. Soon he found himself reading intently about incidents and people he remembered.

After four hours it dawned on him he hadn't found a single mention of Claus Von Wilbert, the Chemist of Death. His random scanning now became a concentrated search. Still, he found no reference, no comment, and no mention of that butcher.

He slammed a book of documents closed and sat for a moment.

"Something is wrong. He killed too many people. Why isn't he mentioned?"

He searched out a curator, ignoring the pain in his leg. "Where can I find more detailed information? I need to find information on a particular person, a Nazi. Can you help me?"

"Yes I can. You need to go to the Archive Building. Everything there is logged and categorized." He pointed out the window to the next building.

Moments later, Abraham stood in the main gallery of the Archive Building. It was large and he didn't know which way to go.

"May I help you?" a whisper came from his left. Abraham turned and found an elderly Jewish scholar, dressed in subdued dark colors with a black yarmulke on his head.

"Yes, I hope so. I was in the other building, the Hall of Names. I was unable to find information on people I knew while I was in Auschwitz."

"A survivor. I was in Bergen-Belsen myself. Have you signed our Book of Survivors?" He stood piously. His hands were clasped one on top of the other in front of him.

"No, I haven't."

"Please, before you leave, do sign it. Come. Let me show you how to access information from our file system. That will tell you where to find the information you want."

Abraham walked quietly behind him.

"Will there also be information about the Nazis who ran the camps?"

"Oh yes." He stopped. "It's very common for survivors to want to look up and read about those who tortured them. It's a natural cathartic healing process."

After being shown how to operate the system, Abraham set about his task. He wanted to find the definitive fate of the butcher chemist. But after three hours he had found nothing. No mention of him. He checked the references of those tried at Nuremberg. Again he drew a blank.

"Excuse me," a soft voice came from behind. "I have to ask you to leave. It is closing time."

Abraham looked up and saw the kind curator standing over him. "He's not here! Why isn't he here? You told me this building held everything!"

"Who's not here?"

"Claus Von Wilbert, the butcher." His fist pounded the desk in front of him. "He forced me to clean the bodies out of his lab. He's not mentioned anywhere! Why? He was known! He should be here!"

"I'm sorry. I don't know what to tell you."

"He was alive and captured during the liberation. The Americans took him away in a jeep."

"Then I can only suggest that you check with the Americans."

"Where?" He stood up quickly, startling the curator who took a step back. "Where should I check?"

"Washington D.C. I know we're supposed to have copies of everything, but who knows, you might get lucky and find what you're looking for there. But now we must go. The building is closing."

*   *   *   *

"Damn! All I want is an open line." Megan McAllister slammed the phone down.

Her co-worker, Maurice, looked up. "Still no luck?"

"No. You know, we're in the god damned C.I.A. It's supposed to be the most sophisticated communication center in the world. Is it too much to ask for just one open trunk line? Abraham could be dead over there in Jerusalem. We should be able to find out."

"Megan, you know how crazy it is over there."

"Well, I have no intention of giving up." She picked up the phone and tried to route her call through a different country as Maurice turned back to his work.

A half hour later, Megan entered the small room off of Al Niddiem's office. It was a standard conference room with nondescript pictures and décor. There was nothing to distract those in the room from their primary purpose, meeting with the head of the C.I.A. She sat alone for a moment, waiting for Niddiem to arrive. Megan was thirty-two and single, and had risen quickly within the ranks of the C.I.A. Typically dressed in soft feminine styles that highlighted her shoulder length auburn hair and green eyes, her co-workers knew not to underestimate her for she was a ruthless tenacious fighter. She'd worked with Abraham Feinstein for the last year and had learned a lot from him. Megan had also grown very fond of him. Now everyone was so wrapped up in the turmoil surrounding the massacre that she figured they'd all forgotten about him. She had tried the phone service for close to an hour but the influx of overseas and domestic calls had overloaded the system.

Al Niddiem finally entered the conference room from his office. "Al, you look awful," she said. "Didn't you get any sleep?"

Niddiem's white shirt was ruffled up and overhung his pants, which made him look even heavier than he was.

"This crisis kept me up all night. I'm exhausted." He flopped in his chair.

"You know, Abraham was visiting his son in Jerusalem."

"I know," he said. Although his surprised look made Megan suspect he had forgotten. "Unfortunately, Abraham will have to fend for himself. There's such turmoil over there, I doubt we could even find him. And if he's dead, well, there's nothing we can do for him."

Megan decided to drop it. She knew there must be something else eating at him to make him so indifferent. She'd seen him in many other crises, and had always admired his calm, clear-headed way of handling things. Today, though, he was an obvious wreck.

Niddiem covered his mouth and gave a big yawn. "You've been briefed on every bit of information we have concerning the massacre in Jerusalem. I need you and your team to find the gas that remains in Iraq. In Abraham's absence, you'll head the team. We have minimal amount of time."

"How minimal?" she asked.

"The President wants to know the location within three days. But I'm sure if needed we could squeeze a few more out of him."

"You've got to be kidding me!" Megan shouted shaking her head. "We get three days to find what military intelligence couldn't during the entire '91' Gulf War."

"Megan, I need you to help me on this one, not fight me. We already know what the gas was, and the chemicals needed to produce it. We've pinpointed this plant as its origin." Niddiem pushed a button on the table in front of him and activated a slide projector recessed in the wall. A photo projected onto the wall. "This was the Baqubah Chemical plant six months prior to the Gulf War." The projector advanced to the next slide. "This is what it looks like now." The slide showed rubble and twisted metal. "The gas originated here. This is as good a starting place as any."

"You're sure it originated there?"

"Yes. Military intelligence talked to their own R & D on chemical weapons. It seems the Russians developed a similar gas. This is the only plant in Iraq that held the components and equipment needed to make it. But, it's obvious they moved it prior to the war. That means it could be anywhere." He shut the projector off.

Megan's eyes caught his for an instant, but he quickly looked away. That confirmed her intuition. He hadn't told her everything.

"My team and I will need access to the Brain and the Seven Dwarfs," she said.

"Without question." He handed her a plastic security card the size of a credit card.

"We'll get started immediately. Why don't you get some rest." She stood and left.

On her way down the hall, she put her security card in her pocket. It carried personalized data on her, her palm and fingerprints along with her retinal scan. All were digitally encoded in it. After placing it into the appropriate slot and firmly pressing her palm against a hand contour reader, her palm and fingerprints would be matched against those encoded on the card and the mainframe computer. At the same time she would lean forward allowing a beam of light to scan her retinal image. Then and only if both scans matched the data on her card and the data in the internal system would she gain access to 'The Brain'. It was without doubt currently the world's most sophisticated spy technology.

The Brain of the C.I.A. was a room the size of a football field. In it sat a massive computer disc storage facility. The Seven Dwarfs were large silos that each held over six thousand high density computer disks. Automatic robots loaded and unloaded these disks. The data was then accessed by one of the Brain's Cray 4-MP Supercomputers. Millions of satellite photographs were stored in this collective farm of information, along with an incredible amount of written material. That information, along with the formidable power of the Cray 4-MP's, gave a person with the right security clearance an enormous ability to access top security information.

Thirty minutes later, Megan's team converged in their conference room. She had already briefed them on their tasks and now they would quickly formulate a plan.

Megan started the meeting. "First of all, I know you're all concerned about Abraham. So am I. Believe me when I tell you I've tried to find out anything concerning him. But it's a zoo over there. Let's hope he's safe. In the meantime, we have an important job to do. I've been asked to be the acting team leader. If no one objects I'll accept, but only until Abraham returns."

She looked around the room to see only nods of encouragement. "I know you've had only thirty minutes but I want to know the main resources each of you and your teams will need. Tim, why don't you start."

Tim, thirty-one years old, was a master at electronic surveillance. Single and a graduate of M.I.T., his knowledge of routing and re-routing systems to get them to do what he wanted was invaluable. N.A.S.A. had called upon him more than once to reprogram a malfunctioning system deep in space. He spoke quietly. "At present, we have a surveillance ship fifteen nautical miles off the coast of Kuwait. It has the ability to intercept all radio traffic throughout Iraq. It can pick up the entire radio spectrum from commercial signals through microwave pulse bursts. After I've tied it into the Brain we can track over five thousand simultaneous calls. I'll tie into it on a live feed through a commercial satellite in a synchronous orbit over the gulf. That, along with the CI92 we installed in Baghdad, should cover it all. If they say it, we'll hear it."

"What's the CI92?" Megan asked.

Tim broke into a broad smile. "CI92, stands for Communication Intercept 1992. We knew the North Koreans were helping Iraq rebuild their infrastructure. They were giving them a main telecommunication trunk line to rebuild their telephone system. On the way from North Korea to Baghdad we updated it. We installed an intercept, which gathers all traffic passing through the main line at any given time and digitally compresses it. It then sends out a high frequency radio burst, which we pick up."

"So we have all the telephones lines in Baghdad tapped." Megan returned his smile.

"Basically, yes."

Megan looked at the two other members of her team and felt confident in their ability.

To her left was Raani. He was a forty-one year old balding second-generation Pakistani immigrant. He had a PHD in spatial physics. Raani was an expert with puzzles and had the ability to see the big picture. He could take a piece here and a piece there, put it together and make sense of it all. His team was to sift through and review intercepted messages just prior to and during the Gulf War. If even the slightest reference were made to the gas, his team would find it.

Next to Raani was Maurice. An African-American born in Kenya, his family moved to the United States when he was twelve. He still spoke formal British English with a Kenyan accent that made him sound like a stuffy scholar from Jamaica. He was twenty-seven and wore a ponytail along with a diamond stud in his left ear. He would work the closest with Megan. His greatest love was photography, and he was an expert in photographic analysis. His skill lay in being able to decipher the natural from the unnatural, and in detecting manmade cover. He and Megan would work together reviewing satellite and aerial photos, to try and track the transfer of the gas.

One hour later the meeting ended. They had agreed on how they would proceed. With time at a premium they all knew they had no time to spare for idle chitchat.

Minutes turned into hours, which dragged on into the evening for Megan's team. They had had no luck yet, and decided to work straight through the night with only short naps to tide them over. Every hour that passed raised the pressure from Israel demanding results.

Megan rubbed her eyes as she stood up from her workstation. She had spent the last seven hours looking through a small magnifying glass at blown up photos of the Baqubah chemical plant. Reams of photos of the plant sat stacked next to her. The only difference in each photo was the time and the day it had been shot.

"Sore eyes, boss?" Maurice looked up from his view screen. His eyes were also bloodshot. He'd been scanning a monitor, looking for different routes of transport from the plant site. The shot chosen could then be downloaded to a printer for closer analysis.

"I'm becoming cross eyed. I need a cup of coffee." She stretched and walked to a small table in the corner.

When she returned, she gazed again at the photo that had occupied her for the last twenty minutes. "Maurice, come here, I want to show you something."

"What?"

"Look at this barge. Follow it downstream on the next few photos." She moved out of the way.

Maurice bent down over the table and eyed the photo through a square magnifying glass. The barge rode high in the water. Its cargo hold was empty.

"It's an empty barge, so what?" He looked up.

"Follow the barge downstream past the plant." She handed him five more photos.

He methodically examined each photo. He spent the longest time on the last one, the one of the barge downstream of the plant. Then he went back and forth three or four times between the last two photos. He looked up and smiled. "This barge is not the same as this one."

"You're right. It's subtle, but they're different." She took the magnifying glass and looked at the last two pictures again.

"I think we can assume the switch was made at the plant. But how?" For the next few minutes Maurice leafed through other photos. He found the ones he wanted, then he and Megan sat for the next half hour and examined the surrounding river bank.

Megan stood and arched her back trying to take the kinks out of it. "I don't see anything abnormal with the river bank."

"I don't either."

"Maybe we're going about this wrong. What are we looking for exactly? A place they were able to switch barges. It doesn't look like it's a natural hiding place. So it must be man made."

"Right," Maurice said. "There's basically no way to alter a natural setting and get away with it. It only looks unnatural."

"So, let's assume for a moment they understand that concept also. Given that, if you were them, how would you hide the barge?"

Maurice leaned back in his chair and thought for a moment. "It's actually very simple. We can't alter any natural setting, so I'd alter a pre-constructed manmade structure."

"A structure the barge has access to," Megan said.

"You're right. And the only one is the dock by the river. You'd have to alter it so it would still look normal from above."

"Build it raised, so a barge could hide under it. From above it would look like a dock at the river's edge."

"Exactly. Nothing out of place, nothing hidden."

"I need a break," Megan said. "You want something to eat?"

"Sounds great."

They walked off satisfied they had the first piece of the puzzle.

Forty minutes later, they sat down again at their desks. Megan had briefed the other groups on the progress they had made.

"Anything from the group?" Maurice asked.

"No, just hundreds of dead ends." She shuffled through some photos.

"We can assume the gas was moved by barge. But was it moved up or down stream?"

"Up." Megan said. "First we have a barge, high in the water, which means it's empty, heading downstream to the plant. We'll call this the Chemical Barge. In this next picture, taken a few hours later the barge is now downstream from the plant, still high in the water, still empty. For the moment let's assume they're different barges. We'll call this the Decoy

Barge." She handed him a new photo. "This was taken two days later, three days before the air strike."

He looked at it for a moment. "The Decoy Barge is low in the water, carrying heavy cargo. It is downstream from the plant and traveling back upstream towards the plant. The Decoy Barge is returning to the plant."

"Correct."

He held his hand out for the next obvious photo in the sequence. "Again a barge, still low in the water upstream from the plant and traveling away from it. This is the Chemical Barge. Empty when it was traveling downstream towards the plant but now full of Chemicals traveling upstream away from the plant."

"Again correct."

"They made the switch at the plant. So your hypothesis is the Decoy Barge was sent downstream to load up with unimportant cargo, while the Chemical Barge was loaded at the plant."

"With the gas," Megan interjected. "The dock at the chemical plant was the switch point for the barges. The Decoy Barge was sent back to the plant and stayed there hidden from view while the Chemical Barge took its place on the river, traveling upstream. The next question is, where upstream did the chemical barge deposit the gas?"

"Man, oh man. I don't think we've got any other choice. We have to inspect the river's edge from this point north," said Maurice, tugging at his ponytail.

"We're gonna need help on this one. I'll pull Frank and Tony who are working on another project and have them join us. They're both good."

"Fine, I'll take Frank and the left side of the river bank. Tony and you can have the right side."

The night sky gave way to the early morning rays of the rising sun, but those inside the building at Langley Virginia hadn't noticed. Their attention had been focused on every inch of the river north of the chemical plant. Megan had pulled six others in to help them. They progressed under the assumption that the Iraqis had hidden the barge upstream in the same manner as at the chemical plant. But north of the plant were hundreds upon hundreds of docks and cement walls up to the river's edge. Any one of which could have been altered.

It was Tony who first noticed something. "Megan. I think I've got it."

"Put it on the wall so we can all see."

Tony inserted the photo under an overhead projector and the image was projected onto the wall screen. He walked over to the screen and started to explain. "The first thing that caught my eye in this picture was these four kids jumping and swimming off the dock in the river. Now look here." He pointed with a laser pointer. "Two of the kids were captured mid jump off the dock. But it's not a small jump. Look at the length of the shadows that are cast on the water. We know the time of day, so the angle of the sun is also known. We can measure the length of the shadow. Simple geometry tells us the length of all the sides of the triangle. Applying that to this picture tells us these kids are jumping off something high. That could only happen if the dock was raised significantly. Looks like that dock is raised and there's an access under it. It has to be."

"Is there any structure nearby?" Megan asked.

"You bet. The Minaret of Samarra is only one hundred yards from the dock. It's a very old temple of worship to the people of that region."

"Well, people, I think we just got lucky. Thanks, Tony. Frank, I want you to pull all the photos we have of this Minaret. Maurice, you and Tony pull all the photos you can find of this dock area. Try to find some angled side views. I need harder proof that the barge was hidden and unloaded here. The rest of you, keep reviewing the river bank for any other areas that might hide the barge." Megan stood and left the room.

In years gone by Maurice's task would have been extremely difficult, but prior to the Gulf War air attack, the U.S. Air Force had photographed every inch of Iraq at least ten times over. It wouldn't be hard, just time consuming, to find multiple shots of the rivers edge from far away angles. And with the help of technology even a far away angle shot could be brought into clear crisp view.

*　　　*　　　*　　　*

Niddiem sat in his office and was pleased. He had gotten some sleep and physically felt better though the emotional strain of his dilemma was still there. "Two days. That's all it took. That's great."

"Whoa!" Megan held up her hands. "This is just a preliminary report, not the definitive one. I thought you should be updated, but based on the information so far, I wouldn't call in the Marines. We have to look at it from all angles, literally. When we're sure this target is the end point for the gas, we'll let you know."

"I understand what you're saying, Megan. But I need to inform the President of this finding anyway."

"Al, if you take this to the President, you and I know it'll snowball! They'll be storming the site before we have definitive proof."

"Believe me, I understand what you're saying. But I need to get him off my back. I promise I'll present it as only a shred of evidence." She wasn't going to talk him out of this.

"Wars have started on just a shred of evidence in the past," she said. "I don't want to be held responsible if they jump the gun."

"That's why I need to give the President something. We have to avoid a war. Anything to help the President persuade Israel not to avenge this massacre will be helpful. You won't be held responsible."

Moments after Megan left, Niddiem had Gordon on the phone and told him the good news.

"How are you proceeding on the other problem?" Gordon asked.

"We'll talk about that in person. I have an idea I want to discuss with you, but let's make sure we're on the right track before we worry about other issues."

Niddiem hung up the phone and sat back in his chair. His eyes fell upon the wall plaque that held the Agency's Motto, **"YOU SHALL KNOW THE TRUTH AND THE TRUTH SHALL MAKE YOU FREE"**. He shook his head and finalized in his mind what he would tell Gordon.

9   Chapter Nine

Maurice sat at his desk, pleased with himself. The search hadn't taken half as long as he had expected. When he saw Megan approach, he smiled and gave her a thumbs up. "We've nailed it down. The Minaret is where the gas was off loaded." Though excited, he still had a British reserve in his voice.

"That's great. How'd you find it?"

"We were lucky, plain and simple. We combed all the Air Force's recon photos of the area, and by chance we got a side angle shot of the riverbank. Not only does it show the dock elevated off the water, it also shows a small amount of the barge." He held up a photo.

"You found a barge hidden under a dock? Can we prove it's the same one?"

"Yes, without a doubt. We digitally enhanced the photo along with the one of the barge north of the plant." He spread both blow-ups on the desk and pointed. "Here on the side of the barge is a two foot long red paint mark. And here's the same streak on the same side of the barge in the recon photo. If the barge had been turned around, the red streak would've been on the inside and we wouldn't have been able to make a positive I.D."

"Maurice, thank you. You just made my day a lot easier. Do me a favor?"

"Sure."

"Make slides of everything we have here. I'll need them soon, say half an hour."

"You got it, boss."

Moments later, Megan was back in Niddiem's office. "We found the proof we need. The Minaret is absolutely the place where the barge dropped off the gas."

"No doubt in your mind?" He motioned her to a seat.

"None, none at all," she replied without hesitation.

"Fine, I'll want you to give the presentation. It'll be at the White House with the President and the National Security Council. They'll have some hard questions and they'll want answers. Can you handle it?"

"When do we go?"

"I'll call John Gordon and tell him we'll be there in an hour. Will that give you enough time to assemble a presentation?"

"It's being assembled as we speak."

Five minutes later, Megan stared at her reflection in the washroom mirror. Her hair was tangled, her makeup long gone. The dark circles under her eyes were testimony to the hours she'd put into the assignment.

She shook her head. "This will not do. You will not give your first briefing to the President looking like this."

Moments later, she returned to the washroom with a towel, a face cloth and soap in hand. After a good scrubbing, fresh makeup, and brushing of her hair she smiled at the reflection.

"That's much better. Except..." She looked at her clothes that were hopelessly wrinkled. "Nothing you can do about it, I hope they've been living in theirs as long as I've been in these." After one final brush of her hair she left.

Ten minutes later Megan rode down Pennsylvania Avenue in the back of Niddiem's official black limousine. Beside her sat Niddiem. She sat quietly, reviewing her notes. When they turned onto Executive Drive Niddiem finally broke Megan's concentration. "I think you should put your notes down for a moment and relax. It won't be that bad. I've already asked you most of the questions I think they'll ask. You've convinced me.

I don't think you'll have any problem convincing the President."

"That's what I'm nervous about, trying to convince the President. He's such a formidable person."

"Yes he is. But never forget he's still a person, no different than any of us. Remember, you're going in with information he needs." He put a comforting hand on her shoulder. "You're just there to present, not to sell. It's up to him to accept or reject it, and make decisions accordingly. But you should know, he has two moods in meetings. One where only he talks asks questions and demands answers. Basically, you only speak when spoken to. The second is a free-for-all with open opinions from everyone. But I warn you, you won't be greeted too kindly if you jump in. You're an outsider. Good advice is for you to speak only when asked a question."

The limousine pulled through the White House gates and stopped near a side entrance. They stepped out under the watchful eye of the Marine Guard assigned to this entrance. With the recent massacre in Jerusalem, security throughout Washington's federal buildings had been heightened. Without comment, the Guard opened the door for them to enter. Niddiem acknowledged this with a nod, but the Marine kept his stoic stance, not making eye contact, or responding in any fashion to them.

"Is this your first time in the White House?" Niddiem asked Megan.

"Yes. Believe it or not, I've never even taken the tour."

"Well you can bet this tour will take you places no tourist would see."

They approached the security desk and a Secret Service agent had them sign in and gave them badges to wear.

"We'll take the stairs," Niddiem said. "I need the exercise." Niddiem patted his belly.

The Shoe Shine Boy

They descended three flights to a small corridor that led
them to the Situation Room. Built during the Truman
Administration, it was a pseudo bunker with concrete walls,
originally designed to protect the President and his Cabinet
from a nuclear attack. Because of today's more accurate and
powerful thermonuclear weapons the room isn't a safe haven,
so now it is used now for highly sensitive meetings. Niddiem
and Megan signed another register at a second security desk,
and then entered the Situation Room.

National Security Advisor Bob Tillman, Chairman of the
Joint Chiefs of Staff Ben Wildemen, and the Secretary of
Defense Steve Albridge greeted them with tense smiles and
nods. A large pot of coffee sat on a credenza, and all three had
full cups in front of them.

"Give your slides to him." Niddiem pointed to a non-
cabinet official in the corner. "He'll get you set up."

Megan looked around. She instantly felt intimidated by the
seriousness of the gathering. After handing her slides over she
walked back to where Niddiem had already taken a seat, but
stopped and hesitated. She didn't know if she should take the
seat next to him. She didn't have to wait long for direction.

"There's a seat by the podium for you," Niddiem instructed
her. She turned and saw where he was pointing. She sat and
observed those at the small mahogany table in front of her.
There was none of the good old boy bantering back and forth
she had half-expected. The group sat stoic and just looked
tired. She fully understood the seriousness of the crisis, but the
toll it was taking on them shocked her.

The door in the back of the room opened and John Gordon
entered. Despite his suit he still wore a string tie and shiny
cowboy boots. "The President will be down shortly." His eyes
locked onto hers. "Are you ready for your presentation, young
lady?"

"Yes sir, but please call me Megan." She read his reply in the scowl on his face.

Gordon took his seat and at that moment the door opened and President Rhodes entered. She instinctively stood up as everyone else in the room rose, and then waited with the others to sit down again until the President was seated.

She was instantly impressed with the President. His presence alone projected authority. He brought the meeting immediately to order. "Let's make this short and to the point. Al, I understand you have pinpointed where the gas is."

"Yes, Mr. President. I feel we have. I've brought Megan McAllister to conduct the briefing."

"You may begin." Without even a courteous nod the President looked at her.

Her pulse raced and suddenly she felt she couldn't get enough air in her lungs. She stood and moved in front of the podium. The few seconds it took for her to find the wireless control and the button on the electronic pointer felt like an hour. When she looked up she saw all eyes impatiently fixed on her. The lights dimmed and she pushed the button advancing to the first slide.

"Thank you gentlemen," she paused and took a deep breath. "This is a picture of the Baqubah Chemical plant just outside Baghdad. This picture was taken just prior to the beginning of the '91' Gulf War. Through prior analysis it was felt this plant was the only one in Iraq capable of developing and producing the gas that was responsible for the massacre in Jerusalem."

Megan advanced to the next slide. "This is a picture of the Baqubah Chemical plant at the end of the Gulf War. Notice the complete destruction. It is reasonable to assume the gas had been moved prior to the bombings."

"Mr. Niddiem approached me with these two pictures and asked me and my team to trace the gas from this plant to its end point. I won't belabor the ways we tried that were fruitless. But let me preface what I am going to show you by saying that it is time lapsed photography. This type of photography provides the evidence needed to be confident in our findings."

The next slide projected onto the screen. "This is a barge traveling south on the Tigris River. It is north of the plant. This next slide shows the barge south of the plant. Both barges are riding high in the water indicating they carry no cargo. But in this next slide we have placed both barges side by side. Nothing too striking until you blow up and enhance this area here." With the electronic light pointer she circled an area in both pictures.

"The next slide shows the enhancement of both areas. Again, side-by-side for comparison, you can see the planking is different. This barge, the one that was north of the plant, has a red streak of paint that is missing on this one. These are two different barges. In the next slide the later barge is traveling north on the Tigris but still south of the plant. It is low in the water, indicating it's carrying some kind of cargo.

"The next picture is north of the plant. The barge is still low in the water carrying cargo. But on the enhancement the red streak is back. Again two different barges attempting to look like the same one."

She stopped for a moment and took a sip of ice water, then continued, "Next we looked at the plant itself to determine how the switch took place."

Twenty minutes later she had finished with the final slide. The projector was shut off, and the light rose. Her confidence had returned, and she stood at the podium awaiting questions.

"Let me get this straight," the President began immediately. "You want me to base all my diplomatic and possible military decisions on a small streak of red paint that you think you see under a dock?" He looked over the top of his glasses at her.

"Mr. President, I can only report to you what my team's final analysis was. Based on all the data available to us, it is our opinion that this barge moved the gas. Our decision was also based on the degree of covertness in which they switched the barges. Something that they didn't want anyone else to know about was moved north on that barge. Unless they had something more secret and deadly at that plant worth protecting, it would be my opinion that it was the gas that was moved."

"So you're advising me to attack and level a holy Muslim Minaret based on your analysis?" The President looked around the room and gave a slight roll with his eyes.

After all that work, she thought, he rolled his eyes? Her face began to burn. "Mr. President, I am not advising you to do anything. I was asked to give you a professional analysis in less than three days on something the entire military intelligence community couldn't give you during all of the Gulf War. I have done it. You can take it or leave it."

Stunned by her outburst she looked down, realizing she'd blown it. She told herself, you don't tell off the President, not even in private, and expect to have a long career in government. The room was dead silent and she could hear her every breath.

"We will move this meeting into executive committee now," was the President's only response.

Megan stood silently at the podium and looked around the room, until Gordon spoke up. "Young lady, executive committee means you are excused."

Megan picked up her notes and left unceremoniously. She shot Niddiem a piercing glance then forcefully closed the door behind her when she left. She stood in the hallway for a moment, not knowing where to go.

The Secret service agent posted outside the doorway looked at her with a smirk on his face. "It looks like they were kind of rough on you in there."

"That's an understatement. Well, it was a fun career while it lasted."

"Don't take it personally. First, these meetings have been going on day and night, and everyone's exhausted. Second, despite all the good P.R., the President's basically a chauvinist. He doesn't like to be told what to do by a woman. Just walking in the room and seeing you probably raised his blood pressure ten points. Here, have a seat."

"No. I think I'll pace and fume for a few minutes. It'll help me lower my blood pressure if I walk it off.

For the next twenty minutes Megan paced back and forth and chatted with the agent. The door to the Situation Room suddenly opened and the President walked out. He passed her and ignored her. He then boarded the elevator at the end of the hallway and was gone. Within a minute the rest of the room emptied, each one of them walked by her without a glance.

She waited for Niddiem to exit, but to her surprise he spoke from the doorway, "Megan, I'll be out in a minute." He shut the door, leaving her again to her thoughts.

Inside the Situation Room, Niddiem and Gordon faced each other across the large table. "Okay, John," Niddiem said, "I've located the gas. I'll give you any and all intelligence information you need. But, I will not, and I'm serious, I will not arrange for our boys to be slaughtered over there. If you want it done, you arrange it." He held on to his suspender straps as he talked.

Gordon let out a snort. "So you think by turning your back you're absolved of this mess. Bullshit, mister. You helped cause it, and by God you will help us get out of it."

"I won't kill our boys."

"No, but you helped kill how many in Jerusalem?"

"You can't blame me for that. I didn't bring that Nazi over from Germany, and I didn't involve him in our R& D program. All I did was carry out a policy 20 years ago as the Assistant Deputy Director of the C.I.A. That policy seemed right at the time. It was a policy that at the time was in our country's best interest, ath that time."

Gordon swung around the table and placed a finger at Niddiem's chest. Niddiem pulled back. "You are involved no matter what," Gordon said, "and you know it. I want that perfectly clear."

Niddiem gathered his paperwork. "This is the bottom line. I'll give you information. I'll help you. I'll load the gun and even aim it. But I'm not pulling the trigger."

"If you don't have the balls to do what needs to be done, then by God, I will. I don't like sending our boys to the slaughter, but I have to look at the big picture."

"Sorry Gordon, your speech won't work on me. The deal is this--tomorrow you and the Vice President are leaving for Jerusalem to attend a memorial service. I assume you'll also make a side trip to reassure the Saudis and Kuwaitis, apprising them of the situation."

"That's right."

"Okay. Here's what I've set up. From Kuwait you'll take another side trip, by yourself, to the town of Mityahah. Just outside that town you'll meet General Kazem Malek of the Iraqi military. Now, that's it. I'm out of the picture."

"And how will you arrange the meeting?" Gordon asked.

"He'll find you. But you, you'd better think about what you're doing." Niddiem waited a moment for a reply, but when none came, he left the room.

Megan looked up at Niddiem with a sorry face, but was relieved to see his smile of reassurance. "Your briefing was fine, but your follow through left a little to be desired. You did okay. They agreed with your analysis and will act on it. Are you ready to go?"

"Definitely," she replied with a sigh of relief.

When they reached the stairs, Megan heard Gordon's Texan drawl call out from down the hall, "Young lady."

She stopped in her tracks but didn't turn around.

His voice boomed down the narrow corridor, "Let me tell you, you have big brass balls. You're one of the few people I know who in the same meeting was able to piss off the Secretary of State and the President of the United States. Yes, young lady, you have big brass balls."

Megan slowly pivoted to face him. "One of us had to have balls in there and it obviously wasn't you. And the name is Megan, Megan McAllister, not young lady."

For the first time in days Niddiem found himself chuckling as they drove back to C.I.A. Headquarters in Langley. "Megan, you do surprise me at times. Besides being good, you're one tough scrapper. Just glad you're working for me. I must say you impressed the President."

"Even though I'm a woman?" she asked cocking her head.

"Yes, even though you're a woman. The President himself has cleared you for the next aspect of the plan. We're sending in a small Delta squad to destroy the gas. At three-thirty this afternoon you'll have to be at the Pentagon to brief Colonel Burnhall, the Commander of Delta Special Forces, on what you've found."

"I know the Colonel. He's a nice guy." She smiled.

"How do you know him?"

"My boyfriend works for him. The Colonel and I meet occasionally at social functions."

As they drove back, Niddiem appeared immersed in his paperwork. But his mind was planning the meeting between

Gordon and General Kazem Malek. Underneath it all was grief for the inevitable deaths of the Colonel's Delta Squad.

10   Chapter Ten

The trans-Atlantic flight had seemed unending to Abraham. He hadn't slept one moment of the flight. Instead he stared at the in-flight movie, oblivious to it, the headset paid for but unopened. Though the movie showed scenes of a beautiful spring day, his eyes saw only terror, death and hatred. His mind was miles away, wrestling with the past.

After he landed in Washington D.C., he mechanically passed through customs and took a bus to a local Inn. Although close to home, he felt too exhausted to drive himself there. Only when he finally lay down in bed did his mind and body, give way to a deep sleep. The kind of sleep that allows the body to forget the pain the mind is facing.

When he awoke, the bedside clock showed 1:19 P.M. He'd slept for almost eighteen hours. Despite that he was still exhausted. Stress was a strange and dangerous thing. It could debilitate and cripple the body as fast as the most serious illness or physically traumatic event.

After a shower, he changed into clean clothes and set out. He hadn't eaten since leaving Israel and was hungry. He walked outside and saw a small diner across from the Inn, which in addition to an meager menu, happened to have tourist booklets on Washington D.C.

Abraham ate a sandwich, sipped coffee, and leafed mindlessly through a guidebook. The words "United States Holocaust Memorial" grabbed him. He read about it:

The privately funded United States Holocaust Memorial Museum is a sobering tribute to the six million Jews and other victims of the World War II Holocaust. The story is told through documentary film, photographs, artifacts and oral histories.

It was just after three in the afternoon when Abraham entered the Holocaust Memorial. Though it was reminiscent of the Yad Vashem Memorial in Israel, it lacked the same intensity. He entered a small theater, found an empty seat and watched one of the continuous documentaries about the camps. The Nazis had shot much of the footage taken while the camps were up and running, killing at full capacity. The graphic scenes shocked a few in the audience but for Abraham it stiffened his resolve to learn the fate of Claus Von Wilbert. Forty-five minutes into the documentary, Abraham realized the perspective of the cameraman had switched from that of the Nazis to that of the liberating Allies.

Finally his own camp was projected on the screen. The camera panned back and forth and his tired eyes slowly sharpened. The picture in front of him triggered deeper olfactory memories of the smells that had long ago been burnt into his nostrils. The memory of death and the rotting corpses that had been defiled and abused in both life and death, again came to the forefront of his mind.

"That's him!" Abraham gasped as his hand clutched his chest. The Commander who had liberated the camp walked in front of the lens. The same Commander he'd taken by the hand and walked through the barracks, the same Commander who stood off to the side when the jeep that carried Von Wilbert drove up. He would know what happened to Von Wilbert.

The commentary on the documentary rolled on and related the living hell inside the camp. Suddenly the Commander approached the camera and answered questions.

A teenager in the audience started to talk loudly to his companion. Abraham nearly stood up in his seat. "Shut up, do not talk!!"

"Hey, mister."

"I said be quiet!" Abraham snapped back. The boy threw him a dirty look, but Abraham turned his attention to the screen.

"Commander Steinman, could you give us an assessment on the condition of those still alive in the camp?"

Abraham couldn't believe his luck. "Commander Steinman. That's him." He jumped up, ignoring the angry voices around him and hurried out of the theater, repeating like a lunatic, "Commander Steinman, Commander Steinman."

Without much thought, he set off for the Pentagon. He knew people there who'd help him track down this commander. At the moment his focus wasn't broad enough to think of returning to C.I.A. Headquarters and accessing the appropriate military file there. A taxi ride and twenty dollars took him to the entrance of the Pentagon. He walked through the glass doors and approached the information desk.

"May I help you?" a young soldier asked.

"I hope so. I'm very tired. I'm looking for Lt. General Weatherby. Could you tell him Abraham Feinstein is here and would like to see him for a moment."

The soldier looked up the extension, and then dialed it. Moments later he looked up at Abraham. "I'm sorry. The Lt. General has left his office for the day."

"Well maybe you can help me. I'm trying to find the whereabouts of a Commander Steinman."

"One moment." Before Abraham could continue the soldier had typed the name into a computer and was scanning the monitor. In a short time he looked up. "I'm sorry sir, I don't have a Commander Steinman listed in our register."

"Yes, I know. I'd be quite surprised if he was actively working. He'd be quite old. I'm sure he's long since retired. He was the Commander of the unit who liberated the concentration camp I was in at the end of World War II. I'd like some information on how to find him."

"I'm sorry, sir. I wouldn't know how to begin to help you."

Abraham pulled himself up to full height. "Young man, somewhere in this massive building there's a file on Commander Steinman. Where would it be?" His jaw tensed and his teeth clenched.

"One moment, sir." He dialed the phone and spoke softly. Abraham couldn't make out what he said. The soldier hung up and turned back to him. "One of our public relations officers will be down in a minute to assist you. Would you have a seat over there."

*   *   *   *

The Special Operations Division for the Joint Chiefs of Staff was tucked down a small corridor on the second floor of the Pentagon's B ring. Behind an inconspicuous locked door worked a highly compartmentalized planning cell for the nation's Delta Force.

In a few moments, Megan would brief Colonel Burnhall and his immediate superiors on the same information the President and the National Security Council had listened to only a few hours before. From here, the Special Operations Division would formulate its plan for the next phase of the mission. For this mission a small unit of commandos would penetrate Iraq and destroy the deadly nerve gas arsenal.

Megan sat at this briefing and thought how much more comfortable she felt around military men than around politicians. Military men dealt with the reality of a situation, whereas politicians were so concerned with appearances that they often completely lost sight of reality. She cringed when Ben Wildemen, Chairman of the Joint Chiefs of Staff, who had been at the White House for her previous briefing, entered along with Colonel Burnhall.

Wildemen sat down, smiled at her and said, "Megan. First, I know enough not to call you young lady. I have never enjoyed a briefing as much as the one you just gave. I thought Gordon and the President were going to rupture blood vessels. Well done Megan, well done."

"Thank you," she replied with a nod. She turned to Colonel Burnhall, "Hello Colonel."

"Megan, how nice to see you again," the Colonel said.

"You two know each other?" Wildemen asked.

"We've met at a few social functions," Megan replied. She and the Colonel smiled at each other.

"Ben tells me you and your team has done a fabulous piece of detective work," the Colonel said. "I've asked Generals Wells and Baker to join us. They'll work with the team on Operational Planning. The basic plan has already been approved by the President and the Security Council."

The meeting began shortly after the two generals arrived. They all seemed impressed with what Megan's team had uncovered. Forty minutes later the briefing was drawing to a close.

General Wells asked, "How long do we have to develop our concept plan?"

"Twelve hours," Wildemen replied.

"None of us are pleased with that time schedule," Colonel Burnhall said when he saw the General's displeasure. "I can tell you I don't relish sending my men into a situation that's not well thought out or practiced. We were lucky at Sun Moon Lake a few days ago, but I'm not happy risking the lives of my men on luck. However, we developed the Delta Force to handle situations on the fly. Gentlemen, I want your Operational Plan on my desk in twelve hours. I want my men in place in the Persian Gulf in thirty-six hours, ready to go."

They all nodded.

The meeting ended and Megan walked down the hall.

"Megan!" She turned to see Scott Ashland, Colonel Burnhall's aide approaching.

Megan had hoped she wouldn't run into him. It was always difficult to run into ex-boyfriends. Especially when the ex had decided he wanted to rekindle the relationship.

"Hello, Scott." She tried to appear in a hurry and make her way around him, but he had strategically placed himself in her path.

"You haven't returned my calls."

"I've been busy."

For an awkward moment they stood there. He was still as attractive as ever, standing there lean and tall with short brown hair. He had always exuded confidence in everything from his stance and walk to the way he smiled, showing off his pearly white teeth. In conversational exchange he typically controlled the flow and direction...until now. Now he had a nervous smile and appeared quite anxious.

"What is it Scott? I'm in a hurry," Megan said.

"I know I made a mistake and hurt you, but..."

"We've been over this too many times." Megan glanced around uneasily. "Look, this isn't the time or the place. I'm not interested in seeing you again. Anyway, I'm seeing someone else."

"Who, Sam Davon?" he asked.

Megan was surprised to see Scott openly display jealously.

"Yes. Look Scott, I don't want to talk about this with you, especially not here. I've already come close enough today to blowing my reputation. Maybe we can talk later, after the crisis is over. But basically, as far as Sam and I are concerned, our relationship is none of your business. Goodbye."

Megan walked briskly down the hall to the stairwell, feeling it was better to walk down four flights than continue the conversation in an elevator.

The Shoe Shine Boy

*   *   *   *

Abraham watched the public relations officer scroll through his computer screen for Commander Steinman's name. Not finding it on the active or inactive list, he opened up the retired file. "Well, I've found him here. He retired in 1954."

"Where is he now?" Abraham asked.

"I'm sorry, sir, but that information is not listed. And to be honest, if it was, I wouldn't be able to give it to you. We do have to protect the privacy of our soldiers, active or retired."

"You mean you won't give it to me." He stared without blinking at the officer.

"No. That's not what I said. I said that information isn't here. But if it was, I still wouldn't be able to give it to you. I'm sure you understand."

"No, I don't understand. Neither do you. Let me repeat myself."

"Sir, there's no need to. I do understand, and I am sorry."

"No, you don't understand." Abraham beat his chest with open palms. The dead ends, the frustration, it was all becoming more than he could bear. "I'm the only one alive of my entire family. And all I ask is the name of a man who can answer a question for me, so when I die I can rest in peace. I need to know if one of the butchers from my past got what he deserved. I need to know justice was done so I can go off and die with peace of mind. Do you understand me?"

"Yes."

"Then what is Commander Steinman's address?" Abraham screamed. His neck veins were bulging and his breath was fast.

"Sir, I told you I don't have it. Really, if I did, even though I wouldn't be allowed to, I'd give it to you."

Standing quickly, Abraham knocked over his the chair. "Why, dear God, why? What have I done?" He started pounding his fists on the desk in front of him.

The officer quickly picked up the phone. "I need security in AC 104 immediately."

"What is this? You call guards to throw me in jail? This is America, not Nazi Germany!" The guards arrived quickly.

"We're not going to arrest you sir," one of the officers said approaching him. "But we have to ask you to leave the building." He reached out for Abraham's arm.

"Don't touch me! I was manhandled by the Nazis and I will never allow anyone to manhandle me again." He threw the soldier's hand off of him and abruptly limped out of the room then down the corridor. The security team was close behind him.

*　　*　　*　　*

Megan opened the door to the hallway from the stairwell when a security team blocked her way. They seemed to be capturing a troublemaker, though she couldn't see who it was.

"I'm sorry Miss. Please step back for a moment." He turned back to the troublemaker. "Sir, you will come with us now so we can escort you out of the building or you will be arrested."

Megan was unable to see the man as they spirited him away from her down the corridor. All she heard were gut-wrenching sobs, and she shook her head in pity at the poor man's anguish.

The traffic back to Langley was horrible. Megan hated the bumper-to-bumper rush hour. She was tired and was looking forward to going to bed early. That and a long hot bath were the only things that motivated her at the moment. But first she had to get back to C.I.A. Headquarters.

A little after five thirty, she walked into her team's working area. She emptied out her briefcase and prepared the material that needed to be stored in the safe for the night. Maurice sat at his desk with his feet up, reading the latest issue of Time. "Hey, Maurice."

"Hello Megan, there was a call for you a few minutes ago from Sam. He said he tried to call you on your cell phone but you didn't pick up. He wants you to call him. Said it was extremely important he see you tonight."

"Shit." Megan looked at her cell phone. "Dammit," she muttered. It was turned off. She dialed him quickly.

Maurice was too engrossed in his magazine to see her trembling. As she waited for Sam to answer she crossed her arms and shivered. The message 'extremely important' was their code signal. They had to get together for a meal or just a quick walk, depending on the time he had. He was going on a big mission, and she knew what it was. It had to be Iraq. They're sending him to Iraq. It was a very dangerous assignment. She knew because she had helped develop it. There was a good chance some of them would die over there. She shook her head and wondered how she would react if he were one of those who didn't return.

On the third ring he answered. "Hello."

"Sam, it's Megan." her voice quivered.

"I think we should go to dinner tonight."

"Okay. I'm scared," her voice cracked, giving away her concern.

"Everything will be okay. Don't worry. I'll pick you up at 8:00."

"Sam?"

"Yes."

There was a short pause before Megan continued, "I love you."

"I know. I love you too."

She hung up the phone then turned to Maurice. "Why aren't you home relaxing? What're you doing still hanging around?"

"I'm going in a minute. Unbelievable, did you see this?"

"See what?"

"The Special Edition of Time Magazine, it's devoted completely to the massacre in Jerusalem. They have some pretty nasty pictures. I'm amazed they even published some of them."

She walked over and he handed her the magazine. Her eyes locked onto the cover photo. It was that of a man lying on the street with the partially wrapped body of his son in his lap. The man's hands were raised in the air, and the anguish on his face as his eyes pleaded with the sky above sent a chill down her spine.

"Oh my God!" She looked closer at the face.

"What?" Maurice took the magazine back and stared at the photo. "Abraham!"

"He needs our help," cried out Megan.

"At least we know he's alive," replied Maurice. "I'll try to get a line to Jerusalem and track him down. Where will you be?" He was already reaching for a phone.

"Sam and I were planning dinner. But after seeing this I'm not sure I should." She thought about Sam and knew she had to see him.

"No, go. Only one of us is needed to place the calls. Anyway, it could take all night." His feet came off the desk and planted firmly on the floor.

She looked at him and tried to smile. "Thanks, I'll have my cell phone on. Contact me if you hear anything."

"I will. Now you go."

By ten o'clock Megan couldn't eat any more. She had barely touched her food, although they were at her favorite restaurant.

"Sam, I'm sorry, my heart's not in this tonight. I can't get Abraham out of my mind and I'm so worried about you. You leave tomorrow. You deserve better company than this."

"It's okay. I'm not at my most entertaining tonight either. Look, when Abraham returns we'll all rally around and help him. But there's nothing we can do for him until then."

"I know, but I still feel horrible."

"I know you do. That's why I love you so much." Smiling slightly, she accepted his hand in hers.

"So tell me about your day at the White House."

She quietly discussed her findings and the briefings she had conducted earlier in the day.

"I can't believe you said that to the President," Sam chuckled.

"Neither could anyone else in the room. Poor Al, he didn't know what to do. He couldn't decide whether to support me or throw darts at me. It was pretty funny seeing all those pompous asses with their mouths hanging open, and the President sputtering." Megan smiled at the memory and then stifled a yawn.

"Listen, I'm exhausted. But it's such a nice night, let's drive down to the Mall and walk for a few minutes.

"Okay. But just for a few. Tomorrow will come too soon for both of us."

For a long time Megan and Sam walked in silence holding hands. Finally Megan said, "I'm scared."

"About what?" he asked.

"I'm afraid something bad is going to happen to you...to us. Sam, I want to settle down. I want to have a family. I want a normal life. I'm afraid our life styles...your life style won't allow it. I don't want to get hurt. I don't want to lose you. I'm afraid you might get killed." She stopped and turned to him with a tear running down one cheek.

Sam wiped it away and kissed her softly. "I won't apologize for what I do. I can only tell you that I love you and will always be there for you."

"But what if you get killed?" she asked.

"One day we're all going to die. For me it might be tomorrow, or sixty years from now. Either way it doesn't matter. The only things that matters are today, and the legacy we leave behind us. Come on. Let's walk." He took her hand and they walked on.

On their way to the Lincoln Memorial they walked through the Constitutional Gardens.

"Do you believe Nixon wanted to make this area into an amusement park?" Sam said.

"It doesn't surprise me in the least. What surprises me is that they turned him down."

They walked a path that slowly wound its way beneath the shade trees and then paralleled the artificial lake. Lovers kissing, and homeless people wanting to be left alone so they could sleep, frequented the benches lining the path.

Megan spotted him first. Up ahead, a man in his early sixties, his head in hands weeping. She looked at Sam and kept walking, wondering if they should stop or not. But the man lifted his head and she saw his face.

"Abraham!" She ran to him. "Abraham, are you all right?" She knelt down so their eyes were on the same level. She touched him gently. "How did you get here?"

"How can I ever be all right?" he spoke between sobs. "My heart's been ripped out of my chest."

She saw his hands were shaking.

"Even our own military won't help me. All they do is call guards and throw me out of the Pentagon."

"You were at the Pentagon today? That was you I saw being escorted out?"

"You mean thrown out. All I wanted was information about the butcher, the killer of my people." He looked at his empty palms.

"Abraham, you know the government and the agency are doing everything possible to find and punish them." She took one of his hands.

"How can they punish unknown people when they refuse to help me find one butcher they had in custody. They just won't tell me."

"I don't understand. What are you talking about?" She looked up at Sam, puzzled.

"I'm talking about them protecting the murderer, the one who gassed them all."

"Are you saying the government is protecting those responsible for the massacre in Jerusalem?"

"No, no, no! At the end of the war, when I was liberated from the Nazi death camps, the butcher Claus Van Wilbert was captured. The American soldiers took him into custody. I saw him in handcuffs. He made me work in his lab cleaning the bodies out of his experimental gas chamber. But where is he now? I need to know he was punished. Why won't they tell me?" Abraham looked at her in despair. "All I want to know is that justice was done. That he was dealt with, that he's dead and not living and hurting people anymore."

"Is that why you were at the Pentagon today?"

"Yes. I just wanted to find an address."

"Of who, the chemist?" Megan asked.

"No...Commander Steinman's address. He's retired now. He was the commanding officer who liberated the camps. All I want to do is talk to him. To find out what happened to this Nazi chemist he had in his custody. Don't you see, I must find out that there's justice in this world for the victims, for my family." His whimpering turned into open sobbing. "How can

I believe they will help the poor victims now if they refuse to help a victim from the past?"

"I'll help you, and so will the Agency." She didn't understand fully but she needed to reassure him somehow.

"Come, we'll take you home. You need to get to bed." Megan stood and helped him up.

The light went out in the back bedroom of the small brick Tudor in Chevy Chase. Abraham finally lay on his own bed, exhausted and alone.

Megan had sent Sam home. He had wanted to stay, but Megan knew he needed to get some sleep before his mission. Now she rested on the couch in the living room, determined to protect Abraham from any intrusion. She looked about for something to read, and saw a magazine poking out of Abraham's still packed flight bag. She pulled it out, only to see it was TIME, the issue with Abraham on the cover.

"My god, he bought it and carried it with him." The tears welled up then she broke down and sobbed silently.

*   *   *   *

Al Niddiem sat across from Abraham and Megan as Abraham explained the horror of the last few days. When he was done they were silent for a few moments. Then Niddiem rubbed his eyes and looked up. "Abraham, I don't know what to say. I'm heartbroken by your loss, but I'm thankful you're alive. I want you to take some time off. You know we're working with the military to identify the people and government responsible for the attack in Jerusalem."

"Yes."

"I'm going to recommend you take a leave of absence. You're too close physically and emotionally to this."

"Yes, I know. I need the time off. I need to find Steinman. He's my only lead to that butcher chemist."

"Why couldn't we do a search on both of them?" Megan asked. "Jonathan Green can help. He's a strange guy, but he's a computer wizard. Abraham, do you remember the chemist's name?"

"How could I forget," Abraham said. "It's a name I'll take to my grave...it's Claus Von Wilbert."

Niddiem's heart stopped, and he suppressed a curse. *Oh shit*, he thought. How much more complicated could this get? A bead of sweat formed on his forehead. None-the-less he stood and calmly walked them both to the door. "Help him out in any way you can Megan. But remember, Abraham, I want you to take time off. Please take care of yourself. We still have a lot of work to do on this one, and you're too close."

After they left Niddiem raced into his side office. It was filled with the latest and most sophisticated computer terminals designed. He ran his I.D. card through a groove, and then placed his right hand on a scanner. The computer screen came to life. Niddiem sat down and typed:

CLAUS VON WILBERT

The requested file opened up and he typed.

PLACE FILE: CLAUS VON WILBERT IN VOICE PROTECTED LOCKED FILE.

The computer monitor then read:

: VOICE ACTIVATION SYSTEM: please type in your name.

Niddiem typed in:

: AL NIDDIEM

The computer monitor then displayed:

: AUTHENTICATION CODE: Welcome Al Niddiem please type in your Authentication code.

Niddieam typed in:

: 57987BBALNIDDIEM

The monitor then displayed:
: SPEAK VOICE ACTIVATION CODE YOU WILL USE
Niddiem leaned over the console to project his voice into the small microphone built into the console. "Al Niddiem 7894AACA."
The computer displayed"
: AL NIDDIEM 7894AACA ACCEPTED
Instantly all access to Claus Von Wilbert and any file mentioning his name was placed in Al Niddiem's protected file.
"Sorry, Abraham. You can search all you want, but it'll be in vain."

*   *   *   *

Abraham and Megan walked slowly down the hall towards Jonathan Green's office. Abraham's limp became more pronounced and his mood more pensive the closer they got. It was difficult to believe that after all he had been through he simply had to ask Jonathan to do a simple computer search, something no one else seemed capable of doing. They found Jonathan with his back to the office door, dark sun glasses in place, typing on his keyboard at a furious pace. The monitor he faced was dark and turned off. After he would type for a moment he slid his hands onto a Braille display that his keyboard sat next to. The raised bumps flowed under his fingers as he absorbed the words. Jonathan was a unique person who lived by his own rules. Blinded in an accident at the age of seven he had never let his lack of sight be a disability for him. He was a portly man in his forties with soft toneless arms. Jonathan loved to eat and he was very particular about what he ate. Only the best gourmet food would satisfy him. "If you're going to be fat you might as well do it with style", he would often say. Attention to his personal grooming was another story. Though always clean, neatness was not Jonathan's forte. His hair was usually disheveled, flat and bodiless and his bushy mustache was in dire need of a trimming. He wore pants that were constantly two inches too high and his white gym socks were always tucked into a pair of black tie shoes. When he walked down the hallway there was no caution in his stride. Jonathan walked with gusto in each step, his fluorescent red cane bouncing quickly on the floor in front of him. At least once, if not twice, a week he would have his cane catch a passerby and upend them onto the floor. Instead of an apology Jonathan would reply, "Look where you're going and get out of my way. You'd think you where blind and I had eyes."

Without turning around in his seat Jonathan asked, "Is that you, Megan?"

"Yes, and Abraham is with me." They walked in and sat down.

Jonathan spun in his chair and faced them. "Hello Abraham. How are you doing?" Though he stared in Abraham's direction, his gaze was slightly high.

Abraham replied with a soft voice, "I'm doing okay. Thank you."

Megan had called ahead and explained Abraham's plight. While Jonathan couldn't visually see the pain on Abraham's face he could feel his despair.

"I'm going to do my best to help you. What's the man's name you want to find?" Jonathan asked.

"Commander Steinman. He was in charge of the unit that liberated the death camp at Buchenwald. Shortly after the liberation I saw that butcher in his custody. To find him I need to find Steinman, because all records have disappeared."

Jonathan spun back to his keyboard and started to type. "Let's try the military's central records facility in St. Louis.

Every man and woman who has served in the military since 1934 is on file there."

He typed in Commander Steinman's name then pressed enter. Jonathan gently placed his fingers on the Braille display and sat quietly for a moment. Then without looking up he said, "I've found thirteen Steinman's. Let me print them out." He hit the print button and his Braille printer along with a standard printer came to life. Handing Abraham the printed page Jonathan took the Braille one and started to read it with both hands.

"The fourth one down is a Steinman, Commander of the Fifth Light Infantry in 1945. He retired in April 1953. He was cited with a commendation for his compassion in the liberation of the death camp, Buchenwald is specifically mentioned."

"That has to be him," Abraham replied.

Jonathan spun around and typed in Steinman's service number that was also listed. A moment later he lifted his fingers off the Braille display and wrote an address on a piece of paper and held it out for Abraham to take. "He lives at 1037 Washington Street, Woburn, Massachusetts."

"I can't believe it was that simple, especially after what I've been through." Abraham took it and shook his head. "Thank you so much. Now hopefully I can find Von Wilbert and put this behind me."

"Von Wilbert. Hold on a moment." Jonathan again spun back to his keyboard and ran a search on Claus Von Wilbert. He had the agency's highest security clearance. He had access not only to the Seven Dwarfs, but top-secret files that didn't even show up under Megan's clearance.

Jonathan's fingers read the Braille display then he hesitated a moment before saying, "You're right. No evidence of him. I hope Steinman can help you more than I can."

Abraham grabbed Jonathan's right hand and pumped it fervently. "Thank you, thank you. You've been more than helpful. I'll talk to you when I get back from Massachusetts."

Jonathan listened as they walked down the hall. He rubbed his head in thought for a moment, and then he ran his fingers again across the Braille.

Claus Von Wilbert, access denied.

"Huh," Jonathan said. "You do exist. But why the secrecy, especially over a death camp murderer?"

One of the benefits of having written the security code program was that he knew his way around it. Typing again, he opened up the program. This time he printed it on the Braille printer. Taking the page in hand he read it line by line until he found the answer. Claus Von Wilbert's file and all reference to him had been placed in a voice activated secure file. They were locked up, but by whom, and for what reason?

What disturbed him most was the time of the order. They had been locked less than thirty minutes before Abraham and Megan entered his office. He exited the file and then sat for a moment in silence, pondering the coincidence. He decided that for now he would leave it at that, a coincidence.

11   Chapter Eleven

A ir Force Two taxied into position for takeoff on the far side of Andrews Air Force Base. On board, the Vice President, various members of Congress and John Gordon sat in somber silence. The engines were barely heard through the well-insulated body of the plane and the tension of the situation was somewhat relieved by the plush accommodations in the 747 jumbo jet.

Gordon sat immersed in his own thoughts. He was not focused on the memorial service they were on their way to attend, or the tragedy that caused it. Hell, he thought, the people in Jerusalem had been killing each other for centuries and probably would be for centuries to come. Nor were his thoughts on his upcoming meeting with Mateusz Adar, Israel's Defense Minister. If Adar was a problem, Gordon would stomp him like an ant. His mind was beyond that. It lay in the sands of Kuwait where he would meet an Iraqi General. Despite the desire to choke the Iraqi General to death on sight, he would have to help him. To save the United States he would have to help the enemy. Over and over again he reviewed the situation in his mind.

*   *   *   *

South of Washington D.C., the turbines of the C-130 Transport emitted a high pitched roar that vibrated and shook Sam, Gino and Roger, strapped into their barely padded seats. The Air Force was big on technology and gadgets, but extremely stingy on spending for comfort. The flight crew handed out earplugs for noise dampening, but no pillows or blankets...you had to bring your own on this flight.

12   Chapter Twelve

5000 years B.C., the Tigris River drew nomadic herdsmen of the desert towards its flowing waters. In the centuries that followed, some settled here, becoming farmers. They invented irrigation systems and created history's first surplus of food. Here in this valley between the Tigris and the Euphrates River the cornerstone of civilization was formed. Mesopotamia, the land between these two rivers, had produced overwhelming achievements for mankind, both civilized and uncivilized.

Through the centuries this valley has been under siege by many enemies, from the Mongols in 1258 AD, to the Allies in Desert Storm in 1991. Today would be no different from the centuries of turmoil and strife in the past. Today's battle would be short and decisive. But as history has proved, the size of the siege doesn't always dictate the effect it will ultimately have on the course of history.

In Al Amara, a small town south of Baghdad, Highway 50 crossed over the Tigris River near the town's center. This crossroad had seen many conquerors and defenders try to control this strategic area where the river ran wide and shallow, and the waters flowed slowly. It was no different during the early aerial attacks in the opening hours of the Gulf War of 1991. The sturdy steel bridge that spanned this historic ancient river was easily and decisively destroyed. Soon after the cease-fire, a smaller but functional bridge was erected. Saddam Hussein's elite Republican Guards understood, as did the Allies, the critical importance of this bridge. With Basra constantly under siege by radicals, and Saddam Hussein having to quell any uprising before it spread, Hussein needed a

The Shoe Shine Boy

functioning bridge at Al Amara to ensure the mobility of his troops and supplies.

Ameen and his brother Hamid also understood the significance of this bridge. They and two others worked feverishly in the early morning light, placing explosives under the supporting spans. A convoy of Hussein's troops, ammunition, and supplies had left Baghdad and was on its way south. Ameen had gotten word only a short time ago, thus the haste of his small cell of counter revolutionaries. They planned not only to destroy the bridge, but also to destroy it as the convoy crossed it.

Ameen and Hamid lived in Baghdad with their sister, Atiqa, in a small apartment. Not long ago the three had lived there with their mother and father. That ended one day when Hussein's militia took their father, Yahya, away. Their mother tried in vain to stop them, but her protests were useless. Sent to the front lines in Kuwait, with no military training, he was shoved into a trench in the desert sand and issued a gun. The ammunition was withheld, though, controlled by the local unit commanders.

On more than one occasion Yahya had watched soldiers who had been pressed into service try to leave the front lines, only to be shot by the fanatically loyal commander's staff. So in fear of death he stayed in his trench, and wondered about his fate. He didn't have to wait too long. One evening leaflets rained down upon them. The pamphlet read:

"Tomorrow if you don't surrender we're going to drop on you the largest conventional weapon in the world."

Few slept that night. Some tried to escape, despite the guards the commander's staff had posted.

Early that morning an American MC-130 Combat Talon cargo plane flew over Yahya's area. Out of its belly fell a BLU-82 bomb. Shortly thereafter in the southwest corner of Kuwait an enormous blinding flash lit up the sky, and above it rose a mushroom cloud. So powerful was the sound and shock wave of this explosion that many Iraqis thought the Americans had dropped a tactical nuclear weapon on the front lines.

Within two days of the news of their father's death Ameen and Hamid saw their already depressed Mother collapse unconscious and die. The doctors told Ameen she died from a broken blood vessel in her brain, a stroke. But Ameen knew otherwise. His mother had died of a broken heart. She and her husband had been so much in love that she never recovered from his kidnapping and death.

Ameen's father had died at the hands of the Americans, but Ameen felt no malice towards them. It was Saddam Hussein he held responsible.

Now, turning to his younger brother, he guided him in the placement and wiring of the explosives on the bridge.

"Hamid, remember, make sure all connections are sealed with tape. I don't want any of them not going off because of faulty wiring," Ameen said in a stern voice. He and Hamid were physically opposite of each other. Ameen was muscular with a hard leather worn face despite his young age of sixteen. At the moment his curly black hair was matted and tangled, with beads of sweat dripped off his nose as he concentrated on his task.

"Older brother, you have such little faith in me sometimes," replied Hamid. Hamid's boyish smile and soft features were misplaced in this hard dangerous environment. Even his walk and gestures were so feminine it would be hard to imagine the Iraqi Military considering this fourteen-year old a ruthless terrorist.

While Ameen and Hamid worked methodically under the bridge, their two other companions were busy setting explosives on the road north of the bridge. Without warning a Soviet-built BTR 60 personnel carrier came in view. It rounded the hill not far from them.

One companion panicked at the sight of the army and accidentally touched two wrong wires together, completing the electrical circuit to the explosives that were only inches from him. His dismembered body flew through the air in three directions. His friend, stunned by the blast, struggled to his feet and ran towards the bridge. Ameen and Hamid scrambled out from under the girders.

The Iraqi soldiers in the personnel carrier were prepared. They were watching for this very occurrence. Too many of their convoys had been attacked recently.

Ameen and Hamid watched in horror as their remaining companion ran towards them. The soldier inside the personnel carrier spun the turret and brought the sights of his twenty-five mm cannon towards the running man. The soldier pulled the trigger, and simply walked the line of fire into the running torso, instantly splitting the body in half.

With no place to hide, Ameen and Hamid ran across the bridge. They needed to reach the other side and set off the detonator.

But the gunner was too quick. He adjusted his sights and pulled the trigger again. Ameen jumped to the side but one of the tracers shattered his left calf, splintering the bone. Hamid stopped, frozen with terror.

"Run Hamid! Blow the bridge! Run!" Ameen shouted. But his brother stood frozen, catatonic with fear.

Within moments, the personnel carrier stopped next to them and soldiers surrounded them.

13   Chapter Thirteen

Israel was a nation in mourning. The Jewish nations cry of "Never Again" was silenced by sorrow for the thousands of innocent lives lost and the unanswered questions surrounding how this could have happened. Into the dawn of this sad day Gordon's diplomatic flight, designated Air Force Two, landed in Tel Aviv. It was filled with a diverse delegation representing all branches of the U.S. government and various religious beliefs. They came to mourn, and to offer what little they could in this time of sorrow for this tiny nation.

As Air Force Two landed, U.S. military flight thirty-seven left Israeli air space and continued its flight over the country of Jordan until it entered Saudi Arabia's air space. It was on a different mission. It was on a mission to do something concrete so that this kind of tragedy would never happen again. Three and a half hours later the rear gantry of the C-130 opened onto the tarmac at Dharam Air Force Base in Saudi Arabia. Sam and his two team members, blinded by the searing sun for a moment, shouldered their packs and weapons then walked down the gantry into the hot desert.

"Captain Davon?" An American soldier dressed in flight-clothes and helmet approached.

"Yes."

"You and your men will follow me. We have a short flight to the U.S.S. Nassau. My men will load your gear."

The three of them followed him and boarded a CH-46 Sea Knight Helicopter. They immediately took off and headed out over the Persian Gulf. After a sixty mile flight Sam spotted the U.S.S. Nassau off in the distance. Its superstructure, twenty stories tall and eight hundred and fifty feet long, appeared no larger than a postage stamp off in the distance. The U.S.S. NASSUA LHA-4 was an amphibious assault ship capable of landings from the wet well in its aft section or enlisting its flight deck to send an array of helicopters and carrier jump jets into the air. It was also home to a population of four thousand American service men and women.

Soon the helicopter was positioned for landing. The twenty thousand pound vibrating aircraft hovered in mid-air as a yellow-shirted sailor on the flight deck guided the pilot first to the right, then to the left, then slowly forward to the designated berth. Their landing spot offered twelve feet of clearance between other stationed copters, and gave them less than five feet to the flight deck's edge.

Sam craned his neck to watch with professional admiration as the pilot's skill was tested. He followed hand signals for landing, all the while compensating for the ship's constant forward movement and the dramatic pitch and roll of the deck. Finally, Sam felt the vibrating machine drop to the deck, and the resonance from the rotors changed from an ear splitting whine to a neutral hum. He saw the deck crew run under the deadly whirling rotors and attach the tie down chains to the copter's superstructure.

Once on the flight deck, a tall man in full uniform met the three. "Welcome. I'm Colonel Black, Commander of the 26th MEU. We'll be responsible for your insertion and extraction on the mission. We'll have a short briefing at 1315 hours in the ready room. That'll give you enough time to wash up and rest. The Lieutenant will show you to your quarters. Just a word of caution gentlemen, the general population aboard ship is unaware of your mission. I'd like to keep it that way…for your own protection."

14 Chapter Fourteen

John Gordon stood with the long line of diplomats that represented countries from around the world. The warm breeze flowed off the Mediterranean and through Gordon's silver hair as he stood in the park where the service was being held. Gordon wore his traditional black mourning suit, though he still wore his Texan string tie and cowboy boots. He was a Texan and those two aspects of his appearance were worn with Texan pride. The commemorative service for the victims in Jerusalem was long and drawn out. With his hands clasped together below his waist, and his head bowed, Gordon looked solemn and sympathetic. But all the while his mind ran through the events that led to this terrible moment in time. He still found it hard to believe that past administrations had been so stupid. Now it was up to him to see that their mistakes didn't cause the downfall of this administration. His mind wrestled with the implications.

Gordon's mind raced. Yes, it was a cover-up. But there was no other choice. He wasn't out to protect an individual, but an entire country. The decisions made years ago were voluntary. The decision he had to make today was reactionary. The Delta Team was expendable. They'd taken an oath to protect their country. They knew when they joined that one day they might have to give up their life to protect their country. And on this mission they'd have to do just that. Then his thoughts shifted to a more current problem. He was not comfortable with the lack of a cohesive plan. He was flying blind. How was he going to meet this General Malek? Niddiem had only told him he'd be contacted. Gordon hated not being in control. He reached

The Shoe Shine Boy

for an antacid, but realized he'd eaten them all on the flight over.

After the service, his first official meeting was with Mateusz Adar. Gordon had taken the undiplomatic hard line with the Israeli Defense Minister the last time they'd met and negotiated. Their telephone conversation continued in the same vein, when he informed him of the Israeli Air Force quarantine. There was no reason to think this meeting would be any different, considering the inflammatory issue they were about to discuss. The difference this time was they were no longer in neutral territory. Perhaps he should go a little easier, given the recent tragedy. Gordon realized he was tired emotionally, and was not in a diplomatic mood. He had more pressing problems to consider than the Prime Minister's outrage. Their meeting was held in Adar's office. They faced off over a scarred desk and Adar immediately took the offensive.

"How dare the United States government quarantine the Israeli Air force, and steal our code and operations manuals! This is an out and out open act of espionage." His voice squeaked and his face appeared more mouse-like to Gordon then he remembered.

Gordon countered, "Your country has been spying on the United States for years. How the hell do you think you got the bomb? So cut the bullshit."

"My country categorically denies having nuclear weapons." His hands twitched with nervous anger.

"Yeah, well, we know better. C'mon, Mateusz, we can be productive, or we can argue over things that don't matter. Let's not waste time."

"It is not a waste of time to…"

Gordon cut him off with a wave of his hand. "First of all, we both know the gas originated in Iraq. You had planes loaded with nuclear bombs to retaliate once you located the specific target. Most likely you'd have gone after Baghdad if you didn't find the target. That's why we quarantined you.

"Secondly, I'm officially informing you that my government has located the whereabouts of the gas and is in the process of destroying it. We will not tolerate any interference that might jeopardize the safety of our men, or their mission. We'll bring back evidence, then try and convict Hussein."

Adar shook his head and his pointed nose twitched as his nostrils flared. "Then what? Do you expect him to turn himself in for punishment?"

"Then, whatever retaliation your government wants to hand out against him is up to you. Shoot him in the head for all we care. The world will support you. But they won't support incinerating hundreds of thousands of innocent people. Your country has to stop making political decisions based on revenge. Use your heads for once."

Within two hours Gordon and the Vice President were again aboard Air Force Two heading east towards Rhiyad, Saudi Arabia. The Vice President would brief the Crown Prince on their secret military operation, and on the containment of the Israeli forces. He would then spend the night.

But Gordon would instead board a military helicopter to Kuwait City. There he would brief the Kuwaiti King and return the next morning for the flight back to the States.

*   *   *   *

Baghdad was a sprawling Iraqi metropolis, an oasis in the harsh desert sands. Parts of the city, though, still held the scars of the Desert Storm bombing attacks. On the eastern border of the city sat the Ramad Army Base. Its bombed out structures had quickly been replaced. Its communication towers repaired. Its infrastructure rebuilt. Everything in this dictatorial regime that concerned the happiness and comfort of Saddam Hussein's elite military took precedence over the masses, which were left to their misery and squalor. Hussein understood that as long as the military was content, they would do his bidding and protect him. The powerful hold he had on the common people of his country was based on fear, not loyalty.

In the middle of the base sat an unpretentious Quonset hut much like the other base buildings. However, one level below the dirt floor was a room carved out of the hard packed dry desert sand. This unassuming building held the base's only prison. The prisoners locked up in this underground hell were deemed important enough to deserve interrogation rather than execution, though few survived the interrogation. Those that did survive could count on a swift termination of their lives shortly thereafter.

In this subterranean dungeon a thick wooden chair was bolted to a four by four slab of cement. Ameen sat motionless, his hands and feet strapped tightly to the chair. His chin rested on his chest. Dried blood had long since crusted on his nose and split lip, the result of what his captors considered a light beating. His leg had flies hovering and landing on the raw darkened muscle and exposed bone caused from the bullet that hit him during his run on the bridge.

Two guards stood in the corner talking quietly together, smoking non-filtered cigarettes. They quickly dropped them to the dirt floor, crushing out the burning embers, when General Malek descended the small stairs and entered the poorly lit room. Without saying a word, he walked over to Ameen, grabbed a fist full of his thick hair, and raised his head until their eyes met. Ameen was powerless to respond. He simply looked into the General Malek's eyes with contempt.

Malek bent over and spoke into his left ear, "You think you are strong."

Ameen's glazed eyes stared into Malek's face.

"You're not strong," General Malek continued. "You're weak. You think you're strong and that you'll win. But your arrogance will be your downfall. I'm the one who controls your future...your destiny...your life. And most of all, I control your death." He grabbed Ameen's throat with his left hand and squeezed until he heard noisy gasping respirations.

"Yes, I control your death. You will die. And I'll win. Your strength will be your downfall. I'll make your death so brutal and painful that I'll win."

Suddenly he released Ameen's throat and stood up. Ameen gasped and coughed for air as his lungs filled between spasms. "I'll never talk. I'll never help you."

Moments later his brother, Hamid, descended the stairs. His hands were bound tightly behind his back. The guard pushed him down the last four steps, and he flopped onto the dirt floor. He was then dragged to his feet, and led over to a second chair, a few feet from Ameen. They looked at each other but didn't speak. Each tried to gather strength from the other's courage, though Hamid was visibly scared and had difficulty keeping his body from shaking.

General Malek walked over to Hamid and viciously grabbed his face. His fingers dug deep into his cheeks. "Do you think you're as strong as your brother?"

Hamid's eyes were frozen on Malek. "I'll show you how weak you are. You hide behind buildings and kill my men. You blow up my equipment. Every time you do this I have to execute a commander for sloppiness. I've lost many good men. Now it will end, and you will help me, you worthless dung of the earth. You will help me because your foolish brother thinks he's strong. He very well may be, but that doesn't matter because you are weak."

He let go of Hamid's face and picked up a pair of pliers. "Do you know what pain is?" He stared into Hamid's eyes without blinking.

Hamid nodded his head yes.

"No, I don't think you really do! Let me show you." He raised Hamid's right hand and ripped off the thumbnail with one tug. Hamid's face contorted with agony and he let out a horrendous scream.

"Leave him alone!" Ameen called out in a horse dry voice.

"So our brave soldier finally speaks." Malek kept his back to Ameen. "That is pain. It's quick and simple. But there's something far deadlier than pain." He knelt in front of Hamid, and grabbed a second finger. He held it in the pliers, but applied only minimal pressure. Hamid shut his eyes and held his breath, but nothing happened.

"The evil of pain is fear," Malek said. "And before I finish with you, you'll understand fear."

Malek released the finger and walked back to Ameen. He kicked him viciously in the crotch. Ameen opened his mouth but couldn't scream. The pain was too intense.

"I want you to be strong! Show your brother how a man dies!" Malek spun, pointing a finger at Hamid. "And you will understand the consequences of your actions."

"We now begin!" One by one, he took Ameen's fingers and bent them back until each snapped, and hung limp. Ameen's hellish screams echoed in the small room. As Malek slowly deformed Ameen's body, he continued his verbal abuse, promising Hamid more pain, and a lingering death. This beating continued unabated for close to one and a half hours. As the beating progressed, Ameen flowed in and out of consciousness.

"I am tired of this game. It is time to end it." Malek stood behind Ameen and lifted his head by the tuft of matted hair on his forehead. His voice echoed in the small room. "Hamid, you will watch and remember. From this day on, you'll help me because you fear me. Do you know what it is to die? Not by a bullet in the head, but slowly. Watch and you will see."

Hamid stared in shock at the dirt floor. Malek motioned a guard to hold his head, forcing him to look at his brother. Malek placed a razor under Ameen's left ear and slowly pulled it across his throat. A gurgling sound rose as air rushed in and out of the hole in Ameen's throat with every breath he took. Red blood ran down around his neck.

Malek leaned over and whispered in Ameen's ear, "Be strong, and die in agony. But before you die, I want you to know that your brother is weak and with your death, your proud death, he will help us."

Ameen struggled for consciousness. His eyes darted around. But Malek was not content simply to let him die. He walked over to Hamid and stood behind him. "You can kill a man two ways by slitting his throat. If you go deep enough you cut the artery and he bleeds to death very quickly. But I prefer slicing the neck a little shallower, cutting only the vein. The blood trickles out and the victim bleeds to death slowly and stays awake. The victim stays alert until moments before death. I want you to watch as your brother struggles with his last thoughts of life. And, as you watch, I want you to fear me. Because if you don't help me, you will not be next, your sister will. And I will make you watch as I violate every aspect of her body. Then you will watch her blood slowly drip onto the dirt. And lastly, you will die the most painful death of anyone at my hands. So watch your brother and decide." He grabbed Hamid's head from behind and forced him to watch his brother's final moments.

Ameen's head bobbed up and down. It took nearly five minutes, but his eyes finally glazed over as his awareness faded into blackness.

15   Chapter Fifteen

Sam sat on the edge of his bunk and rested his feet on the cold steel floor. He had managed a short nap, and felt somewhat refreshed. Each of them had been given private quarters, which surprised him. Aboard a ship, space was at a premium, with twenty-five to thirty men sharing living quarters only slightly larger than a motel room. He had spent many missions in one of those rooms with bunks stacked five high to the bulkhead. But this mission was special. They were under orders not to discuss it with any of the crew.

Sam washed up then left for the ready room. Roger and Gino were already there. They were sitting in large comfortably padded leather chairs when he entered.

Colonel Black greeted him from the front of the room. "Welcome. Now that we're all here, shall we get started? Please help yourself to coffee and rolls." He pointed to a side table.

Sam listened to the information that was delivered in a straightforward manner. "Gentlemen, your mission is not an easy one. We have no real proof that your destination, The Minaret, actually has underground storage chambers. Unfortunately the structure is located too far upstream for you to be inserted by submarine. We have no choice but to fly you in. We have a CH-53E Superstallion helicopter standing by. You'll refuel over Kuwait. Two AH-1T/W Cobra Attack helicopters will escort you to and from the L.Z."

The men reviewed the equipment and firepower they needed. Next they decided on their pickup zone. Less than two hours later they adjourned. Sam and the rest of the team had thirty hours to acclimate themselves to the time zone and weather, before the mission would actually start.

Back in his quarters, he changed into gym shorts, a tee shirt and sneakers. Moments later he joined Roger and Gino on the flight deck. After some light stretching and calisthenics, they joined the multitude of Marines running mile after mile around the now quiet platform.

As they ran, they kept to themselves. Though their mission was classified as top-secret Special Forces, the word had traveled fast through the ship that a three man special team had arrived to kick some ass. It hadn't taken long for rumors to abound, some way off base and others remarkably accurate. So they ran a distance from the others and the crew respected their privacy. Finally they sat on the deck and did cool down stretches.

"What are the odds on this one, Sam?" Gino asked.

"Don't know. I wish we had more intelligence information. We can't worry about that now. See you at dinner." He got up and headed below deck.

16   Chapter Sixteen

Abraham hailed a cab at Boston's Logan International Airport. Then he sat staring at the nameless streets they passed during the forty-minute ride to Woburn. He hadn't called ahead. He simply hopped the first flight he could get. He rationalized that at their age, the Steinmans probably weren't very mobile. So they were likely to be home.

The cab pulled up to a modest cape style home surrounded by a meticulously manicured hedge. Abraham paid the cab driver but asked him to wait. After ringing the door bell the wait was agonizing. Eventually the door opened. A woman in her eighties stood there. "May I help you?" she asked.

Preoccupied with his own feelings, Abraham hadn't even thought about what he'd say or how he'd explain himself. "Yes I hope so," he said, his voice cracking. "I'm looking for Commander Steinman. I met him many years ago at the end of war. I was hoping I could speak to him."

"Please come in. I'm his wife, Carol." She opened the door wide and he saw that she had gentle eyes that reminded him of Clara's. He waved the cab away, and then followed her into a comfortable, old-fashioned home. The furnishings, though long out of style, were meticulously clean and preserved. Hand made Afghans lay on the couch in the living room and the easy chairs. "Please sit down. How do you know my husband?"

"I was at the death camp at Buchenwald when it was liberated. My name is Abraham Feinstein. I was a boy when your husband liberated us. Is he home? I'd really like to speak to him."

"I'm sorry, but I buried him three days ago." Her voice was apologetic, and her eyes were bright with tears. "He was sick for so long. I'm grateful he's finally resting peacefully."

Abraham slumped. It was too much to bear. "This is unfair. What have I done? Why must I live through such pain?" He broke down and sobbed.

Carol stood up. "Please, you're frightening me. What's wrong?"

Abraham took a few deep breaths and wiped his eyes. "I'm sorry. This is wrong of me. You have your own loss. I shouldn't burden you with mine. I'll leave." He lifted himself out of the chair onto his injured leg. His face winced with pain and he fell back into the chair.

"You're hurt. Please sit for a while and talk to me. I'd like someone to talk to. Stay for tea."

"You're very kind. Thank you."

The minutes turned into hours as he sat, sipped tea, and ate finger sandwiches with her. Abraham told her about his life in the death camps. Nothing was left out. When he tried to jump ahead she would stop him and ask questions, forcing him to relate the most intimate details. Finally he reached the part when her husband entered the barracks.

"So you're the Abraham he spoke of."

"What do you mean, he spoke of?"

"For years after the war he talked about you. That walk you took him on through the barracks had such an effect on him. You were so young and lived through such horror. You forced him to come face to face with the worst evil. It affected him. It made him more compassionate. You gave him strength in situations that would've made other men crumble. He talked about you often. I only wish he was alive to see you again." She looked down and shook her head.

"Me too. It seems I'll never find the answers I need."

"I don't understand."

Abraham sighed. "Before I left the camps, the chemist, Von Wilbert, was in his custody. I can't seem to find out what happened to him. I was hoping your husband could help me. It's important I put that part of my life to rest."

"Maybe I can help. Please, give me a few moments." She stood and slowly walked into the next room.

He sat quietly looking around the tastefully decorated room. Less than five minutes later she returned and handed him an old leather bound book. "Please look through this. It's my husband's diary of the war. The last fifty or so pages were about the liberation of the camps. I'm sure you're mentioned in it."

Abraham flipped through the pages until he found the section detailing the camps. The rawness of the emotions on the pages gave him goose bumps. Steinman's words captured the revulsion of what he found and the true misery the survivors and those deceased had gone through. Sights, sounds and smells came to Abraham as he read on.

Turning a page, he read about meeting a little boy named Abraham.

I felt the touch of this boy's hand in mine as he led me deeper into a place I didn't want to go. His hand felt like a chicken bone. No softness at all. His eyes were sunken and his skeletal arms and hands were covered with sagging skin. At one point in my tour this boy took a moth-eaten blanket and tucked it under the head of a dying man. He looked at me and told me how they all tried to ease the dying, to give them a little dignity. Those chicken boned fingers had more softness and compassion then one could ever imagine.

Abraham read on, tears streaming down his face. "It's here! I found it."

On the second day of liberating camp Buchenwald, I came face to face with a captured Nazi chemist. I met him only for a moment, but I've never before seen such calculated coldness. Chills ran up and down my spine. He boasted to me how he had invented the perfect killing weapon. And that it would save his life. How ironic, an instrument of death would save a life. But he was right. Despite my desire to put a bullet in his head, I was forced to turn him over to the intelligence group. I'd heard they were scurrying throughout Germany rounding up the intellectual elite. They wanted to get them before the Russians did.

It burned my soul to turn him over. Their thoroughness was impressive. All documentation of his capture, and existence, were destroyed. I can only hope after our government extracts what they need from him they'll kill him the way he deserves. But deep down inside I know he's too valuable. Our military will cherish him.

Abraham closed the book and trembled, with rage and disbelief.

"Did you find what you were looking for?"

"My...my god, how could I have been so foolish to have trusted them." He held the diary in front of him and stared at it.

"If what you need is in there, please take it."

17   Chapter Seventeen

"Stop ringing the damn doorbell. I'm coming! I'm coming!" Megan called out as she stormed through the dark. She tied her terrycloth robe as she walked. Her auburn hair was twisted and tangled and she rubbed the sleep out of her eyes.

The bell didn't stop.

Megan reached her front door and looked through the peephole. "Abraham." She unlocked the door and threw it open. "It's midnight. Come in. What happened?" She looked closely at him. The sad pitiful look was gone. It was replaced with white-hot anger.

"Read this!" He thrust the diary at her. "It's all here. Von Wilbert's alive! He killed, maimed, and plotted the death of countless Jews. And instead of being stopped by a bullet in the heart he was rewarded with a place in our government. Read it!"

"What is this?" She took the diary from his shaking hands and led him into the living room.

"That is Commander Steinman's diary. He's dead. He died a few days ago. But he wrote it all down, all of it. Our government saved that bastard. Read it! I marked the places."

"Okay, okay. Give me a moment. Please sit."

"No, I'll stand." He paced nervously back and forth.

Megan opened to the first marker and started to read. She shuddered at Steinman's description of the death camps. As she read she felt Abraham watching her intensely. She trembled for a second then looked up.

"Don't stop. Keep reading." He pointed at the diary.

She was aghast at what she read. By the time she reached the description of Abraham, tears were rolling down her cheeks. Fifteen minutes later she finished.

"Now you see. I'm not an old paranoid fool swallowed up in grief. Why would they do this? Why? I believed this country was different. That's why I live here. Why?" Abraham clasped his hands together to stop them from shaking.

"I don't know what to say. We expect better from our country. But I think they did this out of fear."

"And what did they have to fear by giving him the justice he deserved?"

"I guess it was the loss of knowledge. For all they knew, the Russians had someone also working on the same type of experiments. They had to keep up. It doesn't make it right. But the question is, what do you want to do?"

"Find him." The answer came quickly.

"And then what? Shoot him in the head? You're no murderer."

"I know. I thought about it long and hard. I'd love to walk up to that bastard, make him get down on his knees and beg for his life. Then I'd put a gun to his face and pull the trigger. Pull it for all those corpses he forced me to drag out of his death chamber.

"You couldn't do that."

Abraham paused, then his shoulders dropped slightly. "You're right, Megan." Then after a long moment in thought he said, "Instead I'll expose him. But I need to find him first. I'll photograph him to prove his existence. Then I'll turn the evidence over to the Israeli government. They'll act. They'll demand justice, and carry it out. That's what should've happened decades ago. Will you help me?"

She took only a moment to reply. "Yes, I will. But we do it my way. I don't want you charging into Niddiem's office tomorrow and stirring up a hornet's nest. We don't know who's involved and this will obviously step on some toes. We do it my way or not at all."

"Agreed."

18   Chapter Eighteen

Ismail was thirty years old. He was the leader of a small group of Iraqis fighting for their country's freedom against Saddam Hussein. Ismail was a robust vibrant man with the vision of a free Iraq. He walked and talked with an infectious enthusiasm that allowed others to believe in him and the risk of their cause. Ismail turned from the window overlooking war-scarred Baghdad. In front of him seven young men sat on the floor around a small coffee table. They were in a modest apartment on the west side of the city. Only days ago there had been ten in this small cell of terrorists but with the unsuccessful raid at Al Amara three important members, Ameen, Aziz and Rashid had been lost. Hamid had also nearly been lost, but he had managed to escape. Hamid told them how he jumped off the bridge and swam to safety before they could capture him. His story of how the other three had been shot at the bridge had inspired the group. They mourned the loss of their three friends. It reminded them only too well how dangerous this game was.

Atiqa, Hamid's sister, finished serving tea. Despite the hardships, she always found a way to be hospitable to the group. Since her parents' death, she and her brothers barely scraped by in the family's small apartment. The monthly stipend from the government helped, but it was now harder to find supplies to purchase. And now without Ameen to help, things would be tighter still. Her eyes filled with tears every time she thought of Ameen.

"Then we agree," Ismail said. "It will be tonight."

Two and a half miles west of Baghdad sat an electrical transformer station they planned to blow up. The Americans had blasted it out of existence during the early hours of Desert Storm. But the Iraqis had rebuilt it, of course under the strict control of the United Nations.

"It is time we reminded the government of Baghdad how vulnerable it is. The Government has forgotten and takes for granted things as simple as electricity. We will change that," Ismail said.

He looked around the room and felt confident. They had talked and re-talked through every step of the plan. They knew where the explosives should be placed for maximum effect. They had memorized points of entry and escape. With everything set, the meeting ended. They left one by one, so as not to arouse suspicion.

Two hours after the meeting Hamid left the apartment. "Atiqa, I'm going for a walk. I need to calm my nerves." He looked down at the bandage on his finger. It covered the raw open nail bed that until recently had been covered by a nail.

Hamid walked aimlessly for the next half hour, alone with his thoughts and his terrible dilemma. He had to make a decision, but what real choice did he have? Finally he stopped at one of the few remaining telephone booths in town. He dialed the number he had memorized not too long ago and talked for a few moments.

After listening to the reply he answered, "General Malek, I've told you all I know." He hung up. Hamid walked away from the telephone with his shoulders drooped, and his heart aching. He had betrayed his friends, but he had to protect his sister at all costs. He didn't care if they called him a traitor.

19   Chapter Nineteen

"Son of a bitch!" Gordon paced around the fifth floor hotel room in Kuwait City. Exhausted and on the verge of physical collapse, he was operating on nervous energy. The muscles in his legs shook due to fatigue, but he continued to pace. His head pounded from lack of sleep.

"It's 11:00 at night," he ranted. "What am I supposed to do? Call the front desk and tell the concierge to send a car to bring me to the desert to meet an Iraqi General? Shit! Or maybe I'll just call that asshole, Niddiem!"

A knock on the door interrupted him.

"What! Who is it?"

"Room service."

"I didn't order any room service." He opened the door and faced two robed Kuwaitis. "What's this? I didn't order anything."

They ignored his protests and wheeled the food cart in anyway. Once in, they shut the door behind themselves. The tall one uncovered his head.

"I have been instructed to drive you to a meeting northwest of Mityahah. The two of you will trade places." He pointed to his companion.

"What is this, a B rated movie?"

"We don't have much time. Please cooperate."

The shorter one took off his robe and pulled it over Gordon's head. Then he took his scarf and wrapped it around Gordon's face, allowing only his eyes to show.

The tall one looked at Gordon. "You need to take those off." He pointed to Gordon's cowboy boots. "You will wear these sandals.

Gordon did as he was asked. The tall one nodded. "Good. We will go now. Two people in, two people out. The guard at the end of the hall will not be suspicious. Come, we have a long night in front of us."

"It's been one long night for days. I just keep waiting for the morning to arrive."

"Please, no talking now. Follow me."

Gordon complied and followed him, shaking his head.

They walked down the hall past the guard and stopped at the elevator. While they waited Gordon kept his eyes on the carpet. The stranger turned to the guard and said, "Mr. Gordon wishes not to be disturbed by anyone until morning. He is extremely tired. We will return with his breakfast at seven in the morning.

They entered the elevator and rode it to the kitchen. Outside, they climbed into an old sun-baked Toyota and drove off.

"Do not take your scarf off. Keep your face hidden until we are well out of the city."

"Who do you work for?"

"That is none of your concern, just as your meeting is none of mine."

With that, silence ensued as they made their way into the barren desert. The city lights disappeared and the night sky and the sand in front of them blended into a dark void broken only by the headlights shining a few feet in front of them.

*   *   *   *

The evening was still. The moon intermittently illuminated the Baghdad countryside through passing clouds. It was not an ideal night for a terrorist attack, but Ismail didn't want to wait three weeks until the new moon.

He looked at his watch: 11:45. There would be no signal. They had their plans. They'd place the explosives around the electrical station and in fifteen minutes they'd be gone. He moved to the left of the station, with his backpack that was laden with explosives. Suddenly he stopped. Where was Hamid? He was right behind him a moment ago. Ismail quickly retraced his steps to the bushes. There he found him cowering close to the ground.

"Hamid, what's wrong?" At that moment the moon broke through the clouds. The light illuminated them and Ismail could see the terror on Hamid's face. "It's all right to be afraid. Stay here, I'll be right back." As he turned the night exploded into chaos with the sound of automatic weapons. Ismail dove to the ground, and pulled Hamid even lower. "Hamid, it's an ambush! Follow me!"

While the Iraqi guards, only yards away, shined their lights on four dead terrorists, Ismail and Hamid made their escape back to Baghdad.

* * * *

"Wake up. We have arrived." Gordon felt a light tap on his shoulder.

Gordon rubbed his eyes and looked at the desert landscape of sand in front of them. "God, I must've been more tired than I thought. How long was I asleep?"

"About two hours. It is almost two-fifteen."

"Shit, I'm covered with sand. What'd you do, drive with the windows down?" The inside of the Toyota had fine desert sand coating everything.

Gordon looked out the front window and saw the outline of a solitary tent sitting in the middle of the desert. The Toyota pulled next to it and stopped.

"We are here. I will wait for you while you have your meeting."

Gordon hesitated for a moment.

"You are safe, Mr. Gordon. Your people arranged this meeting. We work for you. If I had wanted to kill you, your dead carcass would be lying in the desert feeding the sand rats at this moment."

"Thanks for the encouraging thought."

Gordon coughed the dry sand out of his throat. He stepped out of the Toyota and walked into the small upright tent. Inside he found a kerosene lamp illuminating it with flickering rays. The pungent odor of burning kerosene instantly irritated his already dry nostrils. Two chairs sat in the tent's center. A military officer dressed in an Iraqi uniform occupied one. The stranger didn't rise. Instead he sat and stared at him. Gordon saw they were alone, so he walked over and sat down.

"Are you General Malek?"

"Yes. Who are you?" His accent was imitation British.

Gordon saw a liter of bottled water next to his chair. He opened it and drank long and hard before he spoke. "John Gordon, Secretary of State for the United States of America."

"Such an important man to come out into the hot desert wishing to meet me. How flattering. To what great honor do I owe this visit?"

"Cut the bullshit. It's not an honor. It's not a meeting of allies or friends. You and your kind are murderers. I'm only here because I had no choice."

"So," Malek shrugged, "you travel all this way to insult me?"

"Let's get down to business. The sooner I leave this flea-infested place, the better. The United States Government and the Israelis know Iraq produced and provided the nerve gas for the attack on Jerusalem."

"You are wrong, we…"

"Don't waste my time." John raised his hand. "What the President and I are trying to do is stop the Israelis from retaliating."

"And what exactly can the Israeli military do to my country that yours couldn't do during your heinous air strike in your Desert Storm?"

"How about a strategic nuclear attack?" The words hung in the air.

"Ah, I see. So it is true the Jews have nuclear bombs."

"Cut the crap, I'm tired. The bottom line is I'm trying to save your country's ass."

"No, I don't think so. The only bottom side you are trying to save is your own. Let me ask you, Mr. Secretary of State." Malek leaned forward. "Did you help Israel develop their nuclear bombs like you helped Iraq with the nerve gas?"

"The nerve gas was the responsibility of a prior administration. And this administration is not going to be blamed for it!" Gordon replied.

"Yes, well, so tell me how you will save my country from ruin."

"The Israelis have agreed not to launch an offensive nuclear attack on Baghdad if the gas is destroyed and those responsible brought to justice."

"So you expect us to destroy the gas and turn those responsible over to the Jews, so they can be shot or hung."

"The plan is this. A U.S. Special Forces team will destroy the gas and plan to return with evidence implicating Iraq. Then Israel will try your leader Hussein for war crimes, based on the evidence."

"Do you expect this to be acceptable to us?"

"No, and it isn't acceptable to us either. We will destroy the gas. But we can't have the Special Forces leave with any incriminating evidence. You must stop them, but only after they've destroyed the gas."

"Let me see if I understand you." Malek stopped for a moment and rubbed the back his neck. "You are asking my government's help in killing your own men."

"Yes."

"What stops me from killing them prior to the destruction of the gas?"

"A nuclear attack on Baghdad."

"So this is nuclear blackmail."

"I don't give a fuck what you call it! The gas will be destroyed and if we don't get confirmation of a successful mission, believe me, there'll be a line to see who gets at you first. I don't think you or your government understand how outraged the world is, or how isolated your country is at this moment."

Malek stood up and looked out the tent opening. His hands were clasped behind his back. "The arrogance and duplicity with which you talk overwhelms me." He turned to Gordon. "You talk about saving Baghdad from nuclear attack. But you are not man enough to admit that your only concern is covering up your own country's involvement."

"Fuck you!"

"You know, Mister Secretary, my mother always told me that the person who loses an argument is the first one who uses vulgar language, or raises his hand to strike the other first."

Gordon stood and walked to Malek until they were nose to nose. "You can think whatever you want. But like it or not, you will allow the gas to be destroyed. Then you will eliminate the attacking team. Your country doesn't get nuked and mine doesn't get implicated. And personally I don't give a shit if it's nuclear blackmail or not." He walked past Malek and stormed out of the tent.

Malek remained for a moment alone lost in thought. He pulled a flask out from his pocket and took a swallow. "Ah, Mr. Secretary of State, how little you understand. How little you have learned. We will never give up such a weapon. So you think I, or Saddam Hussein, care about the peasants in Baghdad? If you want to drop nuclear bombs on them, go ahead. It will cause such condemnation of the Jews that everyone will forget about the gas attack. And in one blinding flash the Muslim world will be united as never before. I encourage you to bomb us."

20   Chapter Twenty

Megan stared intently at Jonathan, silently willing his fingers to move faster over the Braille on the page in front of him. She had stayed up all night reading and rereading the diary while Abraham slept on her couch. In the morning she had passed the pages through a scanner for Jonathan, converting the printed words into Braille. Now she fidgeted in her chair, all the while trying to guess where he was in the diary. The expression on his face indicated to her that he was becoming as overwhelmed as she had been. With a sigh, he finished the last page and sat silently.

"It made me cry," she said. "I couldn't sleep after I read it. So I got up and read it again and cried some more."

Jonathan nodded. "We hear about this. We read about it. But this is beyond comprehension. I can't believe someone in our government dismissed what that bastard had done and granted him safe haven."

"Abraham intends to find him. What do we do? Do we help him? We'd be exposing a very sensitive and embarrassing decision made years ago. I've been chasing these thoughts all night."

"How high is your security clearance?" Jonathan rubbed the back of his neck.

"As high as yours. You know that."

"Well, more or less. Here's the deal. When I did my search for Von Wilbert, I used my clearance code. It's different from yours. It allows me a different access. Don't ask. I was allowed into a file that you and most others are excluded from. I found that Von Wilbert does exist. But all files that reference him had been placed in a locked file that can only be opened via a voice-activated code."

"That doesn't surprise me. They've probably protected that file for a long time."

"Actually, no. That file was secured thirty minutes before you and Abraham first visited me."

"Thirty minutes! Thirty minutes before, we were in Al Niddiem's office! We were talking about Von Wilbert."

"And who do you think secured those files?" queried Jonathan rhetorically.

"Niddiem?"

"That's right."

"You think he secured those files right after we talked to him?" Megan asked as her mouth hung open.

"I'm open to any other suggestions. But personally, that's exactly what I think. And you know I'm right."

They sat there in silence for a long time.

"Well, what do we do from here?" Megan finally said.

"We could storm into Niddiem's office," Jonathan said. "Tell him we know he hid past files protecting a war criminal. Then we tell him that under the rules of the Nuremberg trial he is now an accomplice to war crimes, aiding and abetting a fugitive. Somehow though, I don't think he'd be too receptive to that."

"Get serious. You know that's not an option. They'd find a way to keep it quiet. Somehow we have to get into that file." Megan stood and began to rock from one foot to the other.

"There's no way," he said. "I helped design this system. Believe me I know we've gone as far as we can go."

"So we just forget about it and let Abraham die of grief and self pity. We can't do that."

"I'm sorry. I just don't have an answer for you."

"Fine! I'll remember this when you need help. Have a nice day." Megan stormed out of his office.

Immediately after Megan left Jonathan returned to his keyboard. The decision to help Abraham was one of morality, not security. The implications of opening this file were enormous. But in spite of what he had told her, he knew it would be an easy process. He had written the computer code for the agency's security system years ago. He knew he could break into it in a moment. No one else knew he had the ability, and he wanted to keep it that way, even from Megan. Why divulge his secret? What if the file held no value?

Once he typed his clearance code, and his special access code, the program opened. His left hand read the code off the Braille system reader while his right index finger advanced the program line by line. He scrolled down until he found the code that allowed individuals with specific clearance to insert voice activated security locks. Next he opened the sub file and found Niddiem's latest access code. It was time and date stamped. It matched the time and date Von Wilbert's file was secured.

His finger ran over the code and he made a mental note.

: AL NIDDIEM: AUTHENTICATION CODE: 57987BBALNIDDIEM

He typed it in and Niddiem's file opened up. This revealed his voice-recorded code. This had to be exact. Not only did the system check the spoken words it also matched the voice frequencies, which are as distinct for individuals as their fingerprints.

He inserted a disk into his console and downloaded Niddiem's voiceprint of the code. He listened for any background noise for a moment. One couldn't be too cautious. Satisfied no one was around him he typed: 57987BBALNIDDIEM

PLEASE ENTER VOICE CODE:

He pressed return and the digital copy of Niddiem's voice was downloaded into the system: "Al Niddiem 7894AACA."

: AL NIDDIEM 7894AACA ACCEPTED

He next typed:
: Claus Von Wilbert Files
The file he wanted opened up.
"Bingo," murmured Jonathan.
He removed the disk storing Niddiem's security voiceprint and inserted a new blank disk. Next he burned a complete backup of the Von Wilbert files onto the disk. That took fifteen seconds. Then he instructed the computer to print an entire copy of the Von Wilbert file. Instantly his Braille printer came alive. Seventeen minutes later it finished the last page. He placed the one hundred and forty-seven pages into his briefcase. Next he re-entered the program code and erased the logged presence of him being in Von Wilbert's file. As he removed the disk copy of the Von Wilbert file from the external disk drive, Jonathan knew he would have to put it in a safe place…just in case.

The next morning Megan joined Jonathan in his office.
"I'm sorry I blew up at you yesterday." She sat down. "It was wrong of me. I took my anger out on you."
"No. I'm the one who owes you an apology. I was able to get at the files all along. I didn't want to tell you until I checked them myself. If they held nothing, there was no point in you knowing I could do it."
Ordinarily Megan would have been insulted, but today she was too ecstatic by the news. "So you found something?" she asked.
"Yes I did. I made a copy and started reading it last night. I finished about half of the file before I fell asleep." His voice was pensive and low key. "It's amazing what they got away with. They justified things that should have sent them in front of a firing squad."
For the next twenty minutes Megan sat and listened. Jonathan described the orders that first brought Von Wilbert to

the United States, and changed his name to Arnold Jones. "He was very instrumental in the development of certain nerve gases that now fill our army's arsenal."

"So where is he now?" She slid forward in her seat.

"At the moment he's back in Germany."

"Germany?"

"I was surprised also. I ran his name for a current address and it was flagged by Immigration. He left the country three days ago on a flight to Germany."

"Why would he go to Germany?"

"It's interesting. Throughout his tenure as a chemical technician for us he made lots of trips to Germany. Homesick I'd guess. He was watched pretty closely but it still would make me nervous, given his Nazi background. He always stayed at Von Riechbrand's estate. He was most likely a friend from before or during the War."

Jonathan understood Megan's silence. After a long pause he spoke. "I wondered the same all night. Do we tell Abraham or not?"

"There's no doubt in your mind about this?"

"None at all. He's the killer Abraham is searching for."

He knew her eyes were shut and she was weighing the pros and cons.

"I think we have to tell him," she said. "He has the right to know."

"I agree. But I also think you should tell him since you're closer to him."

Four hours later Abraham settled into a first class seat for his third flight across the Atlantic in less than a week. Megan wanted to join him but with the ongoing Special Forces mission she was unable to. This time Abraham was not drifting aimlessly. He was focused on one thought, to identify and expose Claus Von Wilbert, and to see justice handed out.

David Mucci

Minaret at Samarra, Iraq

21   Chapter Twenty-one

Megan sat at the head of the conference table and addressed her team, "I know I told you I'd only be running things until Abraham returned. But he has a lot of grief to work through, and he's taken an extended leave of absence. In the meantime, if there are no objections, I'll continue as acting head of the team."

She saw only nods of encouragement. "Okay. Thank you. Our next task is to monitor the progress of the Special Forces Team. They'll be landing in approximately seven hours. Maurice, I want you constantly monitoring the airwaves. When that Minaret blows I want to know about it. Tim, you'll monitor the Iraqi military. I want to know if they make any attempt to intercept or intervene in the mission. Maurice, you'll analyze satellite photos of the Minaret. After they blow it I want to know the damage and how they respond at the site. That's it. The mission starts in four hours. Let's get set up. It's gonna be a long night."

Without comment they filed out of the room to dial in and calibrate the electronic eyes and ears that watched over the Iraqi sands thousands of miles away.

At 22:30 hours Sam's alarm clock woke him from a deep sleep. Showers aboard ship were usually quick because fresh water was not as plentiful as on land. But today Sam indulged himself for a few extra minutes. He let the warm water soothe the nape of his neck, and fall down his back. He had no idea when he'd shower again. Half an hour later, fully dressed, he met Roger and Gino in the Officers' mess for a thick, juicy steak. They would need the protein load to carry them through the mission. They ate in silence, keeping their thoughts to themselves.

Full but not stuffed, Sam returned to his quarters and donned a camouflage suit of desert sand colors. Then he applied colored paint to his face and hands. When finished he sat and meditated. Death didn't enter his mind, only pleasant memories.

"ATTENTION. SET CONDITION ALPHA ONE, SET CONDITION ALPHA ONE." The public address system reached every corner of the ship.

Sam took in a final deep breath and let it out slowly. Then he stood and looked into the mirror at his reflection. "Let's do it."

He grabbed his pack and assault rifle and walked into the corridor, Roger and Gino were waiting for him.

"Just once I'd like to do this during the day so we can get a good nights sleep," Gino said.

"Yeah, and get our asses shot off in the sun," Sam replied. Special Operations meant being a night owl.

They climbed the ladder to reach the deck just below the flight deck, where they stopped and waited. Above them they heard the increasing roar from the engines of the C53E Superstallion, and the two Cobra Attack helicopters warming up.

Within a few minutes Sam saw the Combat Cargo Captain of the day approach them. It was his duty to escort them across the now dangerous flight deck. The tranquil surface of steel they had jogged on earlier was now awash with rotors and hot engine blast from the helicopters.

"Are you gentlemen ready?"

"Yes," they replied in unison.

"Then follow me. And good luck."

Sam nodded, and motioned for the others to go first. They walked through a dark passageway to a catwalk still below the flight deck. The Captain held an oversized wand, which cast a subdued blue light over the night scene. Everything around them vibrated in the roar of the helicopters overhead. Sam followed them up a ladder to the flight deck next to their Superstallion. The hot blast from its engines assaulted his senses. The flight deck was dark. All visible light was extinguished or covered with blue filters.

They climbed aboard and strapped into their seats. The crew chief came and checked them, then called out orders. "Crash position!"

Sam ducked his head between his legs and held tight with his hands over his head.

"Exits!" was the next command.

In unison they pointed to the nearest exit.

"All clear," the Crew Chief called out.

Finally, the Air Boss granted permission for them to take off.

The quality of the noise changed as the rotor pitch adjusted and the vibration level went up. Sam grabbed his rifle as it bounced from the vibration. The ugly, noisy beast that a moment ago was chained to the flight deck took off and transformed from an ungainly monster to an agile bird.

Within moments, the flight deck returned to tranquil quiet, except for the public address system.

"CONDITION ALPHA ONE COMPLETE."

Miles out from the flight deck the Superstallion, with a Cobra gun ship on either side, flew into the darkness at no more than one hundred feet above the smooth gulf water. All navigational lights were out and the three pilots wore Night Vision System Helmets. The two Cobras flew parallel to the Superstallion.

There wasn't much for Sam and his team to do during their flight towards the darkness of the Kuwaiti sand. All their equipment had been checked, packaged, and loaded onto their Fast Attack Vehicle.

When the three black helicopters passed over the Kuwait mainland a simple radio message was transmitted. "Alpha One has dry feet."

Soon they passed into Iraqi territory. A second transmission was sent. "Alpha One is hot."

Now they flew at one hundred and fifty knots, one hundred feet above the sand. The pilots guided their crafts up and down with the rolling dunes, which were displayed clearly in a green phosphorous hue on their Night Vision System Helmets. They traveled undetected towards the landing zone, thirty-seven miles west of the Tigris River. When they were almost there, one of the flight crew came into the cargo bay. "Three minutes to L.Z."

They each responded with a thumbs up sign. On cue they rose and approached their F.A.V. (fast attack vehicle), nicknamed Ninja Jeep. It was a dune buggy modified with completely silent mufflers, a fifty-millimeter machine gun where a roof usually would be, and a high seat behind it for the gunner. Infrared lights mounted on the front illuminated the desert so only those with infrared Night Vision Systems could see where the vehicle was going. Stored in pods along the sides of the vehicle was all the equipment they would need for the mission.

Sam took the driver's seat, Gino the passenger's, and Roger the gunner seat. Sam pulled the knob in front of him. The engine ignited and a new vibration shot through the frame of the F.A.V. Though the gauge registered engine revolutions, the exhaust was completely silent. The copter's rear gantry opened and extended its jaw to the darkness below. The infrared lights illuminated the sand below as it passed by at a decreasing distance and speed.

In a split instant, the forward motion of the Superstallion stopped as the gantry touched the soft sand. At that moment Sam pressed the accelerator of the vehicle to the floor. They shot forward, and leapt off the metal ramp. The moment they cleared the gantry the Superstallion had lifted off and was returning at one hundred and sixty knots south toward the Persian Gulf waters, again at one hundred feet above the sand. The jeep's tires dug into the sand and instantly propelled them forward until they reached a top speed of sixty miles per hour. From the moment the F.A.V. touched Iraqi soil they raced forward.

The two Cobras that flew along side the SuperStallion spun in synchronous pirouettes one mile from each other, scanning the desert for any heat signatures of danger. Finding none, they turned south and raced to catch the Superstallion.

At sixty miles per hour, the Delta Team quickly closed the distance between themselves and the Tigris River. The F.A.V. hummed as it silently propelled them over bumps, and up and down sand dunes.

Gino kept an eye on the Global Navigation System. Their end spot had been precisely picked to provide maximum protection for the jeep. The G.N.S. would bring them within three feet of their planned destination.

Sam steered them over a dune and into a small hard-packed gully with seven-foot-high walls of sand on either side. The gully was only ten feet wide and seemed to close in on them as they raced through it. They followed it to the right, and then raced down a slight incline into the open desert below.

Gino spotted the campsite only seconds before Sam and Roger did. But it was too late. They were in the middle of it in an instant. Gino threw the safety off the machine gun and took aim, but held his fire. In that instant Sam had guided them through the center of the camp and out the backside without a shot being fired. The camels barked with fright and stood up in confusion. The Nomads lying under the stars were startled by their camels' agitation and jumped to their feet. Sand swirled through the air, but there was no breeze. They grabbed their guns but found no target to aim at. They found no danger, just sand flying and frighten camels. Eventually they calmed their animals and settled down to sleep again.

The F.A.V. had passed through their camp in seconds. It was noiseless. Only the whoosh of the wind and the stirring of sand gave any telltale sign that they had been there. Gino placed the safety back on the machine gun.

Twenty-nine minutes after they had left the Superstallion, the cool waters of the Tigris River became highlighted on their Night Vision System Goggles. Sam guided them to the right. He had spotted the rise of rocks that sat twenty feet from the river's edge. A quick survey found no traffic on the river, and no life in the vicinity.

They pulled up next to the rock. Sam pushed the engine's kill button and the vibrations stopped. Without a word he grabbed his assault rifle, climbed the rock and assumed a prone position. He scanned in all directions looking for any sign of danger.

Meanwhile, Gino and Roger pulled aluminum rods from the jeep. They anchored them in the sand, extended them over the jeep and attached them to the rock. Next they draped a lightweight tarp over the rods, covering the jeep. They then shoveled sand over the tent. In fifteen minutes time a rolling sand dune had been created, hiding their vehicle.

"We're done. Are we clear?" Roger asked Sam.

Sam took one final sweep before he replied, "All clear. Let's go."

They unlatched the underwater sleds that had been attached to the F.A.V. and helped each other carry them to the river's edge.

Lastly, Sam took a collapsible broom and swept the sand from the rock to the river. He'd erased all visible evidence of them being there.

With their Night Vision System Goggles and assault rifles placed into watertight compartments, they donned Night Vision diving masks. The closed circuit breathing systems they now had strapped onto their backs trapped every bit of exhaled breath allowing no bubbles to escape and float to the surface where they might be spotted, thus giving away their position. After donning their gear they submerged a few feet below the river's surface. The hydro-sleds pulled them quietly and unimpeded up the silt-laden river. Passive listening devices on the sleds filtered and analyzed the river's sound. If an approaching boat was detected, a warning light would flash inside their masks.

Despite scientific advances, danger was never completely eliminated. The underwater vision system that allowed them to see with exceptional clarity at night was rendered useless when the bottom of a large silent drift barge floated over them.

Sam and Gino instantly recognized the danger. They drove their sleds to the sandy river bottom twenty feet below. Roger, however, looked up at the wrong moment and smashed his facemask into the rough wooden bottom. The cracked mask was useless as cloudy water spilled through the breach and filled it. His sled rolled over and one of the steering fins hit the bottom of the barge and bent. Instinctively he pushed off the sled and swam blindly towards the river bottom. He was followed closely behind by the sinking, disabled, hydro-sled.

Roger waited on the river bottom until the barge was well downstream. Then he surfaced and swam to shore. He stayed mostly submerged by the rivers edge until Sam and Gino soon joined him.

"Are you alright?" Sam asked.

"Yeah, but my mask's broken and I think my sled's damaged," Roger said.

"Here's a spare mask." Sam took one out of a compartment. "It's just a standard one, but it'll do. Let's find your sled."

David Mucci

Roger held onto Sam and the three submerged to the river bottom. After a short time they located the sled. One look at it and they knew it wouldn't travel in a straight line. They detached the pods that contained Roger's equipment and lashed them onto Sam's sled. With that done they set off piggyback style upstream towards their target.

They slowly made their way up the Tigris until they were at a bend in the river on the outskirts of Samarra. Another hundred yards upstream their navigational systems flashed the proper coordinates onto Gino and Sam's masks. They had reached their mark. Nearby sat the eleven hundred year old Minaret. They swam towards shore. There they found the river's edge had been dredged out, creating a small channel. They followed it. Gino held up his hand and they stopped. He raised a thin periscope and surveyed the dock. It was empty. Together they surfaced.

With caution they floated quietly on the surface scanning with their infrared systems for heat signatures. Finding none, they climbed onto the soft sand bank beside the wooden dock.

They quickly unloaded their equipment and returned the sleds to the water, hiding them from view on the sandy bottom. When Sam finally looked around, he saw they were in a crude cavern that had been cut at water level under the desert above them. At the rear of the cavern he could see a corridor cut into the hard packed sand. It was a simple but effective ruse. A barge would come up river, and then it would be floated into the cavern where its illegal cargo could be unloaded away from curious eyes.

The group moved quickly out of the docking area and into the corridor that was the only other way out of the cavern. Night Vision System (N.V.S.) Goggles now replaced their diving masks. The floor was hard packed dirt and the walls were reinforced with stone and brick. No obstacles were available to hide behind.

Sam led the group. He scanned constantly from top to bottom, left to right for a trip wire, or booby trap that would signal the end to their mission, and most likely their lives. A hot infrared image darted in front of his view. He spun, quickly took aim but stopped. It was too small for a human. It was a rodent, most likely a river rat. Only his instincts had saved him from shooting, and most likely revealing their presence.

"Good spot, Sam. Good eyes," Roger whispered.

The air was stale and musty, with a wet fungus odor to it. They rounded a small bend and came across a set of narrow stairs that ascended to the Minaret above. Sam scanned up it but saw no heat signatures. They continued forward down the corridor leaving the stairs behind them. Thirty feet down the same corridor they found their objective, a closed, locked steel door. Without discussion, Sam removed a fine piece of wire from a side pouch and placed it in the locking mechanism. He motioned the others to protect their vision. They turned off their N.V. S. goggles and turned their backs to the door. Sam did the same, but before turning he touched the wire to the inside of what looked like a lipstick container. It contained a chemical catalyst. In a chain reaction, the wire ignited with a burst of intense heat and light that melted through the steel lock on the door in five seconds. The flash faded instantly and the door swung open. Sam burst in, swung to his right, and dropped to one knee in a firing position. Roger mirrored him on the left side. Gino covered the retreat, scanning backwards from the opposite side of the door. A small bare light illuminated the room. It was bright enough to illuminate the otherwise dark room, but not enough to overwhelm their sensitive goggles.

"Right's clear," Sam called out.

"Left's clear," Roger called out.

"Rear's clear. I'm entering the room." Gino slipped into the vault.

The room was packed with canisters stacked in haphazard rows. There seemed to be approximately four hundred, and at this point they had to assume it was the nerve gas. They quietly went to work. First they swept the room for alarms or booby traps. Finding none, each of them set about their designated assignments.

Sam searched the room for an alternate escape route in case the need arose. He found an air vent on the wall three feet above the ground that was large enough for a man to crawl through. Popping off the grill he sat it on the floor.

Roger placed himself in a defensive position near the door to repel any attackers from the corridor. Gino unloaded his backpack and proceeded to place the explosives around the canisters.

Sam searched the room for any evidence to implicate the co-conspirators in the development of the gas. Anything would do, markings on the canisters or serial numbers on equipment.

Suddenly there was the muffled sound of footsteps on dirt. Roger heard them first. Before he could react the steel door was kicked open and three soldiers dressed in Elite Iraqi Republican Guard uniform burst in. The Iraqis died instantly in a hail of gunfire from Roger.

Roger tried to close the door but a dead body blocked the way. Instantly more lead flew from both sides of the door as he tried to repel the attack.

"Kill the light!" Sam yelled as he dove into the air vent, taking his weapon and backpack filled with explosives with him. From the tight shaft he shot an attacker who dove through the partially open door. The Iraqi's skull exploded with a loud pop.

Gino continued to place the explosives quickly and carefully, under the greenish hue of his N.V.S. Intermittently the light from the muzzle flashes would add extra illumination.

Unmoved by the firefight he concentrated on his task, relying on his teammates to protect him.

The room filled with the tang of spent gunpowder. The noise of the rifle shots echoed in their ears. The Iraqis, protected by the steel door, fired their weapons blindly around it. Random bullets flew in all directions, barely missing the lethal gas canisters on more than one occasion. Sam fired from the air vent at the hands and arms that would reach around the door and fire off into the room.

Gino hooked up the last charge and called out, "I'm finished!" He retrieved his weapon and helped with their defense.

Roger pulled the pin on a stun grenade and tossed it through the partially opened door. It exploded with a blinding flash and a thunderous bang. The concussion and echo subsided and the room fell quiet. An Iraqi tumbled through the door and onto the dirt floor unconscious. His finger was pulled tightly against the trigger of his gun. A final burst of lead flooded the room, slamming into and puncturing several canisters.

"Gas! Gas!" Gino screamed. Unable to react fast enough, he fell instantly to the ground in a spasm of death.

Sam grabbed his auto-injector from his vest pocket. With no time to spare he jabbed it into his thigh and pressed the release button. He felt the sharp prick of the needle pierce his skin and the hot burn of the antidote as it flooded into his thigh muscle. He scanned out of the vent and saw Gino slumped over a canister and Roger laying on his side with his auto-injector laying next to him. Sam became increasingly lightheaded and nauseous. His hands began to twitch uncontrollably. Fighting to stay conscious, he reached out of the vent. He had to close the vent. He clawed at the grill cover, barely lifting it between spasms, and pulled it back into place. Then he fell backwards as darkness descended upon him.

21 Chapter Twenty-two

"My God! What kinds of lunatics were running our country?" Jonathan lay in bed with a plate of apple crisp next to him that was three quarters eaten. He licked his fingers then wiped them on a napkin before he ran them over one particular memo from the last administration. As he read he ate and talked to his cat, which was paying no attention to him, as usual.

"They used Von Wilbert to help Iraq develop nerve gas to use in their war with Iran. What were they, blind?"

The more he read the more he understood the enormity of their deception. "They're trapped," he said, "It's a catch twenty-two. They're forced into uncovering and exposing themselves. And they'll never do that."

He dialed Megan but got only her answering machine. "Shit, she's at the agency."

There was no answer at Langley either. "I'm sorry, her line doesn't answer. Would you like to leave a message?" the operator asked.

"No. Shit!" He slammed the phone down. "Of course she's there. I'll have to speak to her in the morning. I'll be damned if I'm going to the agency now." He rolled over and eventually fell asleep.

22   Chapter Twenty-three

Sounds buzzed and swirled with increasing intensity inside Sam's head as consciousness slowly and painfully returned. Suddenly his eyelids jumped opened. His eyes twitched from side to side, distorting his vision. Confused and disoriented Sam involuntarily vomited searing bile. His limbs twitched with spasms and every heartbeat pounded inside his head. The whiff of bile that a moment before had jetted through his nostrils made him gag. Holding his head in his hands he waited for the tremors to subside. His breathing came in slow deep gasps as he slowly tried to collect his senses.

Slow down, slow down. You're alive...barely, but alive.

With the back of his sleeve he wiped the vomit off his face and cleared the fog from his mind. After ten minutes he found his N.V.S. Goggles and activated them. The cavern was silent. Roger and Gino were gone, as were the explosive charges they had set. He would mourn them later, for the moment he had a mission to complete.

Slowly and cautiously, he applied pressure to the grill and popped it off. It broke free and fell towards the dirt. Sam lunged and grabbed it before it crashed to the floor. Again, his head pounded and his body trembled with spasms.

Sam eased himself out of the shaft back into the room. There he momentarily crouched on the dirt floor and aimed his assault rifle at the door. He desperately hoped no one would enter. Finally, he pulled charges from his backpack and went about setting them in the same places Gino had. His pace was slow and arduous. He found threading the wire ends into the detonator extremely difficult. His fine motor hand dexterity had not yet returned.

A shudder started deep in his gut and became so violent he fell to his knees and retched with dry heaves. He clenched his hands over his mouth in an effort to stifle any sound. After the spasm subsided he moistened his mouth with his canteen, afraid to take a drink, afraid of vomiting again. With all charges set, he made his way to the door, but stopped. He heard voices. Sam backed up quickly. His only choice was to re-enter the air vent. Bending down he picked up the grill and quickly climbed back into the air. With a tug he snapped the grill back into place and sat still for a moment to think.

"Shit! Trapped!" he muttered.

Sam crawled through the air vent until it abruptly stopped fifteen feet in. There the vent turned 90 degrees and went straight up. He looked up and saw an opening with light pouring in. The shaft was over one hundred and fifty feet straight up and Sam was uncertain if he had the strength to make the climb. With the reality of the situation staring him right in the face he knew he had no other choice.

With his back pressed against one wall of the vent and his legs against the opposite, he shimmied inch by inch up the shaft. At the top, he looked down. His head clouded up and he started to fall. He instinctively jammed his feet hard into the wall and pressed with all his strength. His fall stopped ten feet down. Moments later he restarted his upward shimmy. Finally, breathless and exhausted, he reached the top. He was relieved to find that at the top of the shaft there was no grill barring his way. He poked his head out of the opening and looked around. It was a small room that appeared to be a small prayer area at the top of the Minaret. After determining it was empty, he rolled out of the vent and onto the floor.

Sam lay still for a moment while his head spun. Finally, he crawled on his stomach to the far wall and gazed out over the top of the hot clay bricks of the Minaret onto the desert below. The sun was high in the sky. He wondered what time it was. He looked at his watch for the first time and saw it was almost noon. It had been almost eight hours since the ambush in the cavern below.

Off in the distance under the blazing sun he saw the town of Samarra. Its low single storied buildings were clustered together, surrounded by a sea of sand. Peering over the edge he saw that the only route down to the desert floor one hundred and fifty feet below was a spiral path three feet wide that wound along the outside of the circular Minaret. Unfortunately he also saw that two worshipers were making their way up it. They and others below were gathering for noon prayer.

A guttural shout behind him caused Sam to spin around. An old man who had just reached the top and stepped into the small worship room was shouting at him in Arabic. Sam jumped up and mercilessly swung his foot, kicking him in the groin. Wide eyed with pain, the old man let out a moan, cupped his genitals with his hands and fell gasping to the hot clay floor.

"Sorry, but you'll survive," Sam said. He quickly gagged the old man, then removed his robe and wrapped it around himself. Though still unsteady on his feet Sam made his way down the three-foot wide path. The ground was one hundred and fifty feet below. One mistake and he would plunge to his death. Three spirals from the bottom he reached the two elderly men he had seen earlier. He kept his face covered by the robe and refused to make eye contact.

The first elder addressed a question to him. Sam ignored him and tried to push by. Angered and not willing to be disrespected the old man grabbed Sam by the shoulders. As quickly as he could, Sam grabbed the old man under each armpit and lifted him off his feet. He spun the old man around him and placed him on the upside of the path. He then repeated this with the second elder. It was either that or throw them off the narrow path to their death. Both elders responded by shrieking at him in Arabic.

Sam broke into a run down the last spirals. As he ran, he reached for the detonator and activated it. In an instant a shock wave reverberated through the Minaret and the surrounding desert. One of the elders he had just passed stumbled and fell to his death.

The blast rocked the Minaret. In moments Sam saw soldiers appear from a room at its base. He wasn't surprised to see them jump into vehicles and drive away. They were afraid of the gas. He knew there was no danger. The gas was heavier than air, and would sit harmlessly in the cave until it decomposed in about an hour.

Sam used the confusion to his benefit and struck out across the desert toward the town of Samarra. He judged it to be about three miles away. Less than a third of the way there he realized he was weaker than he thought. The blazing sun quickly exhausted what strength he had left.

A mile from the Minaret his legs started to wobble and his calf muscles went into spasms as he fell to his knees. Parched he took a long drink of water, and then looked at his watch. He needed to get to the dune buggy. There he could make contact and arrange a new pickup. Looking over his shoulder he knew reaching the hydro-sled was out of the question. Most of all he needed to rest and find shelter. He turned away from the Minaret and struck out across the sand again. He managed to take only two more steps, when suddenly his vision blurred and his world spun out of control. He landed face down on the hot sand. The lingering effects of the nerve gas had won.

23   Chapter Twenty-four

"Megan, you better have a look at this!" Tim waved for her to come over to his communications station.

"What is it?"

"Bad is what it is. We have two separate reports, one by radio, and the other by telephone. Both report an American assault team being successfully ambushed and destroyed at Samarra. All Americans were reported killed."

"Oh no! Sam!" Megan covered her mouth and fell into Tim's desk chair.

"Sam was on that mission?" Tim asked.

Megan could only look at him, unable to respond. Tears welled up in her eyes.

Tim moved closer to her and spoke softly, "It could be a mistake. I'm sure he's alright."

A voice called from a cubicle in the corner of the room, "We have something going on over there!"

Tim walked quickly to Raani's cubicle. Megan stayed in the chair for a moment trying to compose herself.

"What have you got?" Tim asked. Megan entered, but stood off to the side, just wanting to listen.

"We have a flurry of radio intercept between Samarra and Baghdad. At the moment all this is rough. There was an explosion at the Minaret and all the gas was destroyed."

"My intercepts didn't mention any of that." Tim turned to Megan with a hopeful look. "I told you it was a mistake."

"What's a mistake?" Ranni asked.

"I got two intercepts that the entire had been ambushed and killed."

"That still might be true," Raani replied. Megan's face contorted as Raani continued, "I got seven intercepts so far. Compressing them, it appears the team was killed. It wasn't until about five to six hours after the battle that the gas was blown up, probably by delayed charges. One intercept states the soldiers at the Minaret had removed all the charges along with the bodies. Or so they thought. Baghdad is screaming back about their incompetence and demanding those responsible for missing the hidden explosives be executed. And a third party is screaming at all of them to stop broadcasting over the radio because the Americans might be listening. If they only knew," he snorted, and then looked at Megan. She turned away and stared blankly at the floor.

"What's up?" Raani asked Tim.

Tim whispered, "Her boyfriend was on that team."

Raani bit his lip and sighed, "Sorry, Megan, I didn't know."

She took a tissue off his desk and wiped her eyes. She desperately tried to hold onto her professionalism. She needed to at this moment. Otherwise she would be a basket case. She took a couple of long deep sighs, but it didn't help.

"I'm sorry, I just can't do this." She turned and ran out of the room, and down the hall.

Half an hour later, Megan entered Niddiem's office. She had cried uncontrollably in the ladies room for ten minutes. Then she'd forced herself to regain control. She had a job to do. Now she sat in the soft chair opposite Niddiem's desk. "Sam's dead. We lost the team. They're all dead."

"What!" He leaned forward, almost climbing over the desk towards her his suspenders sliding off both shoulders. "What do you mean they're dead?"

A long sigh rolled out of her before she continued in a flat tone, "We intercepted ground and radio transmissions...the team was caught and killed in a gun battle at the mosque."

"What about the gas?"

"It was destroyed, by delayed charges."

"So the gas is gone? Destroyed?" His eyes bore down on her making her feel uncomfortable.

"Yes." She paused for a moment, thinking what Sam's final moments must have been like. Then she jumped up and slammed her fist on the desk. "And so those Iraqi bastards are going to get away with it. The proof is gone, and Sam is dead. I want revenge! I want those Iraqi bastards to rot!" She slammed the desk again. "But it'll never happen! Because your precious gas was destroyed! I guess that makes Sam's death acceptable. Well fuck you! And everything all of you stand for!" She turned and charged out of the room.

Niddiem was silent. He couldn't agree with her more. One at a time he pulled his suspenders back into position.

Once outside Niddiem's office, Megan walked blindly. Soon, she found herself at Jonathan's office. She entered, knowing she'd find some sympathy and support there.

"Oh good, you're here. We need to talk." He motioned her in. But she just stood frozen in the doorway.

"Sam's dead. The team was ambushed," Megan blurted out. "I just can't believe he's dead." She fell into a seat.

"What do you mean?"

"The team...they were ambushed and killed. I just came from Al's office. I guess I took it out on him."

"He may have deserved it."

"I'm tired and need someone to talk to. You know a sympathetic ear?" She looked at her shaking hands.

"Then you didn't get my message?"

"No."

"Shut the door." He pointed in the general direction of it.

For the next half hour she sat with her mouth open as Jonathan related the details of what he had read, and learned, the night before.

"Those bastards!" she responded when he finished. "We helped Iraq develop the gas that killed the people in Jerusalem? And we used Claus Von Wilbert! Unbelievable! He killed Jews in World War II, and now we help him kill Jews in Israel."

"Nasty, isn't it? But it gets worse!"

"What?"

"First, did they destroy the gas?"

"Yes. God…" she looked at the ceiling. "That's all anyone wants to know, was the gas destroyed. What about Sam? Doesn't anyone care about him?"

"Think about it. We send in a team to destroy the gas and bring back evidence as to who helped produce it in the first place. But, it was us who helped produce it! Do you think they'd be allowed to bring back evidence implicating the U.S.?"

Megan's eyes widened. "My God! You mean we helped the Iraqis ambush and kill Sam and his team?"

"That's exactly what I mean. Our government murdered their own people to keep the truth a secret."

"Who could make such a decision? What bastards? It's so cold blooded."

"Open your eyes, sweetie. You've been hidden back in that closet of yours too long. You're surrounded by cold-blooded murders."

"We need to prove it. I want them to pay." She stood and leaned over his desk. "How can we prove it? How?"

"Use your team. You're already set up for deep electronic surveillance. Keep looking, and eventually they're bound to make a mistake."

"And what about Niddiem? What do I tell him?"

"Not the truth, that's for sure. From what I've read, he's in the middle of this."

"If he was responsible, I'll kill him myself." There was fire in her eyes.

Megan walked down the hall. Her mind avoided thinking about Sam. She couldn't let herself get lost in misery. This was too big. She was spying on her own agency and government. She would be digging for information that might implicate people. Implicate them in murder. This was a dangerous game she was entering. A game she vowed to win...at all costs.

24 Chapter Twenty-five

The buzzing waxed and waned, then finally reached a crescendo before abruptly stopping. Sam opened his eyes. He was lying on a straw mattress on the floor of a small room. An opening near the ceiling allowed for a thin stream of air to circulate, aided by the turning wooden fan blades and the open windows.

Sam sat up slowly. His head spun. His parched throat, coated with sand, cried for relief. To his right on the floor was a pitcher of water. Slowly, he drank it all. Finally his eyes focused and he was able to look around. Over in a corner all his equipment was stacked, including his rifle. The quiet that surrounded him was not what he would expect from a bunch of Middle Eastern zealots.

Sam stood and tried the door. It opened swiftly in his hand. On the other side stood a man about to enter, his hand on the other doorknob. Sam's first thought was to lunge for his rifle, but he knew he didn't stand a chance if his visitor was armed. So instead, he simply stared at the stranger, who did nothing but stare back. Then Sam noticed he was carrying a tray.

He walked in past Sam. He appeared to be in his early thirties and he wore a clean white linen shirt that flowed to his ankles in a dress fashion. On his feet were open sandals. He showed no open concern having his back turned to Sam as he bent down and placed the tray on the floor beside the straw mattress. Finally the man spoke, "I see you're awake. Good. How are you feeling?"

Sam watched him for a moment, confused by the man's easy attitude. Then he decided to respond, "Weak and tired, but grateful to be alive. Thank you for your help."

"We'll talk about who thanks who later. I made you some broth and tea. Please take them both. You're probably very dehydrated from your desert journey."

Sam sat back on the mattress, reached for the broth, and began sipping it. Energy slowly returned to him. "Thank you again."

The two were silent for a few minutes as Sam finished the broth. Finally he looked up over his tea, his eyes questioning. The man smiled. "You're wondering who I am, and why I helped you."

"Yes, I am."

"My name is Ismail. I am Kurdish. You are American. We therefore have a common enemy...Hussein."

"Your English is excellent. You speak with a slight British accent. You couldn't have learned that in Iraq."

"That's correct. I was raised and schooled in England."

"So you returned to fight for the cause."

"It was more like the cause reached out and grabbed me by the throat. I'm a lawyer by profession. Years ago when I was a young boy my parents realized there was no future for Kurds in Iraq. What Kurd had any hope of advancing or simply bettering his life under Saddam Hussein? So with the help of family friends in England I traveled there to be raised and schooled." Ismail walked closer then sat Indian style on the floor in front of Sam. "After I earned my degree I stayed in England. With the large influx of Arabs and Palestinians there was always a need for another Arab lawyer. I hoped to save enough money to move my family there.

"But one day I happened to be watching the international CNN news station. It reported that everyone in my hometown of Halabjah was dead. They'd been killed by a deadly poison gas. I was born in that town. My parents lived and died there. So," he shrugged, "here I am. Fighting for those who can't, against a madman."

David Mucci

Sam absorbed what Ismail had said and knew he could trust him. But he also knew he couldn't reveal any information whatsoever about himself.

Standing slowly, Sam walked over to the window and looked out at the desert. "I need to find a way to get to a point in the river. I have equipment there."

"You'll need my help. I've no need to be here anymore. You accomplished the task I'd been planning."

"What was that?" Sam asked as he turned to look at Ismail.

"The gas, you destroyed it. It took me a while to locate it, and I had no idea what I was going to do next. But you accomplished it for me. I am beholden to you," Ismail bowed his head, "and will gladly help you. I just hope someone helps your friend."

"What do you mean 'my friend'?" Sam walked back to the bed and stood directly in front of Ismail.

"While I was at the Minaret trying to plan an attack, soldiers dragged a man out from the base of it. He was dead. They tossed him into a truck. Then a second was half dragged and half walked to the truck. He was very much alive. They were both camouflaged like you. About thirty minutes later you came running down the outside. The ground and the Minaret shook moments later. I followed you into the desert. Lucky for you I did. Your friend won't fare as well, I'm sorry to say. He already looked badly beaten and they punched and kicked him every moment they could."

Sam returned to the window and leaned against the open sill. Off in the distance he saw the Minaret. Though feeling disconnected and very weak, he was certain of one thing. If even one team member was alive he would rescue him, or die trying. "I need to find out where they've taken my friend." He turned and faced Ismail.

"Are you going to attempt to rescue him?"

"Yes."

"The truck that took them away was from the Ramad Army base. At least that's what the insignia on the side read. We can only assume they went there."

"Where's the base located?" Sam asked.

"It is on the eastern border of Baghdad. But if you are planning a rescue, you'll need the help of me and my friends."

"It will be too dangerous. I can't take the responsibility." Sam turned back to the window to think.

"You can't take the responsibility! I don't remember anyone making you responsible. Listen, Mister American Special Forces Hero, Kurdish people have been fighting Saddam and his kind, and dying doing so, long before you knew what responsibility was. We don't need you to protect us."

Sam turned and faced him. "I just don't want any of you to die because of me or my men. I can't accept your help. I'm trained to work alone or with a small highly trained team. It would be safer for you and me if I did it alone."

"So, you know Baghdad? It's a very large city. You can't just walk down the street in your camouflage uniform. Where will you sleep? Where will you eat?" Ismail stood tall and proud in front of Sam. "And your friend, where is he? In what building? And say you find him, how will you escape? Do you think there are helicopters over the horizon to take you to safety? No my friend, you need the help of my friends and me. Accept it, if not for you, then for your friend."

Sam looked at him and knew he was right. Reluctantly he said, "I accept on one condition."

"Which is?"

"I have final say over any plan"

"Good. We will leave in a few hours. We will stay with my friend Hamid and his sister Atiqa in Baghdad. Rest for now, I'll be back in two to three hours. I have to make arrangements for others to join us there. We'll need twenty-five to thirty men with weapons.

Moments later Sam found himself alone. He returned to the bed and there sat sipping tea, contemplating what was behind him and what lay before him. Then, knowing he'd need to be well rested, he laid down and fell into a deep sleep.

26   Chapter Twenty-six

"I need your help," Megan addressed her team. Her voice was full of resolve. "I want all of you to continue monitoring Iraq as intensely as before the mission. I want to know how and who was responsible for the ambush. Anything you find you report to me, and only me. Someone will make a mistake and say something over an open line. When that happens I want to hear it. We go around the clock for now. Pick your teams and shifts." Without any further explanations she dismissed them

The day dragged on for Megan. She finally had time to think about Abraham, to wonder where he was and how he was doing. She had forgotten about him in her pain and anger. How quickly all their lives had changed.

She wondered, was this the anguish Abraham had learned to live with, to accept in his own life? He'd been through so much. Now he was in Germany, hopefully finding Von Wilbert and putting his life in order. What would he do when he was face to face with that butcher, who had destroyed so many lives, including Sam? She hoped that Abraham would find him and kill him.

27   Chapter Twenty-seven

Sam and Ismail drove south towards Baghdad along the one-lane paved road. They both wore traditional white desert pull over robes made of cotton. Both of them appeared harmless, and unarmed. However, in between the liner of the car doors Sam's weapons were stored along with the ones Ismail had brought.

As Ismail drove, he occasionally glanced over at Sam. "You could easily pass for an Iraqi with the color of your skin. Do you have some Arab ancestor?"

"No. I'm one hundred percent American Indian."

"You are American Indian That's interesting. Then you do understand my people's plight. Your people have been as persecuted as mine. Your land was taken, your people slaughtered."

"Yes, but we're getting back at them now." Sam smiled broadly.

"How?"

"Over the past centuries they took our land and put us on reservations. But we're building casinos on reservations and now they're making Indians very rich people. White men love to gamble." They both laughed.

For the next hour Sam listened to Ismail recount the recent plight of his small group of revolutionaries and how the select group he'd chosen were all eager to help. Soon they reached the outskirts of Baghdad. The streets were wide, paved, and spotless.

"I'm surprised. I thought I'd see more destruction from the bombing."

"They've been rebuilding twenty four hours a day, seven days a week. Except for a few stray bombs, your Air Force was very precise in what they hit. The destruction wasn't as widespread as Baghdad wanted you to believe. We were more devastated by the lack of goods and amenities then by the bombings themselves."

Ismail pulled over. "We have arrived."

They were on a side street, just off one of the ostentatious main avenues. The house was in a row of small two-story brick buildings. It was similar to those found in any inner city.

Sam and Ismail climbed a dark flight of stairs and entered a small apartment. Soon Sam was sitting on a pillow on the floor, again being served tea, but this time it was by Hamid's sister, Atiqa.

"Ismail!" A young man burst through the door and embraced him. "You return so soon. And you bring a guest."

"This is Sam. He is an American. Sam, this is Hamid, an important man in our group."

"An American! What is an American doing in Iraq?"

Sam hesitated but Ismail held nothing back. "He and his two friends were sent here to destroy the chemical weapons hidden at Samarra."

"You found them?"

"Yes, but as I was scouting a way to destroy them Sam and his group blew them up. One of his team was killed. The other was taken prisoner. I think they took him to Ramad. I've offered our help rescuing his friend."

"What, with just the three of us? You're crazy." Hamid shook his head.

"Of course not, that would be suicide. Before I left Samarra I contacted the group there. There are twenty-seven others making their way to Baghdad at the moment. I know what safe houses they'll be in. After we confirm the American is at Ramad we'll coordinate an attack to rescue him."

For the moment Sam had nothing to add. "I am grateful for your help." He wondered what he could do to repay them. "It will be dangerous. Are you sure you want to do this? Some of you could get killed."

"Hamid, myself and all who will help us are Kurdish." Ismail replied. "That gas you destroyed would have been used against us in the future. You and your team saved many Kurdish lives. All Kurds have a moral obligation to help you in any way they can. I hope that ends any discussion on that matter."

"My father and mother died because of Hussein's craziness," Atiqa stated as she unexpectedly entered from the small kitchen. "My brother was shot down like an animal by his soldiers. Only by luck was Hamid able to escape. I can assure you, everyone who will be helping you has a similar story. My brother and I will help you or die trying."

"Thank you." Sam graciously bowed his head. "And yes the discussion is closed. I accept your help."

"Good. Then it is decided." Ismail smiled. "We'll eat, then rest. By morning I hope to have confirmation your friend is indeed on the base. If he is, we will scout it out tomorrow and develop our plan. Come, my friend, join me and Hamid for tea and Atiqa will fix a meal."

28   Chapter Twenty-eight

Maurice stood a few feet from Megan. He stared blankly at the pages in front of him.

"Tell me, what is it? What have you found?" she asked.

Maurice hesitated for a moment then handed her the top sheet of paper he'd been reading. "One of the Special Forces Team is alive. They've captured him."

"What? Let me see that. Please let it be Sam." Megan pleaded to no one in particular as she grabbed the page from Maurice. "Do we have any other confirmation of this?"

"Yes. Two other intercepts." He handed them to her also. "All these intercepts came from intra-military phone lines routed through the C192. We picked them up less than one hour apart."

She read them then stared off into space. Her insides were again twisted in knots, not knowing if it was Sam or one of the others.

"Okay Megan, what's going on here?" Maurice said.

"What? I'm sorry. I was thinking about something," she said. "Anyway nothing's going on. Why do you ask?"

"Sorry, I don't buy it. You know about this and I want some answers." He waved another sheet of paper in his hand. She reached for it but he pulled it back.

"Sorry. Before I let you read it, I want your promise of full disclosure."

An angry look was her reply and she grabbed it from his hand and read it. "Oh my God! Jonathan was right!" She looked up. "Who else knows about this?"

"No one, yet. Okay, now we talk."

She thought for a moment and realized the futility of stonewalling him. He could also help her more if he knew what he was looking for. "Come with me." She led him into a side office and shut the door.

"Sit down and listen. Let's get one thing clear. If you mention anything I'm about to tell you I promise you have no idea how much trouble I'll cause you. Understood?"

"Yes."

Forty-five minutes later the office door opened and they walked out. Maurice returned to his workstation quietly and Megan left to find Jonathan.

For the next five minutes Megan waited impatiently in Jonathan's office. "Where have you been?" Megan said when Jonathan strolled into his office, muffin in one hand his cane in the other.

"I was at the cafeteria. I was hungry. Is that okay?"

"No it's not! I've been waiting for you, dammit!"

"Well excuse me. I've got to eat. I'll call you and ask permission next time. What's gotten into you anyway?" He sat down at his desk and took a bite of his muffin.

"One of the team is alive. The Iraqis have him prisoner at a base on the outskirts of Baghdad."

"Is it confirmed?"

"Yes, by three separate intercepts." She waved them in front of his face forgetting for a moment he was blind.

"Kind of bold of them to think their lines of communication are safe."

"That's not all!" She held up the last intercept. "We have a fourth message. This one is a conversation between a General Malek and a high-ranking Iraqi government official. The General was infuriated. He was calling for someone to be held responsible, someone from his own side. He wanted someone to pay with his life for the incompetent ambush at the Minaret.

He said they had plenty of warning and that it shouldn't have happened."

"Plenty of warning?" He took all four intercepts and ran them through his scanner.

"Yes, that bastard John Gordon met with General Malek and warned them of the attack."

"What?" He pulled the Braille copies off and started to run his fingers over them.

Megan continued, not giving him time to finish reading them. "You heard me. Gordon helped them ambush our team. Dammit, whether Sam's dead or alive, I want that bastard's ass!"

"Who else knows?"

"Just Maurice. He pulled the intercepts. I had to tell him everything. I'm not worried about him. He won't tell anyone."

For a moment Jonathan rocked in his chair. "Now we need to decide what we are going to do with this information. Telling Niddiem is out of the question."

"Right...he's got to be involved. When I briefed the President and the National Security Council he stayed behind after the meeting and talked with Gordon behind closed doors. When they emerged, neither of them looked too pleased."

"I think we have two problems," Jonathan said. "The first is the out and out treason committed by Gordon, and the second is the American being held prisoner in Iraq."

"I'm telling you one thing. We will get that American out of Iraq." Megan jumped up and started pacing in the small office.

"I agree. As for Gordon, I don't think we can trust anyone at this point. We'll deal with him later. We also should assume that everyone from Niddiem right up to the President is involved."

"The only one we can trust is Colonel Burnhall," Megan said. "We tell him everything."

"I agree. Take these and make copies of everything. I'm sure he'll want proof."

"I'll call Scott and tell him I need to see the Colonel A.S.A.P.," she said. "I have this gut feeling Sam's alive, and I'm going to get him home." Her despair over Sam's death was gone. It was replaced by determination and hope.

29   Chapter Twenty-nine

Megan sat on a couch in General Burnhall's office, waiting for him to appear. The office was neat and formal, but somehow friendly. Maybe it was the group pictures of Burnhall's men that hung on one wall, or the individual photos on the other wall of all those who had perished in the line of duty. Megan noticed three new hooks awaiting their pictures.

Colonel Burnhall entered and sat next to her. "I'm sorry we have to meet under such sad circumstances," he said. "The death of men under my command is never easy to accept." He glanced at her. "I'm sorry. That's selfish of me. I know the pain you must be feeling with Sam's death. I wonder, though, if all commanders blame themselves for some little oversight that might have made for a different outcome."

"Colonel, you need to hear me for a moment. I think Sam is alive. I have concrete evidence that one of your men is alive and being held by the Iraqis at Ramad Military base east of Baghdad."

"I don't understand. Every bit of intelligence I've seen confirms their deaths. I have an official report from the C.I.A. corroborating this."

"I'm sorry, but that report didn't come from my office, and I seriously doubt its validity."

"Are you saying I'm being lied to?" His expression became hard.

"Yes. Colonel, your men were ambushed. The Iraqis had advanced warning of the mission. I also have information here that proves John Gordon met with an Iraqi General while on his trip to the Middle East." She glanced at the paper on her lap. "Malek was his name. It appears Gordon informed him of the impending attack." She handed him a copy of the communication intercept Maurice had given her.

Burnhall read it and looked up. "This doesn't make sense. Why would he do this? What was the purpose?

"Let me give you the quick version. I won't tell you how we unearthed all this information. But believe me, it's the truth." She gave one last glance at the empty hooks on the wall, and then began. "At the end of World War II, the United States captured a Nazi chemist named Claus Von Wilbert. During the war he had worked on a highly specialized nerve gas for Hitler. He was a criminal, but after the war we brought him to the U.S. We changed his name and used him to develop our own nerve gas arsenal. During the Iran-Iraq War, our government decided that we wanted Iraq to kick Iran's butt. So we helped them develop a chemical weapons program. Specifically we helped them by sending them Von Wilbert. But the war ended before Iraq could use the gas, so they kept it and last week used it against Israel. When we sent our team in to destroy the gas, any evidence brought back would expose the U.S. That couldn't be allowed to happen so the Iraqis were tipped off. Can you imagine if we were implicated in helping a Nazi, who gassed Jews in World War II, gas them again half a century later? That's it in a nut shell."

"Who was involved with the original decision to help the Iraqi's?"

"The only ones left in office today are our illustrious Director of the C.I.A., Al Niddiem and our Chairman of the Joint Chiefs of Staff, Ben Wildemen."

"Ben Wildemen! I can't believe he'd sacrifice his own men. It goes against everything he's ever fought for." The Colonel stood up abruptly.

"At this point there's no evidence Wildemen was involved in helping the Iraqis ambush your men. Though I have no evidence saying he didn't. But I do have hard evidence of his initial involvement. So I have to assume that even if he wasn't actively involved, he probably knew about it and was helpless to stop it."

Megan stayed seated while the Colonel paced back and forth. She knew how he felt...her reaction had been the same.

"John Gordon wasn't involved in the beginning was he?" Burnhall said.

"No."

"So we have to assume Wildemen and Niddiem, or just one of them, briefed him on the problem. Then Gordon, with or without their help, planned the ambush." He spun to face Megan. "That son of a bitch traitor. He used my men, me, and God knows who else. He wantonly sent my men in there knowing they'd be killed! Slaughtered! He will be held accountable! What about the President?"

"I don't know."

"I can't believe he'd be involved." His tone calmed a bit as his mind started to calculate and plan. "But, to safely accomplish what I want to do, we have to assume he's actively involved. The first order of business is getting my man back. Will you help me?"

"Yes. That's why I'm here." She was relieved at Burhall's reaction.

The Colonel picked up his phone and called Scott to join them. When Scott arrived, he and Megan simply acknowledged each other.

"Scott, Megan will give you a complete briefing later. And Megan, I need to see hard evidence on everything you've told me before anything we decide is implemented."

"It's already on its way over to you, sir."

"Good. Scott, one of our team is apparently alive and being held at the Ramad military base on the eastern border of Baghdad. I'll fill in the blanks later. For now you just have to accept the fact that our government does not want him rescued. We will be flying solo on this one." He wrote as he talked. "I want to put together a team to rescue him. Scott, it is imperative that you understand that what we discuss in this room stays between the three of us."

Scott nodded affirmatively.

"We'll send in a quick response rescue team. Two FAVs, three men on one vehicle and two on the other. One Cobra will support them and a CH-53E will transport them. Orders will originate from this office only, approved by me. We'll use the NASSAU as our launch ship."

"Sir," Scott replied, "the commander of the M.E.U. on the NASSAU will want confirmation from higher up before he releases his copters for an assault. We need to have an answer before that problem arises."

"I know. Confirmation will have to be routed through this office. Your job will be to stonewall them, and leave the rest to me. I'll be going on this mission. I'll have to throw a lot of weight around and bully a lot of people. But the bottom line is, we will rescue my soldier."

"It will most likely cost you your job and most likely a court-martial," Scott added.

"I promised my men I would always stand behind them. I won't abandon one of them to save my career." He glanced at the pictures on the wall. "What good is my career if I ignore my moral obligations? How could they ever trust me again? Here's the roster list. I want them immediately activated. I also want confirmed air routing for them to Saudi and a confirmed pick up from the NASSAU upon landing there. Megan, I need that evidence within the hour. And I trust you'll fill in Scott on the issues at hand."

"Yes, on both counts, sir." Megan nodded.

"Good, we'll meet back here in three hours."

Megan left to brief Jonathan.

30   Chapter Thirty

BAGHDAD, 6:00 A.M.

"Wake up."

"What?" Startled out of a deep sleep Sam jumped to his feet wearing only boxer shorts and a tee shirt. He lurched forward, ready to attack, ready for action. "What's wrong?"

"Nothing, it's morning," Ismail said. "Calm down."

Sam rubbed his blurry eyes and looked around. "Sorry, I must've been out cold. I was more tired then I thought."

"I've received word. Your friend is indeed at Ramad."

"How is he? And do you know who it is?" Sam unknowingly clenched his hands into fists.

"He's alive. That's all I know. Get dressed. Atiqa has breakfast for us."

The rolls were old and stale but Sam inhaled them. The warm tea helped quench his never-ending thirst. In a short time Hamid joined them. After breakfast they sat, drank more tea, and discussed the mission at hand.

"Today we will have a busy day," Ismail started. "Hamid and Atiqa will go to the market. I've made a list of supplies and food you'll need. It should be sufficient to see you and your friend to the Turkish border. You and I will go meet my friends who will help us. We'll go over the plan together. If all goes well, the rescue will be tomorrow."

"Why so soon?" Atiqa asked.

"Two reasons. First, the longer we wait, the greater the chance they'll kill the American. And I'm concerned that somewhere in our group there is an informer."

Hamid froze with his teacup up to his lips, his finger started to throb.

"We've been ambushed during the last couple of missions," Ismail continued. "All of them were planned very secretly. But every time the Iraqi military were waiting for us. No, we go tomorrow."

"I'll go tonight if needed," Sam added.

"No, that's too soon. We have too much to arrange and plan."

A half hour later they all left Hamid's house. Ismail and Sam walked in one direction while Hamid and Atiqa went the opposite way.

The market was overcrowded and hot, despite the earliness of the day. By noon all the stalls would be closed. The heat would be too stifling to sell any goods.

"Why don't we spilt up," Hamid suggested to Atiqa. "It'll take us less time that way."

"Okay. I'll give you half of the list and we'll meet back home when we're done." She said, "I'll take the more difficult items. I know the ins and outs of the market." As an Iraqi woman, Atiqa's main responsibility was to go to market and be skilled at finding what she needed for home.

Two hours later she had all the items except a flashlight and extra batteries. These were a precious commodity in Baghdad. Having no other choice, she knew she had to turn to the black market. There she would end up paying an exorbitant price.

She wound her way through the narrow paths of the marketplace until she came upon a small, unassuming stall. She greeted the elderly vender who sat crouched in a flat foot squat. "Malieka, good morning."

"Atiqa, it is so nice to see you. I heard about Ameen. My prayers go to you and Hamid." He pressed his palms together.

"Thank you. He died a naked death. Malieka, I'm having trouble finding a few items. I was hoping you could help me."

"Gladly, what is it you need?"

She hesitated for a moment. "I need a strong flashlight and extra batteries."

"Hm." He rubbed his beard. "Those are very scarce items."

"It's really important." Their eyes locked in nonverbal communication.

"Yes, I understand." He wrote down an address and handed it to her. "Go here. Tell him I sent you. He will give you a good price and good merchandise."

"Thank you. Allah watches over you." Atiqa turned and made her way across the market.

It was a thirty-minute walk to the address she had been given. It was also in the opposite direction from her apartment. The other items she purchased grew heavier with each passing minute. But she told herself the pain she felt in her arm and shoulder was nothing compared with the pain the American prisoner would be put through if he wasn't rescued.

On her way back she passed in front of the Ramad Military Base's front gate. She glanced in, and then stopped, frozen in her steps. Beyond the gate, in one of the shadowy doorways, she saw Hamid. He was talking very animatedly with a soldier, an officer. She watched his hands gesture wildly until the soldier slapped him in the face. She gasped as he was dragged inside by his shirtsleeve.

What was he doing there? She wondered. Who was that soldier who slapped him? She knew she'd him before, but where?

"Oh no!" She dropped her bags as her hands covered her mouth. It was General Malek! After her father's death they were invited on the base to receive a medal for him. It was General Malek who presented the medal to her mother. She remembered the bitter image of her father being honored after they all but murdered him.

She stood there catatonic, what was Hamid doing with General Malek? There was only one answer. If true, he was the cause of Ameen's death, along with all the others. She grabbed at her bags and blindly ran home through the streets of Baghdad. As she ran her tears mixed with the sweat from the heat, the horrible realization setting in.

*　　*　　*　　*

Sam and Ismail opened the door to Hamid's apartment as they discussed yet another detail of the plan. They were silenced by Atiqa's screams floating down the hall.

"What were you doing there? Tell me," she bellowed.

"I'm telling you, it wasn't me you saw."

"Don't lie to me!"

Sam and Ismail entered the main room to see Atiqa slap Hamid hard across the face.

"What's going on here?" Ismail demanded.

"I saw him on the Ramad Military Base with General Malek, and he denies it." She never turned her eyes from Hamid's face. "It was you! I know my own brother. Or tell me, do you have a double that wears the same clothes? No, it was you and I want to know what you were doing there!"

Hamid looked around the room and saw the distrust. The strain of the past few weeks shone on his face. It was with total relief that he finally confessed, "Okay, it was me. But I was there protecting you."

"Protecting me from what?" Atiqa said.

"I was protecting you from rape, torture and a terrible death. Do you think I did this for me? No, I did it for you."

"Explain yourself," Ismail demanded.

Hamid backed against the wall and began to sob. His weak legs could no longer support him, and he slid down the wall until he was seated on the floor, with his head in his hands. "When we were ambushed at Al Amara, Ameen and I were captured. He was shot in the leg. He begged me to run but I stayed with him. They brought us to a small room and Malek tortured him. I was made to watch." He sobbed and gasped for breath between words.

"Malek slowly broke all of Ameen's bones. He burnt his skin, shocked him with electricity. I was helpless. They wouldn't even let me look away." His eyes pleaded with them. "His screams were horrible. Finally, Malek slit his throat and I had to watch his blood drip onto the floor. He died in agony. Malek promised me that if I didn't help him he would make me watch him rape, and torture, you next." He looked up at Atiqa with swollen, reddened eyes. "Don't you see I had to protect you? I had to help him. Don't you see?"

"No! I don't see!" Atiqa lashed out, kicking his legs in rage. The sharp hard toes of her shoes instantly left red welts where they struck. He offered no resistance. "Our entire family is dead because of Hussein and men like Malek. And you helped him kill our friends! Why am I special? What do I tell their families? I'm sorry your brother or husband is dead, but my little brother was only protecting me! Is that what I tell them? I'd rather be tortured, raped, and killed, then give in to those butchers. Didn't Ameen teach you anything?"

Hamid was now curled up into the fetal position, sobbing. Finally, Sam stepped forward and took Atiqa by the arm. "Stop this. Sit down."

He helped Hamid off the floor and into a seat. Hamid looked at Atiqa, but she refused to make eye contact with him.

"Listen," Sam continued, "I've seen very strong, highly trained men crack under emotional and physical torture. There is no shame. But I need to know, did you tell them about our attack tomorrow?"

"Yes," Hamid's voice was low and thick.

"You told them it was tomorrow night?"

"Yes."

"Then we attack tonight."

"I don't know if we have enough time," Ismail said. He was silent for a few moments, and then said, "But it just might work. Atiqa, you and Hamid will have to leave. They'll come looking for you both. You'll have to go north to the Kurdish refugee camps."

"No," said Hamid, finally looking up. "I will not run. I caused this. I will stay and fight. And if I die, then I'll be rewarded by being once again with Ameen."

"What about Atiqa?" Ismail asked.

"I'll stay and fight, too." She squared her shoulders, and then finally looked at her brother. "Then we'll run north to the camps. We face this together."

"Okay. Then we have a lot to do." Sam added. "First I want to pass by the base and take a look at it as close as I can."

Sam stood and Ismail, having nodded in agreement, followed him out the door.

31   Chapter Thirty-one

The rotors of the CH-46 copter were still turning when the side door opened. Colonel Burnhall and his men disembarked quickly. They removed their personal gear and placed it onto the flight deck of the U.S.S. NASSAU. Colonel Black approached, his hand extended. "Welcome to the NASSAU. Your men will be shown to their quarters. I hope your flight was without incident."

"Yes it was. Thank you."

"Your orders were very vague. I hope you can enlighten me a little more on them."

"Of course I can Colonel. Shall we move this into your ready room where we can talk?" The warm blast of air that rolled across the flight deck took Burnhall's breath away. It would take him a while to acclimate to the heat of the Persian Gulf.

Moments later they entered the air-conditioned superstructure of the ship. Colonel Burnhall followed Black to the ready room.

"What's going on?" Colonel Black asked.

"One of my men from the assault is alive. The Iraqis are holding him at Ramad Military Base, just east of Baghdad. The bottom line is, we're here to get him out. It'll be a quick in and out with minimal exposure. I'll be going myself."

"That's a little abnormal, isn't it?"

"This entire situation is a little abnormal. It's my responsibility to go. I'd rather not elaborate. Here are my orders." He took a sealed envelope out of his pouch and handed it to Black.

"You know I'll have to get confirmation of these orders before I can release the birds to you."

"I'd expect nothing less. You can contact the Rapid Deployment Force office at the Pentagon. They'll be able to supply you with any verification you need." Burnhall stood and rubbed his neck. "If you don't mind, I need to rest. I'm exhausted."

Colonel Black sat for a moment after Burnhall left and reviewed the orders. There was something that bothered him. It was nothing he could pinpoint. He just had a strange feeling in his gut. As a military man, he had learned many years ago to trust his gut feeling. He stood and walked to the communications room.

"Lieutenant, I want you to contact this office in the Pentagon and get confirmation of these orders. I want it P.D.Q. Is that understood?"

"Yes, sir."

The colonel handed him the top order sheet. "I'll be in my quarters."

Two hours later the communications officer knocked on his door and entered. "Here's the confirmation for the orders you asked for. I'm sorry it took so long. There appeared to be a tie up on the other end."

He handed the facsimile sheet to him and was dismissed. Colonel Black read the sheet and became even more concerned. It was nothing more than a copy of the order sheet he already had. It wasn't confirmation.

Moments later he returned to the communication room. "Soldier, patch me to General Weyling at FMFLANT."

"Yes, sir."

Colonel Black sat while the communication officer raised Fleet Marine Force Atlantic in Norfolk, Virginia. The current Commander, General Weyling, picked up his phone and was patched directly to Colonel Black.

"Bob, how are things on the other side of the world?" The General appeared in a light mood. The connection was perfectly clear.

"Fine, General, just fine. Let me ask you, how well do you know Colonel Burnhall?"

"Very well, he's a fine man. He's in charge of Special Forces Delta Team. Why do you ask?"

"He's here with a team. They just arrived a few hours ago. Apparently one of his players from the Alpha One mission is alive, and is being held by the Iraqis. The Colonel's here with his team to initiate a rescue mission. I'm just trying to get confirmation of his orders."

The line seemed to go dead for a moment. Then the General said, "I'll tell you, Bob, I have no knowledge of the mission. It's very unlikely the Pentagon would use our ships as a staging for an assault and not talk to us. I'm sure everything's on the up and up. But I can't imagine the oversight. Whoever caused it will have their ass in a sling, and real soon. Let me look into it and I'll get back to you. Just move ahead as planned. I don't want to hold up the mission and place one of our boys in further danger."

"Thank you, General."

*   *   *   *

"Colonel Burnhall's office, may I help you?" Scott answered the phone.

"This is General Weyling. Where is Colonel Burnhall?" The voice on the other end of the phone sounded extremely annoyed.

"I sorry sir, he's not available at present."

"Damn right, cause he's in the Persian Gulf aboard the U.S.S. NASSAU. I want to know who gave him orders, and permission to go there!"

"I'm sorry, sir, I can't answer that question."

"I don't like being stonewalled! Can't or won't?" the General screamed.

Scott pulled the receiver away from his ear. "Sorry sir, I can't. I do not know the answer to that question." With that Scott signed his own court martial papers. There was no response. The line simply went dead.

"Shit!" Scott quickly dialed Megan, who picked up on the first ring. "Megan, we've got problems. General Weyling just called. He knows the Colonel's in the Gulf with a team. He's trying to find out how he got there. It's only a matter of time. I'd say less than an hour, before the whole plan blows up and the Colonel's caught. We have to notify him. I'm stuck. There's no way I can do it. I'm not cleared for direct communication to the NASSAU."

"I'll take care of it. With the link ups we have here I can basically send him a military fax. Gotta go. Bye, and Scott...thanks."

*   *   *   *

Colonel Burnhall was just drifting off into a long awaited sleep when a sharp knock on the door roused him. "Come in." He rose from his cot, blurry eyed, and met the communications officer.

"I have a communiqué for you sir. It was non-coded and over a non-secure line." Burnhall unfolded the slip of paper.

RE: Walk in the Sand
From: M.G.A.N.

Discussed details with higher ups. Wet feet cause fungal infection. Dry them immediately. Will monitor.

"Thank you, Lieutenant. That's all."

The Colonel was dressed in moments. It was one o'clock in the morning. None-the-less he quickly rounded up the rest of his men. The order was simple. They had to leave now or they'd be stopped. The group dressed in their battle gear and headed out for the flight deck. Timing and intimidation would be everything from this point on. They ascended the ladders to the flight deck and unceremoniously approached their copters. Burnhall walked to the side and approached a Marine. "Are you the night crew chief?"

"Yes, sir." He saluted sharply.

"Are these copters fully loaded and fueled for tomorrow's mission?"

"Yes, sir."

"Fine. We have a change of schedule. We'll be leaving immediately. Please see to it. My pilots are going through their flight checks. My men are checking their equipment."

"Sir, I need authorization to release these birds to you. I'll have to contact Colonel Black."

"Yes, I understand that. Time is critical right now. I'll get the Colonel. I want you to get these birds ready with rotors running. I'll be back with the Colonel and your permission in five minutes. When you get it I want to be able to climb in and leave. I have a man's life resting on time. Do you understand me?"

"Yes, sir."

Burnhall walked off the flight deck. He found himself a head and relieved his bladder. When he heard the roar of the helicopters gearing up he knew it was time. All would quickly hear the vibration and noise and Black would be hot on their tail. Back on the flight deck, the roar from the engines was overpowering and the wind from the rotors felt like a hurricane blasting in his face. Burnhall walked up to the Crew Chief and yelled in his ear. "Colonel Black is on the bridge. He wants you on the flight phone to give you confirmation. Thank you for your help."

"Yes sir. Good luck." They shook hands.

The Chief walked away. Burnhall wasted no time. He climbed into his copter and shut the door behind him. Near them the rotors of an AH-1 Cobra helicopter spun at full speed. The Colonel put on a radio headset and gave an order to both pilots. "Gentlemen, take off now, please."

Burnhall saw Black and the Crew Chief run onto the flight deck. But it was too late. Both copters lifted off and quickly were lost in the darkness of the Gulf.

It didn't take long for the call to come over the radio. "This is the U.S.S. NASSAU ordering flight 290 and 188 to return to the flight deck immediately."

"This is Colonel Burnhall. I'm sorry. We are unable to comply with that order. For the safety of my men and this mission I request radio silence."

"That's a negative. This is Colonel Black. Turn those birds around now."

"I'm sorry, Bob, you'll have to trust me on this one. One of my men is in danger. You know the rules. We never leave one behind. See you when we return."

"You'll see the brig when you return."

"If I get my man out alive, it'll be worth it. Burnhall over and out."

32   Chapter Thirty-two

At three A.M. two stolen trucks, with their lights off, barreled down the road towards the Ramad Military Base. One hundred yards before crashing through the front gate, the canvas covers that had been pulled over the truck beds were discarded. Ten men in each truck took positions. They held their weapons in their hands. There were multiple replacements at their feet.

They crashed through the front gate. The two startled sentries died in a hail of gun fire, and had been unable to sound an alarm. Once through the gates, the trucks split up. One went to the right. The other went to the left. The men fired automatic weapons, bazookas, and threw grenades through windows as they passed. The base rocked with multiple explosions. Iraqi soldiers ran through the dark night confused and disoriented. Explosions seemed to come from all areas of the base. In one corner of the base a tremendous fireball spewed flames in all directions. The small fuel dump that had been there moments before had ignited, illuminating the sky.

For a fleeting moment one of the trucks slowed and Sam, wearing full combat gear along with his N.V.S., jumped out. The truck sped off in an instant. Quickly, Sam ran and crashed through the front door of the nearest building. He rolled to the floor, took aim ready to fire, but the entrance was empty. Rising, he moved forward, quickly scanning in all directions. Still no one. With caution he rounded a corner but stopped. On the floor was a dead Iraqi soldier with three holes equally spaced in the center of his chest.

Sam descended a flight of stairs until he reached the cellblock. Still there was no resistance. Suddenly, to his right, there was the silhouette of a soldier. He spun, aimed, but didn't fire. The Iraqi was sprawled on the floor. He was also dead. Shot three times in the chest. The blood was still trickling from his wounds. It was a fresh kill, less then thirty minutes ago. Quickly, he checked the cells. They were all empty. One lock, though, glowed on his scope. He touched it. It still felt warm. Upon a closer look he saw it had been flash melted. He knew only Special Forces could have done this. They had made a clean rescue, less than thirty minutes ago. They were his ride home and he had to catch them. They didn't know he was alive. He thought for a second. Their landing zone had to be in the desert. If he could get close to them he could attract their attention. Sam took the stairs three at a time and raced to stand outside the building under cover of the doorway.

"Come on, where are you?" Finally the silhouette of the truck rounded the corner. He blinked his flashlight to signal them. The truck again momentarily slowed as he bolted across the dirt and vaulted into the rear of it, next to Ismail.

"What happened? Where's your friend?" Ismail yelled above the noise of machine gun fire next to them.

"He's gone. He's been rescued. Less than thirty minutes ago."

"By who?" They felt the pings of bullets hitting the side of the truck. "Let's go! Let's go!" he yelled, pounding on the roof of the cab. As they accelerated the Iraqis fell in a hail of return fire.

"They were Special Forces. We need to find them," he yelled in Ismail's ear. "What's east of here?"

"About ten kilometers of desert and then a rock bluff," Ismail yelled over the constant report of gunfire.

"That's where they'd be. We've got to get there."

"We can't in this truck. The last four kilometers are covered with jagged rocks. The tires will be ripped to shreds."

They rounded a corner and found themselves in a fierce firefight with a group of about fifteen Iraqis. Two men beside Sam fell instantly from headshots. Sam returned fire, emptying his ammo clip into the group. He then emptied a second one. Next he picked up a rocket grenade launcher, aimed and fired it. The shrapnel from it tore through the Iraqis, ending any resistance. They quickly sped off down the road.

Sam spotted a truck. It was a BMP-1 troop carrier. "There! Take me there!"

"Where?"

"The troop vehicle, that'll get me across the desert and rocks." Sam pointed to the armor-protected troop carrier with tank treads instead of tires.

Ismail pounded on the cab's roof again. "Stop there, and then drive off."

Before they had stopped Sam was on the ground running towards the infantry vehicle. To his surprise, Ismail followed him. "What are you doing? Go with them."

"No! You'll need help. One to drive, the other to shoot the cannon."

"Fine, there's no time to argue. I'll drive. I have the night vision system."

The two of them climbed in and bolted the door behind them. Sam took the driver's seat and immediately started the engine. Ismail climbed into the turret of the 73mm cannon. Throwing the transmission into gear, Sam tore across the open field. The vehicle knocked down a chain link fence then headed out across the desert. Ismail pulled the trigger, sending a few rounds back into the camp at those attempting to fire at them.

Within moments they reached the vehicle's maximum speed of seventy kilometers per hour and were bouncing across the desert sand. The terrain in front of Sam was vivid and detailed. His N.V.S. goggles were working perfectly. He was able to see the tire marks in the sand that had been left by the Special Forces. He hoped he wasn't too late.

Back at the camp, the two trucks exited the front gate and in moments they were lost in downtown Baghdad. General Malek ran out of his quarters and approached his soldiers. "What are you doing? Go after them!" he screamed red-faced.

"The two trucks drove into Baghdad but two men stole a troop vehicle and headed off into the desert. Who do you want us to chase?"

Just then a soldier ran up to them. "General Malek. I checked as you asked. The American prisoner is gone."

"Take a squad and chase them down in the desert. He mustn't escape. Kill them all on sight. Forget the others. They're lost in Baghdad by now."

"Yes, sir."

"What are you waiting for? Move! Now!" Malek grabbed the nearest soldier and pushed him.

Within minutes three BMP-1 vehicles tore out across the desert, their headlights blazing, following the tracks left by Sam's escape.

The General ran into the remains of the radio room. "Do any of these work?"

"No sir. But the telephone does."

"Get me Colonel Abrail at Rashid Air Force Base."

"Yes sir."

Moments later the connection was made. "Colonel, General Malek here. I want two attack helicopters now. An American prisoner has escaped and is moving east across the desert in a stolen vehicle."

"I'm sorry, General. I'll need to get authority first."

"I'm giving you authority! And if the helicopters aren't in the air immediately I promise I'll give you a bullet in the face! You do remember General Akkad."

There was a moment of silence from the other end. "It'll take them fifteen minutes to get airborne."

"Have one of them pick me up. I want to conduct the attack personally." He slammed the phone down and stormed outside to pace, scream and wait.

33   Chapter Thirty-three

"They're off!" Raani called out to the group, with a jubilant wave of his hand. His headphones picked up the radio traffic from the helicopters. "They got him out without any problems. They've left the landing zone."

"Great! Is it Sam? Do we know who it is?" Megan bit her nails nervously as she talked.

"No. Sorry, Megan. As soon as they mention who it is I'll let you know."

"Wait a minute," Maurice called from his cubicle. "Something else is going on over there."

"What do you mean?" Megan hurried over to him.

"I have frantic calls over telephone lines demanding helicopters to chase an American who shot up the Ramad Military Base with a dozen Iraqis. The American stole a troop vehicle and is being pursued on the ground by troops heading east from the base."

"But the Colonel's group was in and out without any confrontation, according to Raani," Megan said.

"That's right. Either this second group was nothing more than a coincidental terrorist attack or there's a second American alive there. And if he knew one of his team was being held prisoner he'd more than likely try a rescue of his own."

"That's Sam!" Megan blurted out. "I'm sure of it. He'd never leave one of his team behind. We have to notify Colonel Burnhall to turn around and help him."

"How can we? We're only capable of listening. We're not set up for transmitting," Maurice said.

Megan looked at Maurice with pleading eyes. "But we sent the fax."

"Yes, but that was over an open non-secure line. That was a simple fax link-up. Those copters are on an ultra high frequency coded channel. Sorry, I don't know how we can make the connection." Maurice's eyes went from Megan's to Raani's then back again. "I'm open to suggestions."

"Jonathan!" Megan lunged for the telephone and dialed his extension. "Jonathan, I need your help..."

"I don't think we should talk over an open line..."

"I don't have time to worry about that. Just listen. Burnhall's team was successful and is on their way out of Iraq. But we have to turn them around!"

"Why?"

"Because there's a second member of the team alive, and he's being chased across the desert towards the Colonel's landing zone. But the Colonel's not there. If they don't turn around he won't survive." The phone went dead.

Moments later Megan heard a commotion from down the hall. "Out of my way! Out of my way! Blind man running! Out of my way! Blind man running! Blind man running!"

Jonathan entered the doorway. "Megan, get me to your main terminal!"

Megan half guided, half dragged him to it. Jonathan sat down and wasted no time. His fingers rapidly typed on the keyboard.

"Whose system has radio intercept?" he demanded.

"Mine." Maurice replied.

"What's its access code?"

"Beta five three five."

"Close it down and reactivate it but don't boot it up. Megan, what's the extension of the nearest telephone?"

"Uh..." She looked around. "7912."

Jonathan continued to type at a frantic pace, issuing commands to the mainframe computer. "Okay. Megan I need your help. I need your eyes. Look at the screen and scroll the curser down to the line that reads Delta Satellite Recon Communication."

She found it and did as he asked. "You're on it now."

"Good." Jonathan pressed enter. "What does it read?"

"It wants an access code."

"Good." He typed in his name and pressed enter.

"It denied you access. It says access denied. Shit!" Megan was becoming frantic.

"Calm down. I wanted it to." Next Jonathan typed in his personal access code. It was the same one he had used to access Von Wilbert's file. Suddenly a program code displayed on the screen, ready to be edited.

"Now find me the line that reads 'Jonathan'.

Megan ran her finger down the screen. "I found it."

"Read me the next line."

"A79411?10"

Jonathan typed that in. Instantly the program code that instructs the computer what to do and where to go within its files opened up. "Find A79411?10," he demanded.

Megan scrolled down the screen. "I've got it!"

"What's the next line?"

"Z5259912."

Jonathan exited the program and again typed 'Delta Satellite Recon Communication'

"It wants your access code again," Megan told him.

He typed 'Z5259912' and pressed enter.

"You're in!" Megan exclaimed.

Lastly he typed Maurice's code/Delta Satellite Recon Communications/7912 and pressed enter. "Pick up the phone. You're tied in directly to the Colonel's helicopter's frequency. All you have to do is talk."

*   *   *   *

"Colonel, I've got something strange coming over the air," the pilot called to the Colonel Burnhall who was in the back of the helicopter with his team members.

"What is it?"

"I think you'd better pick up and have a listen. There's a woman calling for you. Says she's Megan and a friend. She's demanding to speak to you. I don't even know how she got on air."

The Colonel put on a set of headphones and microphone and pressed the online switch. "…need to speak to Colonel Burnhall."

"Burnhall here, go ahead, Megan."

"Colonel you need to turn around. There's another member of your team being chased across the desert by the Iraqis. They're heading east out of the Ramad Military Base. They must be heading for the landing zone you just left."

"Are you sure?"

"I'm one hundred percent positive. The Iraqis are chasing with troop vehicles but General Malek has called for helicopters. You need to turn around."

"Hold on, Megan. Ed," he called to the pilot, "can we make the round trip on our fuel?"

"Negative, Colonel. If we return we won't make it south of 32 degrees. We'll be north of the No Fly Zone. As it is, we'll just make it over the Gulf to refuel."

"Ed, get me Colonel Black on the NASSUA."

Colonel Black's voice was suddenly there. "Burnhall, this is Black. We've been monitoring your conversation. I've got a tanker circling just outside Iraqi air space to refuel you. You are to return immediately to the NASSUA."

"That's a negative, Black. I've got another man in trouble. I need to help him. We will need to be refueled north of the 32 parallel."

"My tankers will not, repeat, will not enter north of the No Fly Zone. I'm only refueling you to get my birds back in one piece and throw you into the brig!"

"If I don't help him, my man will die!"

"Burnhall, if you go back you'll run out of gas and you'll all either die or be taken prisoners. You will return immediately and place yourself under arrest."

"What about my man?"

"I don't give a damn! I have my orders and you have yours!"

*   *   *   *

"I see lights behind us. They're chasing us," Ismail called forward to Sam. Sam scanned ahead. His N.V.S. goggles detailed the landscape better than headlights would.

"If they get close, shoot at them."

Sam scanned the desert in front of him for infrared hot spots. All he had to do was see the team. He'd get their attention. He'd make sure they see him. Looking back for an instant he saw the pursuing BMP-1s matching his speed. It was a standoff for the moment. But that would change if they got to the rocks and the Special Forces were gone.

"Where are the rocks? How far?" he yelled back at Ismail over the whine of the engine.

"You should be seeing them in a minute or two."

Sand swirled around and covered everything inside the vehicle as it was sucked in through the open gun ports like a siphon. Finally up ahead an irregular jagged rise appeared.

Sam scanned in front of them and saw no hot spots.

"We missed them. They're gone," Sam shouted. "Any suggestions?"

"None. Those rocks are the only protection for many kilometers."

"Then that's it. We stop and fight there. It's only a matter of time before they get a copter in the air. We need protection."

They paralleled the rocks until Sam saw the marks in the sand where the Special Forces had landed. He stopped the BMP-1.

"There's a ridge with good cover up there, about twenty feet. That'll be the best spot to fight."

"I agree. There's a fifty-caliber machine gun back here. Let's take it with us."

Sam joined him and the two took their guns and as much ammunition as they could carry to the base of the rocks. Together they hoisted their weapons and ammunition up the rock face to the ridge.

Sam scanned the desert from the ridge. "There are three vehicles coming. I have time to take them out."

He climbed down, re-entered the BMP-1 and mounted the turret. First he activated the tracking system on the AT-3 Sagger Missile System, then he lined the cross hairs on the first chasing vehicle and pulled the trigger. With a momentary blinding throb of light the missile streaked across the dark desert and found its target. It exploded in a fireball.

Thirty seconds later he had loaded and shot a second Sagger with the same deadly effect. With the third and last missile loaded, he took aim at the last vehicle, but hesitated. In the sky to his right there loomed a hot spot. A helicopter was coming right at them.

He raised his sights and took aim but not before the helicopter had done the same. Firing at the helicopter simultaneously, the missiles passed each other mid flight. Sam instinctively dove off the vehicle and hit the sand the instant his vehicle erupted in flames. Searing pain overwhelmed him as a hot piece of shrapnel ripped through his thigh. The helicopter exploded in a fireball and fell to the desert sand.

"Sam! Sam! Are you alright?" Ismail called from above.

"I'm hit in the leg, but I'll survive."

"Can you make it back up here?"

"Yes." He hobbled to the rocks, dragging his injured leg, and started his climb. Each step felt like a knife cutting deeper into his flesh, all the while he felt warm blood coursing down his leg. Ismail pulled him up the last five feet.

"Let me look at that leg." He ripped Sam's trousers, exposing torn ragged flesh and muscle.

"No time. Just put a wrap on it." Sam pulled off his belt and shirt. Bundling up the shirt he pressed it over the wound and tied it tight with the belt. The pain was beyond any he had ever felt.

Within moments their surroundings ignited with hits from machine gun fire. 73mm cannon fire also raked back and forth across the rocks above and below them. Ismail responded in kind with his 50mm machine gun. Sam, ignoring his pain, rolled onto his abdomen and took aim. First, he fired a rocket-propelled grenade, and then he used his assault rifle. His N.V.S. goggles allowed him to see a man mounting the AT-3 Sagger missile turret on the last BMP-1. It took only a moment to aim and fire, killing the Iraqi.

Suddenly a rocket exploded into the bluff above them. Sam ducked his head momentarily, and then looked up. "There's a second copter! We've got to take it out!"

Ismail raked the 50mm machine gun across the sky with no effect. He was unable to see the dark copter.

Sam realized Ismail had limited vision. "Switch weapons! I can see it with my scope. You take out the troops."

The moment they switched positions a second rocket blasted into the rocks above them. Sam instinctively ducked his head, but looked up in time to see a third rocket streak by. This latest rocket came from the opposite direction. He watched it slam into the helicopter, and ignite it in a fireball.

"Yes! Yes! Special Forces! They saw us! That's it, let's kick ass." He held the trigger on the 50mm machine gun and walked it back and forth over the last BMP-1. Before long it was engulfed in flames from an air to ground missile. Some of the Iraqis had already taken cover within the rocks and continued the fight from there.

Sam felt a surge of adrenaline as a Cobra helicopter passed overhead, its gatling gun decimating those hiding in the rocks.

"That's it, we're out of here." He turned to Ismail, only to see the vacant blank stare of death. Part of his head was gone. It had been torn off by shrapnel from the last rocket that exploded in the rocks above them.

With no time to reflect, Sam looked up as a second copter, a C53-H SuperStallion, flew over him and hovered, its guns also erupting. From its side a spy ring hung down, bouncing off the rocks near him. In his first lunge he grabbed it, wrapped it around his wrists and held tight. In moments he was pulled airborne in the opposite direction from the battle. He looked back and caught a final glimpse of Ismail's body.

The Cobra helicopter unleashed one final deadly barrage before breaking off to join them as they raced south towards the Persian Gulf. The cable pulled Sam to the level of the copter's open side door. The downward blast of hot air from the rotors buffeted him as he hung precariously by his wrists. Sam felt blood dripping from his leg at a rapid rate. With every second he felt his strength diminishing. Soon he knew he'd be too weak to hang on. He stared at his wrists. They were numb and blue from the rope looped tightly around them. The buffeting and swirling wind from the spinning rotors above caused him to spin around faster and faster on the cable. The closer he got to the door the faster he spun. His world now was a blur, filled with pain, wind pressure, and the roar from above. He knew he had only a few moments of strength left before he fell to the sand below. Suddenly two strong hands reached out and pulled him into the copter's bay. Exhausted, he collapsed onto the floor. With his hands in spasms he was unable to release his grip on the rope.

"You're safe. You can let go now." A member of the rescue team leaned over him. But Sam's hands were frozen in a death grip. He had reached his limit. Gently, a team member opened his hands and removed the rope for him.

"Here, Sam, have some water."

Sam saw Colonel Burnhall leaning over him. The Colonel placed the canteen to his lips and he took a few sips while others tended to his leg.

To his right he saw Roger. "Gino didn't make it?" Sam asked.

"No, he didn't," the Colonel replied as he sat next to him on the copter's floor.

"I thought you were gone," Sam's weak voice could barely be heard even though the Colonel had his ear right next to Sam's face. "I'd given up hope that you would see me."

"We were long gone. You owe your life to Megan. She and her team did it all. They found you just moments ago. They also bulled Colonel Black on the NASSUA into refueling us over Iraq. She told him she'd implicate him on national television in a government conspiracy of high treason that covered up the development of the nerve gas by our government. Then, she'd implicate him as an active accomplice in your team's ambush and death. And finally, she promised to personally cut off his balls and ram them down his throat in front of his men. I think it was the last one that did it. He ordered the tankers to refuel us in Iraqi air space. Here." He placed a set of headphones and microphone on his head. "She's on the line. I think she'd like to hear your voice."

"Megan?" He mustered enough strength to speak up.
"Sam? Oh, Sam, thank God you're alive! Sam, I love you."
"I love you too, Megan."

* * * *

Thousands of miles away Megan and Jonathan marched down the hall towards Niddiem's office.
"Is he in?" Megan asked the secretary.
"Yes. But he's busy now. Would you like to make an appointment?"
"No," Jonathan said. "We'll see him now. Tell him...never mind. We'll tell him ourselves. Come on Megan." Jonathan headed through Niddiem's office door, with Megan one step behind.

* * * *

Gordon paced outside the oval office. "Did you tell the President I'm here?" he demanded of the secretary.
"Yes, and he wants you to wait outside until he is ready to see you." She turned her eyes from him and back to her work.
This was the first time the President had ever made him wait outside. If only the bastard knew what he was doing to protect him. What a mess. But at least now it was over. The gas was destroyed, the Delta Team killed, and he could put it all behind him. Yes, the end does justify the means. Finally, the door to the Oval Office opened. The President stood there with Niddiem.
"John, I've just had a long talk with Al. I have accepted his immediate resignation from the C.I.A. Come in, I think it's time you and I had a chat, after which I'll be accepting your resignation."

The President led him into the Oval Office and shut the door on Al Niddiem without so much as a good-bye.

"Take a seat, John. No…not that one." The President guided him away from the soft sofa and to a hard wooden chair. "Sit over here."

"And one last thing before we start. If I were you, I wouldn't try to talk me out of your resignation. I'd spend my time, if I were you, trying to talk me out of having you arrested for treason."

34   Chapter Thirty-four

The town of Uberlongen sat at the northern-most entrance of Lake Constance. The dense firs and surrounding hills of the Black Forest added to the majestic sweep of nature that gave this part of Germany its romantic reputation. On a tree-covered promenade overlooking Lake Constance Abraham sat sipping cognac. His camera rested on his lap. He stared at a man emerging from the estate. Yes, Abraham was sure. It had taken two days, waiting on a bench in the shadows outside the Von Riechbrand estate that sat on a plateau overlooking the lake and village below. Now, though, he had him. Von Wilbert didn't notice the man with a limp and cane entering a car and following him down the winding road to the valley below. Why should he? Tourists were common this time of year.

They stopped in the Village and both exited their cars. Soon they sat within twenty feet of each other at an outdoor café on the shore of Lake Constance. Abraham scanned the scenery behind dark glasses. But his gaze always came back to the same person. His face, his mannerisms, yes, that was Von Wilbert. Even after fifty years, Abraham recognized him. Slowly, Abraham raised his camera and took aim. He was merely a casual tourist taking a panoramic picture. He waited until Von Wilbert looked up towards him. Click, click, and click. He saw the look of annoyance on Von Wilbert's face at having his picture taken in this public place. Abraham watched him change seats. He smiled to himself.

"Go ahead, you son of a bitch," Abraham muttered. "Turn your back. It doesn't matter. I've found you."

Every now and then Von Wilbert turned slightly in his seat and glanced over his shoulder at Abraham. Each time he did, Abraham made sure he was staring in his direction. Shortly thereafter Von Wilbert threw some money on the table and left. But not before casting one final glance towards Abraham.

Von Wilbert strolled along the cobblestone street that was lined with furniture and porcelain shops. He was much older than Abraham. His walk was slow and deliberate, with each step carefully placed. That made it easy for Abraham with his limp, to follow Von Wilbert into the town square.

On the far side of the square a church steeple rose towards the sky. It sparkled in white paint and pistachio-green trim. Abraham raised his camera and focused it on the church. But in the last instant he lowered it, refocusing it on Von Wilbert. Abraham quickly finished the roll of film. None-the-less he kept the camera up and stared through the viewfinder. The powerful telephoto lens brought the monster of his past up close and personal. His face filled Abraham's frame and view.

As if he knew he was being watched, Von Wilbert turned and looked directly into the lens. For a fleeting moment Abraham had a front view of Von Wilbert's face and for the first time could look at his eyes. Von Wilbert's eyes were still as cold and dark as they were fifty years ago, with one subtle difference. Abraham noticed a small twitch in Von Wilbert's face.

"Ah, a hint of concern," Abraham said. "You probably remember me from the terrace, don't you? That's okay. You'll be seeing a lot more of me today."

They continued to stare at each other. Finally Abraham lowered the camera, allowing Von Wilbert to see his face in full.

Von Wilbert turned suddenly and walked quickly back to the waterfront. He jumped into his car and drove off in a rush. Abraham's car was nearby and he quickly followed him. They headed southeast towards the town of Meersburg. The road wound tightly along the shoreline. Abraham stayed far enough behind him to avoid suspicion, but close enough to keep him in view. They passed through multiple small fishing villages bordered by the famous Borenesee wine vineyards. This, along with the landscape bedecked with orchids, roses, and bougainvillea, was lost on Abraham. His eyes rarely left the back of Von Wilbert's car.

Von Wilbert slowed slightly as he passed through the town of Meersburg. Abraham's eyes were riveted on the rear of Von Wilbert's car so he didn't notice how close he was following. He found himself close enough to be seen. At that moment Von Wilbert looked in the rear view mirror. Their eyes again locked on each other. Moments later Von Wilbert accelerated, opening the gap between them.

"The chase is on" Abraham bellowed. "You know I'm following you. But you don't know who I am, or why I'm chasing you, do you?" Abraham sped up.

They drove at fifty miles per hour up the winding road. Their days of breakneck speed and screeching tires were long gone. Cautiously, they rounded the tight curves that bordered sharp drop offs and ravines. One moment they were at lake level, the next moment a thousand feet above it. Despite that Abraham never let his prey out of his sight.

They entered Lindau, a medieval town with narrow streets and houses that displayed all colors of the rainbow. The streets were crowded, and Abraham's larger car couldn't take the curves as quickly. He lost sight of Von Wilbert.

"Damn! Don't lose him now," he said to himself.

Abraham wound his way towards the harbor only guessing at Von Wilbert's direction. When he passed the large stone lion that guarded the entrance to the waterfront, he slowed, and finally stopped. In front of him was the entire waterfront with hundreds of boats bobbing up and down at anchor. He opened the car door and half stepped outside, attempting to get a better view, when a sound caught his attention. Nearby came the soft toot of a train whistle. Then three sharp toots. Abraham climbed back into the car and accelerated down the road. He was panicking at the thought of losing him. Suddenly he stopped, his tires sliding in a gravel parking lot, just in time to see a small train pull out of the station. There, off in the far corner of the lot, was Von Wilbert's car.

Abraham slammed his hand on the dash. "Damn! I'm too late!" He hurried out and limped to the ticket window.

"Excuse me. Where is that train heading?"

"To Freiburg," came the reply.

"Freiburg. How far is it by car?"

"About four and a half hours."

"Damn! I'll never catch it."

"If you want to catch the train you should take the ferry."

"What do you mean?"

"The ferry over there." He pointed out the window to the waterfront. "It leaves in two minutes. It goes straight across to a small fishing village across the lake. That's the train's only stop before Freiburg. It has to wind around the eastern point of the lake. The ferry always beats it."

Despite his limp, Abraham ran across the street and down to the waterfront. His cane barely touched the ground as he walked. He climbed the boarding ladder just before the ferry cast off.

Ever so slowly the ferry pulled away from the dock. The large stone lion on a pedestal high above the harbor seemed to cast a benign glance at them. At first Abraham sat on a deck chair, but finding the lake crossing agonizingly slow, he stood and paced the deck.

Finally, in the middle of the lake, he stopped and leaned on one of the railings. He marveled at the tremendous beauty of the landscape. He shook his head and tears welled up in his eyes. "How could such a beautiful land raise such barbarians?" He just didn't understand. Suddenly thoughts, vivid thoughts of brutality intensified. The constant sound of German language barraged him. The beauty and richness of his surroundings were lost in the rage that filled his heart.

By the time the ferry pulled into the small pier Abraham was impatiently poised at the ramp, waiting to disembark. His eyes fixed on the railroad tracks that led to a small rail station.

"Come on, come on! Can't you get that ramp in place any faster?" he said under his breath.

"Finally!" he shouted a few moments later. "Now get out of my way." He pushed people aside as he made his way onto the small wooden dock. He limped quickly up the path to the small rail station. Moments later the ferry blew its whistle and departed.

Indecision swirled over him as he stood on the rail station platform. He wondered if he should get on the train. He pondered. *What if I get on and Von Wilbert gets off? What if he sees me?*

He saw a small alcove on the side of the station. *That's it. I'll hide there. If he gets off I'll follow him. If he doesn't, I'll run and jump on at the last moment.*

He cocked his head and heard the distant shrill of a train whistle from the left. He pressed himself back against the wall of the alcove as the black hulk of an engine came into view. It slowed, and finally stopped, steam hissing from the valves. Ironically, the first two cars were old cattle cars, filled with cattle. Abraham's memories overpowered him. He saw human hands reaching through the wooden slats. The visions of the death camp's rail yard returned to him, mixing with reality.

"You will get off or you will be shot!"

Bile rose in his throat. "No! No! Focus. You must stay focused."

Bang!

He jumped and held his head. "My God, a gun shot!"

"I'm sorry, sir, my son knocked over your box."

Shaking with fright, Abraham peered out from his hiding place. He saw a woman with a small child helping a man pick up a wooden box.

"Stay focused. That was years ago, this is today."

Abraham scrutinized every passenger who got off. He was sure he hadn't seen Von Wilbert. A moment later the conductor looked up and down the platform. Seeing no one else, he signaled the engineer to go.

He started to make a dash for the train. But just as he moved out of his alcove he stopped and jumped back. From the last car Von Wilbert emerged, jumping onto the platform from the slowly moving train. The train pulled out of the station and Von Wilbert stood and looked around. He had a self-satisfied smile on his face. As the rumble of metal wheels faded Von Wilbert called out, "What time does the next ferry arrive to take me back to Lindau?"

"One hour," a muted answer floated by Abraham.

He peered out of his hiding place in time to see Von Wilbert turn and walk across the tracks to a dirt road. Only after Von Wilbert passed from view did Abraham finally move out from his alcove. Abraham followed Von Wilbert down the path deeper into the Black Forest. The thick canopy of evergreens filtered out the sunlight, leaving the ground damp and springy. The path finally opened into a large rolling field. But Von Wilbert wasn't in sight.

Abraham looked across the field. "Where are you?"

"Who are you, and what do you want?"

Abraham spun around and found himself face to face with his prey.

"You are following me. Why?" asked Von Wilbert.

For a moment Abraham just stood there and looked at him. Von Wilbert appeared slightly apprehensive, almost afraid, not the omnipotent individual he remembered from the death camps.

"You don't remember me, do you?" Abraham started in a matter of fact voice.

"No. Should I?"

"You are Claus Von Wilbert."

"I asked, who are you, and what you want?"

Abraham took a step closer, feeling less threatened. This time he used his cane to help his throbbing leg. "You forced me to work for you during the war. My name is Abraham. You forced me to clean the bodies out of your death chamber, to clean your boots, to shine them. Do you remember me now?" He stood only three feet from Von Wilbert.

"Ah...yes. The shoe shine boy, as we called you. Yes, now I remember you. And to think I was running from you. You were weak then and you still are. Go, leave me." He waved his hand in dismissal.

"This time you will not get away," Abraham voiced with venom. "I'll take you to the authorities. You'll pay for your crimes. The United States government won't be able to help you now."

"Ah, so you figured it out. I'm impressed. But since you know so much, do you really think they'll allow you to expose me, to expose them? You are foolish and naive. You are as foolish as you were in the camps. I should have gassed you when I had the chance."

Abraham took a step towards him but winced in pain and grabbed his thigh. For a fleeting moment he had to lean on his cane for support.

"I see you have a bad leg. You are disabled physically and emotionally," taunted Von Wilbert.

"I was shot in Jerusalem, by a Palestinian terrorist. He killed thousands the next day, including my family. I was in the hospital because of my leg or I would have died also."

"Oh my, the irony is beyond me. Let me ask you, did you carry and bury them as you did for me in the camps?"

"Yes. I buried my family."

"So even now you do my bidding."

"What do you mean?"

"Such naiveté. What do you think I've been doing with my retirement? I've always said it's a shame to waste intelligence. It is so nice to see that after so many years you're still cleaning up after me."

"You, you were responsible?" cried Abraham in shock. "You helped them make the gas that killed my family?"

"Yes, I'm proud to say, I did. And it worked far beyond my expectations. Now all that's left is for you to shine my shoes. They are dirty from this walk in the woods. Do you need a rag?"

In a blind rage Abraham swung his cane, striking Von Wilbert in the throat. He fell to the dirt, clutching his neck with his hands. Abraham couldn't stop. He swung his cane again and again.

"You bastard! Killer! This is for all those you killed in the war! This is for their families. This is for those who died in Israel. This...this is for my family! And...and this one's for me...for me...for me! May you die a painful death, and rot in hell!"

He hit him one last time, but there was no need. The first blow to the throat had been the fatal one. Von Wilbert had suffocated, unable to get air into his lungs through his crushed windpipe.

Abraham stood shaking over the still body. Then he raised his eyes and hands to the sky. "El maley rachamim." He thought for a moment then smiled. He finally remembered what came next. He could finish the prayer. The prayer he couldn't finish for Joshua. "El maley rachamim shochen bamromim, Hamtzey..." Now he said it for all those who had died at the hands of the butcher, the butcher who now lay dead at his feet. And when he had finished his prayer he bent down and wiped the dirt off his own shoes with the butcher's sleeve.

Printed in the United States
22673LVS00002B/226-390